More praise for *The Odditorium* and Melissa Pritchard

"Melissa Pritchard's *The Odditorium* is as strange, wonderful, and (most important) as much fun as anything good old Robert LeRoy ~~Ri~~ could ever have envisioned. Passionate, bold imaginings that ~~il~~luminate the darkest, most precious reaches of our lives. Believe it: these stories are a gift."
—Pinckney Benedict, author of *Miracle Boy*

~~Melis~~sa Pritchard has her GPS set to find the *how it is*—out there ~~in t~~he heart—and she makes her way forward with her language ~~on h~~igh alert. The prose is rhythmically astute, finely pitched, serving both imagination and witness."
—Sven Birkerts, Editor of *AGNI*,
author of *The Gutenberg Elegies:*
The Fate of Reading in an Electronic Age

"In this thrillingly protean collection of stories, Melissa Pritchard has done something profound. By imagining her way into historical moments and illuminating their shadows, she amplifies the music of history so we hear beautifully strange, wondrous notes we never knew were there. These stories resound with a fierce yet playful intelligence and a rare, magnificent generosity."
—Maud Casey, author of *Genealogy*

"Fueled by roofless imagination and fearless curiosity *The Odditorium* is a case study in how one writer's wisdom and empathy transforms known facts of existence into something more than magic. Pritchard draws from the cold, deep well of myth, legend, and history to redefine what narrative can do. Each story is a lesson in compassion. Each story is nothing short of genius. Each story was written for you."
—Gina Ochsner, author of
The Russian Dreambook of Color and Flight

"No one is quite so brilliant at voicing the all-but-impossible-to-track interior lives of the most complex human beings as is Melissa Pritchard . . . there is so much energy and inventiveness! Her linguistic flexibility is stunning, comic and gravely substantial. At its heart is always the troubled, often confused but courageous and tenacious human heart."
—Brad Watson, author of
Aliens in the Prime of Their Lives
and *The Heaven of Mercury*

The Odditorium

THE ODDITORIUM

Melissa Pritchard

BELLEVUE LITERARY PRESS
New York

First published in the United States in 2011 by
Bellevue Literary Press, New York

FOR INFORMATION, ADDRESS:
Bellevue Literary Press
NYU School of Medicine
550 First Avenue
OBV 612
New York, NY 10016

"Pelagia, Holy Fool" appeared in IMAGE: Art, Faith, Mystery, Number 61, Spring 2009,
editor Gregory Wolfe; "Watanya Cicilia" appeared in Gulf Coast: A Journal of Literature
and Fine Arts, Volume 23, Issue 1, Winter/Spring 2011, editors Ian Stansel and Zack Bean;
"Ecorché: Flayed Man" appeared in A Public Space, Issue 11, June 2010, editor Brigid
Hughes; "The Hauser Variations" appeared in Conjunctions: 45, Fall 2005, editor Bradford
Morrow; "Patricide" appeared in Boulevard, Volume 21, Spring 2006, editor Richard Burgin;
"The Odditorium" appeared in FANZINE, November 2009, editors Casey McKinney and
Michael Louie; "The Nine-Gated City" appeared in AGNI 70, Fall 2009, editor Sven Birkerts;
a variation of "Captain Brown and the Royal Victoria Military Hospital," appeared in the
fall 2011 issue of Ecotone, Vol. 7, no. 1, editor Ben George

Bellevue Literary Press would like to thank all its generous
donors, individuals and foundations, for their support.

Cataloging-in-Publication Data is available from the Library of Congress.

Book design and type formatting by Bernard Schleifer
Manufactured in the United States of America
FIRST EDITION
10 9 8 7 6 5 4 3 2 1
ISBN 978-1-934137-37-6 pb

For Joy Harris

CONTENTS

The Odditorium

It is the courage to make a clean breast of it in the face of every question that makes the philosopher. He must be like Sophocles' Oedipus, who, seeking enlightenment concerning his terrible fate, pursues his indefatigable enquiry, even when he divines that appalling horror awaits him in the answer. But most of us carry in our heart the Jocasta who begs Oedipus for God's sake not to inquire further . . .

—from a letter of Schopenhauer to Goethe
November 1815

Odds Nipperkins! cried Mother Bunch on her broomstick, here's a to-do!

—from Forgotten Children's Books, *Andrew Tuer,*
Leadenhall Press, 1898

PELAGIA, HOLY FOOL

*. . . we are made a spectacle unto the world, and to angels,
and to men. We are fools, for Christ's sake.*

—I Corinthians 4:9–10

Part the First: Spin, Beat, Spin

Listen, wicked children! When *une jeune* slut-*fille* dirties her
own halo, simple folk cast stones, and it takes the baroque and
obstinate solemnity of God to bring them to their knees before
a creature of such dire humility. Pelagia, born during the pre-
revolutionary era of Tsar Alexander I, was a scoundrel-saint, a
staretz who flipped a convent full of pent-up, quarrelsome
women on its head and put up with having her vile, unwashed
feet kissed by a failing empire of wonder-struck pilgrims.

In 1809, little Pelagia Ivanovna Surin Serebrenikova slipped like
a worm from her mother's fleshy cabbage-cunt in the village of
Arzamas, two hundred and fifty miles miles east of Moscow, that
medieval Byzantine city abandoned by Peter the Great in favor of
a new capital built atop drained swamps and islands by the sea, an
imperial opulence of palaces known poetically as the "Palmyra of
the North," and more prosaically, as Saint Petersburg.

Better looking than average, with strong teeth and an exceptional mind, the child Pelagia Ivanovna Surin Serebrenikova fell
ill one day and lay senseless as a stone upon her pallet of straw.
Upon arising, little Pela was quite gone, and in her place stood
a lazy good-for-nothing who planted herself in the back of the
family vegetable garden, twirling this way and that, hoisting her
skirts shamelessly high above her head. Disgrace! wept the

mother, seeing her child's fine looks and future fortune squandered by this abdication of wits. No longer the apple of her mother's eye, but an *Idiota! Saloi! Yurodivye!* Go ahead, she wailed, beat the girl, hammer at her with fists or switches, pelt her with stewed turnips, fire away at her with macerated apples. She will only whirl on, a brainless top, dervish sport for her six slovenly stepbrothers and drunken stepfather.

Pelagia spun upward into a blond giantess, bewitching all of Arzamas with her vertiginous beauty. Suitors lined up like cannon, like muskrats, like grave-borne communicants. Sick to death of her nitwit daughter, Pela's mother spun her toward the very first muskrat, an Arzamasian upstart with buck teeth and a russet rind of bristly mustache, eager to take Pelagia into his own hands. Sergei Vasileivich was a peculiar fellow, slightly consumptive, a military reject who puttered away, constructing miniature earthen fortresses patrolled by motionless battalions of toy soldiers made of wax. Disciplinary lapses in this tiny army were severely punished.

Sergei once conducted a mock-interrogatory trial in which a field rat was found guilty of gnawing off the wax head of one of his finest officers; the rodent was summarily hanged to the tune of Sergei's improvisatory drumroll and made-up tune, "Alas, there thou hangest. . . . !"

On his wedding day, wearing a handmade linen shirt and too-tight red military-style breeches, with his pointy snout and garland of gourd blossoms on his carroty, disheveled hair, Sergei failed to notice how his bride, towering over him, kept surreptitiously watering the cloth posies on her dress with weak spoonfuls of horehound tea. Gripped by lust, monstrously priapic, Sergei didn't care a fig for Pelagia's watering antics and trundled his bride away in a collapsing wooden cart, steering the reins of a borrowed nag with one hand and grabbing handfuls of tea-wetted flesh with the other, as was his right under God.

Part the Second: Dead Children, Holy Indicators, A Pillow of Iron Shackles

Clap hands over ears, little devils! From this disastrous union Pelagia bore two sons in quick succession, each of whom perished. Rumors flew through Arzamas that she had first squeezed and smothered the infants between her gargantuan breasts, then flung them, salted and boiled, no better than suckling runts, into Sergei's favorite pork and parsnip porridge.

One winter's morning, Sergei's mother came to fetch the unhappy couple and take them to Father Seraphim of Sarov, a man of saintly reputation. As the unlucky Sergei Vasileivich and his mother waited in the monastery's bare, freezing anteroom, Seraphim (reputed model for Father Zosima in Fyodor Dostoyevsky's *The Brothers Karamazov*) closeted the giantess in his cell where they prayed together for long, suspect hours before he came out and commanded Sergei to leave this child of God alone. She was divine real estate. She was His.

Absolved, Pelagia spun ever faster about Arzamas, half-naked, in woolen rags, begging and giving alms away by day, praying and weeping in the Napolny churchyard by night. Sergei, God's cuckhold, took matters into his own hands and delivered his knucklehead wife to a monastery in Kiev for an exorcism. Returning home two days after his wife due to a pesky bout of gonorrhea, he discovered Pelagia had given away all of his belongings, right down to his scarlet wedding breeches, miniature fortifications, toy soldiers, and his favorite pewter spoon. Chanting *I am unafraid of you, I am unafraid of you,* Sergei seized his wife by two fingers and carried her out of doors where he chained her by a rusted length of iron shackle to the side of his sacked and worthless house. *There thou hangest,* he sang, just as he had with the doomed rat, and improvised a military drum roll. But Pelagia escaped three times—unaware she would one day use that same length of iron chain for her anchorite's pillow.

Now everyone in Arzamas began to take a turn at beating sense into Pelagia, even the mayor and the police constable, for it was believed she housed demons, and if these infernal imps could be driven out with stones, sticks, whips, stewed turnips, and rotting melons, Pelagia might yet be an exemplary wife, might yet cook, clean, and scissor out her legs for Sergei at night after all the other chores were done. But beatings proved useless, and what was worse, the mayor had a dream that set the entire village on edge, a dream warning of divine retribution upon anyone who laid a finger on Pelagia. Meanwhile, Sergei happened upon a village girl with a face and limbs far plainer than Pelagia's but who could walk in a perfectly straight line from here to there.

Sergei spun Pela back to her mother. Damaged goods, he muttered. She was a freak and ruining his life, and he had the chance to marry a plain, stupid girl who would ask no questions and bear him children out of her sturdy, obedient cabbage. The stepfather and six brothers warily resumed their beatings, while the stepsister plotted murder, convincing an acquaintance to take aim, yet when the fellow missed his target, he turned the gun upon himself, for what had he done but try to put a bullet in a living saint? The curse of Pelagia lay like a pall over the entire village. No one outside the family dared harm her for fear of having his own skin flayed. Her mother hauled her off one last time to Seraphim of Sarov, who repeated himself. Pelagia must not be harmed, she was God's Fool, Seraphim's Seraphima, and would one day help many climb the ladder to heaven. Half-dead with disappointment, the mother prayed violently for a miracle. Relief arrived in the form of three abbesses passing through Arzamas, who agreed to take the girl back with them to Diveyevo, a forest community in the province of Nizhegorod, founded by Seraphim. The mother leapt at this chance to be rid of her whirligig of a daughter, and at last Seraphim's prophecy that *Matrushka*, or Mother, as he had taken to calling Pelagia, would one day help many, began to take shape.

Part the Third: Dung, Cockroaches, Frogs

Turn a blind eye while looking both ways. Cross over now, petits enfants! Pelagia was rejected by Diveyevo's nuns, scourged and beaten as she twirled about, breaking windows with stones and generally acting completely out of her head. Abbess Xenia assigned her a companion who beat her with a stouter stick than anyone, yet unlike ordinary people, Pelagia rejoiced in her chastisements, for the Holy Fool's fate is to turn the universe upside down, dodge moral lassitude, and rise above the Great Human Myopic. A Fool-for-God liberates herself through humiliation, climbs heavenward up a steep, lonely incline of lunacy.

All at once, Sister Folly stopped twirling and settled into a routine. Squatting in the courtyard of the convent, Pelagia chipped a trough in the dirt, a mock catacomb, using a spoon stolen from the refectory. Filling the niche with manure, she sat down in shit, spooning dung into her gorgeous bosom. When her first companion died, she was given another, Anna Gerasimovna, with whom Pelagia would live out the next forty-seven years in a plain wooden cell on the edge of the forest, at a slight distance from the convent. For a time, Pelagia collected large stones, rolling them willy-nilly into the cell she shared with Anna. She slept in the dirt by the open door, stepped upon, spat at, taunted. Like naughty children, Diveyevo's nuns devised sly tricks and impious pranks to torment their demented sister. No longer was the question how many angels can dance on the head of a pin, but how many evil nuns can jump up and down upon the prostrate body of Pelagia as she howled and whimpered with delight? How scalding can the well water be that they dribble over her head, drenching the foul, unwashed tree roots of her once-yellow hair?

Done with hauling rocks, Pelagia began sailing bricks into a murky frog pond, wading in up to her broad hips before hurling them back onto shore again. She didn't mind the army of emboldened frogs who hopped into her cell and hunkered, croaking voluptuously, in damp, foul corners. One day, Anna, who had had enough, swept the frogs, like so many green, slimy doorknobs, into a pile, tossed them out by their legs, then locked Pelagia inside. Holy Folly retaliated by pulling the door off its hinges, setting it on fire, and sitting in the pond overnight. After that, the two women dwelt in their forest cell, undoored, exposed to brutal Russian winters and insect-plagued summers. Hear, too, that Pelagia never bathed or trimmed her huge, filthy finger- or toenails, and was impervious to cockroaches, those shiny, black revulsions of the devil, skittering across the unhygienic humps and hummocks, the hairy tussock of her unwashed body.

In time, a succession of miracles began to occur. Anna witnessed Pelagia deliberately jump upon a board with a great iron nail sticking up from it, driving the rusted point straight through her high, naked arch. Rushing off to slap together a black-bread-and-onion poultice, Anna returned to find no mark at all, not even a red dot, on Pelagia's stinking, sprouting potato of a foot.

As soon as Pelagia took to roundly thrashing herself with switches and sticks, a second Holy Fool, a fellow Arzamasian, Theodore Mikhailovich Solovyov, showed up, and with Anna looking on (quite terrified but willing to be glorified by martyrdom), the two, matched in girth, began a fierce dueling of sticks and warring words. Like actors in some divine improvisation, they fought with clubs and branches, hurling insults like flaming javelins, like lightning bolts, as they chased one another back and forth through the cell and into the Church of the Nativity cemetery.

When the bruised and muddied Pelagia began uttering streams of pure clairvoyance, pilgrims straggled then elbowed their way into Diveyevo from far and near to be blessed, healed, beaten, and screamed at. She predicted dates of birth and, far more often, death, and on the day Sergei Vasileivich, some hundreds of miles distant, fell mortally ill, Pelagia mimed her old husband's agony and howled like a wolf the instant his soul broke free from his spent, vainglorious body. Even the tsar, dressed in the clichéd disguise of a woodcutter, made his way on foot through the forest to seek counsel from the reputed saint, later claiming she was the one person who would talk with him forthrightly and without guile. Still, when she warned him of his downfall, he did not listen, which proves that even in the presence of a seer and a saint, people hear only what they want to hear.

On they came in droves, day and night, seeking out the vile, stinksome creature sitting on her felt mat, asking their *Matrushka* what they should do about this or that or the other. To one she might scream "Hussy!" and deliver a stinging slap to the cheek along with a riddle; to another she might coo a lullaby, tender a silky caress. Wealth and rank offered no insulation from her unpredictable clairvoyance. When venerable Vladyka Nectary paid an unannounced visit, Pelagia stood waiting faithfully for him in a blinding hailstorm, yet when he named a replacement for Diveyevo's abbess, she boxed both his ears, making of him a perfect devotee, her faithful one.

Eating only raw mushrooms, Pelagia hoarded the many offerings of sweets she received. Candies, cakes, prosphora, all were stuffed into in a lumpy homemade sack, or "storehouse," which hung from her neck, bending her by its dulcet, rotting weight, nearly to the ground. In Pelgia's final years, Anna Gerasimovna began to wake nights to find their cell on holy fire with the terrifying radiance of supernatural visitors. Father Seraphim, many years dead and a venerated saint, arrived to administer the sacraments, and Anna claimed to have seen with her own eyes an angelic being descend through the roof, whisk Pelagia off in its alien arms, and return her, babbling incoherently, at dawn.

In the winter of 1879, Anna Gerasimovna woke one morning to find Pelagia outside, standing near the edge of the forest, in extreme austerity, an orant, arms upraised, wearing only her *sarafan*, a long, sleeveless undergarment, its thin hem nailed by ice to the snowy crown of earth. A caryatid made of flesh and ice, Pelagia upheld, for one complete night, the harsh, sorrowing, human world.

In January, 1884, she contracted a high fever and, enclasped by a dry, withering rosary of nuns, seemed one moment to battle invisible demons, the next to be lifted up in beatific rapture.

At the last, she raised her head a little, its golden nimbus stinking of manure, frogs, and rotten cakes, cried O, *Mother of God!* then fell back, asleep in the Lord, upon her pillow of iron shackles. An ocean of candles flared up throughout Russia. *Panakhidas* for the dead Pelagia were held everywhere, and overnight painted icons, mosaics, carved panels of ivory and cloisonné enamels, images of Pelagia, Fool-for-Christ, sprang up like summer stars. Thousands mourned *Matrushka*, their holy mother. Thousands whirled in keening ecstasy.

In 1927, Communist soldiers, neither toys nor made of wax, closed down the monastery at Sarov, the convent at Diveyevo, and desecrated Pelagia's cell and grave. Late in the 1980s, with Gorbachev's *perestroika* policy (An emperor! Look! Dissolving his own empire!) both churches were restored and reopened. Today, anyone can take the train from Moscow to Diveyevo, walk the same paths as Pelagia, look up at the same vacant sky and admire the forest, little changed.

Three Morals
I.

According to legend, a seventh-century pagan chieftain, Damon, from County Tyrone, Ireland, went mad upon the death of his wife and decided to assuage his grief by marrying his own daughter. Horrified by her father's advances, Dymphna, in the company of her elderly priest and confessor, Saint Gerebernus, fled across the sea to Belgium. The two took refuge and lived as hermits in an oratory in Geel, in the province of Antwerp. Damon's spies tracked the pair down, and after ordering the death of the old priest, the king took up his own sword and beheaded his disobedient child. Locals entombed the two in a nearby cave, and in the thirteenth century, when the sarcophagi were discovered, healings from mental illness and epilepsy began to take place. Saint Dymphna, virgin and martyr, became Geel's patron saint of insanity, of mental illness, of sleepwalking, of nervous disorders, of incest victims, of those possessed, of princesses, of epileptics and runaways. Images of Dymphna depict her being beheaded by her father or praying in a cloud surrounded by a group of lunatics bound with golden chains, or as a princess with a sword holding the devil, fettered, on a leash. Today, Dymphna's remains are in a silver reliquary in Geel's church of Saint Dymphna. Her feast day is May 15. Under her patronage, Geel's inhabitants are known for the care they give the mentally ill. An infirmary was first built in the thirteenth century, and today, the city boasts a first-class sanitarium, one of the largest, most efficient colonies for lunatics in the world and the first to start a peculiar but strangely curative program. First, the insane are admitted to the sanitarium for observation, and then they are placed in the homes of Geel's farmers and city residents where they are treated kindly, welcomed as family members, and watched over without ever being aware of it.

Today, in Geel, you will find the insane living side by side with the sane, eating at the same tables, working in pastry shops, car repair shops, driving buses, and quite often standing in crosswalks, holding out signs to stop traffic so Geel's children can safely cross their streets to school. *(The tale of Saint Dymphna, a narrative variant of the popular legend of a king who desires to marry his own daughter, is without historical foundation.)*

II.

On October 11, 2007, a young man, nude but for one black sock, strolled serenely through Times Square. While speaking into his cell phone, the "curly-haired hipster," later identified as Josh Drimmer, age twenty-six, a playwright and Yale alum from Greenpoint, Brooklyn, zigzagged back and forth along Seventh Avenue between West Forty-seventh and Forty-eighth Streets. After exiting Tad's Steakhouse off Forty-seventh Street where patrons reported seeing a naked man jump up and down on one of the restaurant's tables, Mr. Drimmer was arrested and handcuffed by the police. When his clothing, including a pair of plaid boxers, a blue polo shirt, brown ankle-high boots, and a second black sock, were delivered to him, Drimmer refused to put them on. "He was a pretty strange guy," said a former college acquaintance. "Crazy. He would do weird things, like eat scraps of food people had left around for a couple of hours." Following his arrest, Mr. Drimmer was carted off to Bellevue Hospital. "I have no knowledge of why any of this has happened," said his father from his home in Chicago.

Adapted from The New York Post, *October 12, 2007*

III.

Objects, while appearing solid, are 99.9999 percent empty space. Chaos directs us to a higher order. Past and future do not exist. Dimensions are multiple and time can be traveled. These are the teachings of physics.

Think, child!
Be a spire of light! Go unwashed, speak in tongues.
Idiota! Saloi! Yuradivye!
Look both ways!
Spin.

WATANYA CICILIA

Will you help me pin my frock? The world turns round in a day.

—NOAH WEBSTER, *The Elementary Spelling Book*—
being an improvement on *The American Spelling Book, 1857*

Darke County Infirmary
Greenville, Ohio
August 13, 1870

Phoebe Ann Moses left off sewing cuffs and collars of oil-boiled turkey-red cloth on orphans' jackets and waited in the doorway of the infirmary's parlor. The people who had summoned her, two men and a woman, stood starkly framed inside a square of window light with its short view of a bowed, planked road and longer view of the heat-scorched woodland beyond. They had worked out the details of her fate like a simple sum, and wore somber, drab clothes like leafless trees, dark elms, even in late summer, the tired air outside whirring with the metallic din of cicadas. She had been brought to this poor county farm two weeks before, and today, her tenth birthday, the Edingtons had found someone to take her. Moses-Poses, a worm-riddled crab apple none wanted, passed from hand to hand, the hand about to take her now leading up a plough-muscled arm to a scrawny rooster's neck and face both flat and dipped-in as a pie pan. The man turned his straw hat around and around in his grimed fingers, a nervy, delicate rotation . . . housework she heard him say, farm chores light enough so the girl will have time for her schooling, for the hunting and trapping of small game.

In homes left fatherless and destitute, it was not unusual for children like Phoebe Ann Moses and her baby sister, Hulda, to be given away. Either that or "thee will starve, Annie," her mother's hands settled with resigned weight on her daughter's shoulders. In too-big shoes cut from a calf's tanned hide, stitched with that same calf's dried sinew, she set the filthy pine planks of the parlor floor creaking as she crossed the room for his inspection, a close, scuffing sound set against the disquieting mass of sharp-singing cicadas. She kept her eyes down as the Edingtons offered a relieved farewell (like her mother, one less mouth), and down even more as she followed the man's high, cavalry-like boots, clods of dirt, like an uneven sowing of black seed, dropping away from the worn heels, out into the afternoon's alkaline glare, smelling of gravel dust, souring vegetation, and the pinched vinegar- sweetness of ripe crab apples. The talk was all of cicadas, silver-winged, glistening, the brown-liquor stench of their bodies littering the orchard, legions and legions of them, a Biblical swarm blighting the land, their spirited shrilling in the hottest parts of the day, and of the English-imported sparrows, the crow-blackbirds, vireos and robins, all natural enemies who devoured them.

He urged but did not help her into the buckboard, and not onto the seat beside him, but like a pig hauled for doom, into the straw-littered splintering bed of the wagon. In the man's coiled-tight tones she caught the first chill, like a snap of ice from tree limbs, but worse than ice, for his nature would never warm or thaw toward her. He drove his pair of horses, bloat-bellied, splay-footed bays, away from the red brick infirmary, the kindly Edingtons encoupled and shrinking inside their front doorway, waving as if she were off through bursting cornfields and heavy-laden orchards to something fine, not moving impossibly further from her soft-spoken Quaker mother, from the cool, green, and game-filled woods she loved to roam, hunt, lose herself in. The farmer offered neither word nor water even as he drank, his whiskered throat pulsing in an ugly way when he turned to look back at her.

He unharnessed his sorry team, not helping her step down from the wagon with her little bundle, a secondhand linsey dress, a copy and spelling book, treasures she had found, unused, in the infirmary's "classroom," more a spare place for storage of unwanted chairs, desks, and books unopened than for any instruction. Inside the tenebrous, stifling gloom of his house, he put one hand like an order against her back, drove her toward an unsmiling woman with a lean, long face, in whose pin-elbowed arms was cupped a baby, its pruny face bewildered, its mewling a fretful warning.

What name?

She'll go by Annie.

The drained, ignorant smell of that house, the way sunlight snuck in through the windows, defeated by the time it hung, milky and bleak, over the coarseness inside, never left her. In future years, if asked, she would refer to the man and woman who had enslaved her only as "he-wolf," and "she-wolf." She almost never spoke of that time, though she would be admired for her quiet, constant charity to orphans, much of her fortune given away for their care and for the proper schooling of young, indigent girls.

> *Savage nations inhabit huts and wigwams. The troops march*
> *to the sound of the drum. The sun illuminates our world.*
> —NOAH WEBSTER, *The Elementary Spelling Book*, 1857

Rosebud Creek, Montana
The Moon of Making Fat
June, 1876

Jumping Bull, the young Assiniboin he had adopted as a brother, took up a sharpened awl of buffalo bone. Starting from the wrist, he methodically cut one hundred pieces of flesh from both of Tatanka Yotanka's thick arms all the way up to his powerful shoulders. *A blood blanket for our people.* His older brother's hands were stained dark red with dry buffalo blood; thick blue lines representing the sky striped his shoulders. Chokecherry sticks pierced his bare chest above each nipple, tethering him with rawhide thongs to the tall cottonwood at the center of the

Sundance arbor, the tree glittering silver in the dry, tossing wind, the veins of each heart-shaped leaf in the perfect image of an *inipi* lodge. With other Hunkpapa Sioux warriors, Tatanka Yotanka fasted, pierced, and danced four days beneath the sun in a sacred place near Rosebud Creek named Deer Medicine Rock. Piping on an eagle bone whistle strung on a leather cord around his neck, his breath caught inside the bone of the eagle, highest-flying bird, higher flying than the meadowlark, the chickadee, the sparrow, higher even than the red-tailed hawk, messenger between earth and Wakan Tanka. He piped, his breath emerging differently than it had gone in. Spirit.

On the third morning, Totanka Yotanka left his body. In the vision that came to him, many soldiers and horses fell, upside down, boots and hooves pointed toward the sky, heads to the earth. The bluecoats' hats fell off. They had no ears. Numerous as grasshoppers, dead, they kept falling.

Days later, Major General George Armstrong Custer, with his half-Sioux, half-Ree scout, Bloody Knife—who would be killed on June 26 at the Little Bighorn, his severed head carried back to the Sioux camps and mounted on a stick—rode alongside Rosebud Creek ahead of the Seventh Cavalry, passing through thickets of wild rose, plum, and crab apple trees in scented bloom, spring grass thick and green. They came upon the circular arbor of a Sundance, read the Sioux prophecy of their defeat, Tatanka Yotanka's vision, painted on Deer Medicine Rock, then found the same drawing in one of the sweat lodges. Further on, they found a freshly deserted Sioux camp, and inside a sweat lodge, a row of three red-painted rocks. Spirit warning. Bloody Knife read these signs for Custer and then found another—a stick pointing from a buffalo skull to a cow skull—the victory of all Indians over white men. Oblivious, vain, blindly confident in his luck, Custer pressed on.

Sgt. Flynn

Ten thousand braves are riding, Sergeant Flynn,
In the Black Hills they are riding, Sergeant Flynn,

Crazy Horse and Sitting Bull,
They will get their bellies full
Of lead and steel from men of Garryowen.

All the men are dead or scattered, Sergeant Flynn,
They are bruised and scalped and battered, Sergeant Flynn,
I'll make up your bed tomorrow, and stand o'er your grave in sorrow,
As they play again the taps for Garryowen.

—from *Seventh Calvary Song of unknown origin*
written after the Battle of the Little Bighorn

Respected for his courage in battle, Tatanka Yotanka prepared for war as if for the honor of death. With his flesh offerings and piercings newly packed with powdered goldenseal, he put on a smoke-tanned buckskin shirt sewn over with green-dyed porcupine quills; from its shoulders and arms, like black corn silk, hung long tassels of human hair. He wore a red breechcloth, deerskin leggings, beaded moccasins and in his braided hair, greased with bear fat and wrapped in otter skins, two eagle feathers.

That June, massive camps of Lakota, Hunkpapa, Oglala, Sans Arc, Minniconjou, Two Kettle, Northern Cheyenne, a few Brulé and Blackfeet stretched for miles among the shallow-rooted cottonwoods bordering the Yellowstone and Little Bighorn rivers.

Wolves howl in the woods at night. The devil is the
great adversary of man. The latch holds shut the door.
—NOAH WEBSTER, *The Elementary Spelling Book, 1857*

Darke County, Ohio
January, 1872

She lay unmoving in a hard, blue cleft of snow. Better to sleep here than to crawl back into that cauldron of fists, peeled switches, shrill labors. Better to lie upon an eiderdown of dogwood blossom, seek refuge in the woods, wear a swift-fashioned wreath of sweet wild roses on her long, loosened hair, find where the rabbit hid in the hedgerow, the grouse in gully and ravine, the quail in stubbled golden field, better to raise its weight to her shoulder and aim true her father's old cap and ball rifle, sighting down its gray-blue, polished barrel, the river-grained oak stock cool and flat against her cheek, taking in the smell of burnt gunpowder, better to hear her mother's quiet gratitude—"thee done well, Annie," unwrapping from long, gray-green strands of damp swamp grass the ruffed grouse, the bobwhite, better to lie back, hands beneath her head, tuning her mother's favorite hymn . . . *'Tis the gift to be simple, 'tis the gift to be free, 'tis the gift to come down where we ought to be, and when we find ourselves in the place just right, 'twill be in the valley of love and delight* . . . hidden safe beneath the dappled green and blue-white quilting of sky, hickory and oak, walnut and ash, better to lie hidden in a pool of wild iris, each flower blue as fairies' wings rising high out of its pale green chalice of blades, its petals guarding a bright wink of yellow, better to die, enter a Heaven poorly described than linger here, enslaved.

Stumbling over the girl, small as a stick of kindling dropped in the snow, he carried his fevered waste of investment up the attic stairs to put her down on a burlap mattress of dry corn stalks, tossed over her a cover of pieced, patched burlap. He ordered his wife to bring her neither food nor drink, she could crawl downstairs when she got hungry enough to finish tasks doubled from such rebellious absence. His wife told him she had pushed the slow, idle girl out into the night and bolted the door, reward for falling asleep while darning a yarn stocking, her fingers grown quiet and therefore insolent.

For Annie, now eleven, there would be half a year more of being made to rise at 3:00 AM, perform a hundred repetitive labors made novel by slaps, pinches and switchings, the welts on her scrawny white back a sketch of scars and fresh wounds, greenish-red weals, sore enough so she could neither sit in a chair nor lie down on her back at night. Forced to eat scraps and parings, made to drink what had spoiled, she fell under the blunt scythe of sleep each night, waking in darkness to a more fearful existence than the day before.

Cunning, they sent false, cheerful letters on a regular basis to her mother— Phoebe Ann, "Annie," was healthy, strong, and doing well in school. When her stepfather fell ill, they wrote saying Annie preferred not to come home just yet. When he died, they wrote that she begged to be excused from his funeral so she would not miss precious days of school.

Then came a Saturday in summer when they left in the wagon, trusting her alone. Dropping the long-stemmed, iron house key into a rusted blue tin cup on a ledge above the spring house, an act done more from pride than for their convenience, packing up the same bundle she had arrived with two years earlier, the linsey dress, the red Webster's *Spelling* and the blue copy book in which she had written with a lead pencil every letter of the alphabet, large and small, practicing her signature over and over, *Phoebe Ann Moses*, she walked then ran to the railway and, begging a fare, caught a train toward home. Unable to read, she had penciled over and over the copy book's sayings: *By Its Fruit the Tree is Known, Afflictions Are Often Blessings in Disguise, Disarm Enmity by Acts of Kindness, Elevate Your Affections Above this Earth.* Sometimes she copied the poems, wondering at their meaning, laboring out a neat progression of letters and spacings each night before hiding both little books away, always in a different place. When she had filled up the ruled pages of the copy book, she went back, tracing over and over again, her original efforts. For two years, these books, filled with black shapes vining like sumac and honeysuckle along the paper march of railed fence, were her only treasures. Their meanings remained foreign, obscure, but each letter that she learned to shape and link to the next was a holy, living creature, a sign of curving, black hope.

White is not so properly a color as a want of all color.
An exile is one who has been banished from his country.
It is almost impossible to civilize the American Indian.

—NOAH WEBSTER, *The Elementary Spelling Book, 1857*

After Custer's defeat, after the reported scalpings, mutilations, and deaths of all 265 men in his Seventh Cavalry, an Indian victory that would call down revenge, blood, and suffering on the Cheyenne and the Sioux, Tantanka Yotanka took three thousand of his people north, seeking refuge in the Great Mother's (Queen Victoria's) land. On the bleak, scoured plains of Saskatchewan they lived first on nothing, then on less than nothing. There was no meat, no hides for their *inipis* or for clothing. The government gave them no aid, no rations, no supplies. In Parliament, they were a joke.

> SIR JOHN MCDONALD: *I do not see how a*
> *Sitting Bull can cross the frontier.*
> MR. MCKENZIE: *Not unless he rises.*
> SIR JOHN: *Then he is not a Sitting Bull.*

—*House of Commons Debates*
Session 1878, Canada

So they starved, died of disease, their horses froze. Little by little his followers, even Crow King, even Gall, another adopted son, reluctantly left, heading south for the prison of the White Father's reservation, hoping to save what was left of their families. In July 1881, less than five years after the battle of the Little Bighorn, Tatanka Yotanka, wearing a torn calico shirt and ragged leggings, wrapped in a filthy Pendleton, crossed the Canadian border into the Great Father's land with the remaining 186 of his followers. He made his six-year-old son surrender his only weapon, a Winchester rifle, saying "let it be known that I was the last Sioux to give up his rifle." Imprisoned at Fort Randall, he was now a lurid sensation. Killer of Custer. Bloodthirsty

Savage. Murderous Devil. Newspapermen flocked to interview him. Chiefs and subchiefs traveled to seek his advice; for many, he was their last hope. Two years later, he was transferred to the Standing Rock reservation where he lived on an allotted parcel of acreage with his two wives, Stands With Her Nation and Four Robes, and eleven children in a small cabin near the Grand River. To Standing Rock agent James McLaughlin, he was a permanent threat to the government's beneficent plan for the Indian's adaptation to Christianity, to Western education, to the hoe and the plough, to the farming of barren, worthless, apportioned land no one wanted.

> *My heart is red and sweet, and I know it is sweet because whatever passes near me puts out its tongue to me; and yet you men have come here to talk with us, and you say you do not know who I am. I want to tell you that if the Great Spirit has chosen anyone to be the chief of this country, it is myself.*
>
> —*Sitting Bull*
> *U.S. Congress. 48th. First Session. Senate Report 283*
> *From Dawes Commission Report, 1883, Standing Rock*

In 1885, on the order of Henry Teller, Secretary of the Interior, Sitting Bull, America's most notorious political prisoner, was sent with a small party of Sioux on a tour of fifteen American cities. It was intended that he see and be subdued by the vast accomplishments of the white man, though he had only agreed to go because he had been promised a meeting with "the new White Father in Washington," Grover Cleveland. Instead, the Sioux were put on exhibit at the Minnesota Agricultural Fair and in New York City. After visiting the waxworks and novelties museum, Eden Musee, on West Twenty-third Street, Sitting Bull and his warriors were modeled into life-sized wax figures eternally posed alongside history's most notorious presidents, kings, and criminals.

Der Deutcher's Dog

Oh where, oh where has my little dog gone,
Oh where, oh where can he be?
With his ears cut short and his tail cut long,
Oh where, oh where can he be?

Listen to the Mockingbird

Listen to the mockingbird, listen to the mockingbird,
The mockingbird's still singing o'er her grave;
Listen to the mockingbird, listen to the mockingbird,
Still singing where the weeping willows wave.

Ten Little Indians

One little two little three little Indians
Four little five little six little Indians
Seven little eight little nine little Indians
Ten little Indian boys!

Ten little nine little eight little Indians
Seven little six little five little Indians
Four little three little two little Indians
One little Indian boy!

Olympic Theater
Saint Paul, Minnesota
March 19, 1884

Sitting Bull, guest of the United States government, sat in Box B to watch the Arlington and Fields Combination, "the greatest aggregation of talent" ever to appear in Saint Paul. The "red-skinned fiend" who had murdered Custer eight years before had spent the day touring sights selected by city officials—sampling a cigar made especially for him at Charles Fetsch's cigar factory, visiting Mr. Oppenheim's millinery house where forty white women decorated him with garlands of ribbon and artificial flowers, walking through the offices of the Pioneer Press where he was invited to eavesdrop on a telephone conversation, and viewing two elementary schools, in the first of which he listened to children recite lessons and observed them do calisthenics, while in the second, Franklin School, the principal rang the electric fire alarm to demonstrate how the large brick building could be evacuated of teachers and children alike in one minute and forty-five seconds. Everywhere in Saint Paul that day, citizens lined the streets to watch Chief Sitting Bull pass by, flanked by his nephew One Bull and Standing Rock's Indian agent, Major James McLaughlin, followed by an inflated entourage of city dignitaries. Some hissed and openly jeered at "Custer's killer," an unimpressive-looking man with long, greasy, otter skin–wrapped braids, barrel-chested and stout, wearing a calico shirt, brocade waistcoat, blue trousers bordered with gold braiding and patterned with brass buttons and on his strangely small, tapered feet, beaded moccasins with india-rubber soles. Tonight, he sat in Box B, a Fetsch's cigar in his pocket, a limp paper garland of bluebells and white trillium around his neck, looking impassively down at the gas-lit stage, not applauding after the Wertz Brothers' acrobatics, listening politely to Miss Allie Jackson's medley of Septimus Winner songs, "Der Deutcher's Dog," "Listen to the Mockingbird," and "Ten Little Indians," followed by Flynn and Sarsfield's burnt-cork minstrel show, which failed to amuse him. He stifled yawns and shifted restlessly until a young woman named Annie Oakley, chestnut hair spilling in curls halfway down her back, bounded lightly from behind the red velvet curtains wearing an embroidered jacket, buckskin skirt, and fringed leggings, and with a .22-caliber Marlin rifle proceeded to extinguish a burning candle, then knock corks from bottles and ashes off a cigarette dangling from a man's mouth, apples from the heads of twin white poodles named Jack and George, halve coins tossed into the air, and split a playing card edge-on, putting five or six more holes in it before it plummeted to the stage. Bored silly through Arlington and Fields' "aggregation of talent," Sitting Bull stared at the trick shooter, sat bolt upright on the edge of his seat, then rose to his feet shouting *Watanya Cicilia*, *Watanya Cicilia*, "Little Sure Shot," as the girl took her bows then sprinted offstage amid a swell of shouts and sustained applause. This tiny, fearless young woman named Annie Oakley had a perfect aim and a pure heart; she was blessed by *Tunkashila*, Grandfather Spirit. He sent a message asking to meet her. When she replied saying she was too busy, Sitting Bull sent sixty-five dollars to her hotel room along with a request for her photograph. Returning his money along with her photograph, she added a message saying she would be pleased to meet him the next morning. Two weeks later, an advertisement appeared in the *New York Clipper*: "The Premier Shots, Butler and Oakley, Captured by Sitting Bull." Included in the ad was news that Sitting Bull had presented twenty-four-year-old sharpshooter Annie Oakley with a large eagle feather from the head of a Crow chief, the original pair of moccasins he'd worn at the Battle of the Little Bighorn, and a publicity photograph of himself. The article did not disclose that Annie Oakley had agreed to be Sitting Bull's adopted daughter, or that his own daughter, who had died soon after the Little Bighorn battle, had made the exquisitely beaded moccasins.

After the trip to Saint Paul, Agent McLaughlin returned Sitting Bull and the other Sioux men to the Standing Rock reservation. His fifteen-city tour had ended, and the promise to meet the "Great Father" in Washington, like all *wasi'chu* promises, had never been kept. Annie Oakley and her husband traveled on to Ohio to begin their season's tour with the Sells Brothers circus. Frank Butler and Annie Oakley, "champion shots," were a minor subheadline in circus advertisements boasting "the greatest array of arenic talent," "a whole world of wonders, greater than the greatest, larger than the largest, better than the best," with over fifty cages of live, wild animals, ". . . embracing every known type of beast, bird, reptile and deep-sea monster." The circus boasted hippopotami, rhinoceri, an aquarium of "amphibious monsters," and the smallest star of the circus, Chemah, the Chinese dwarf, "the smallest adult body that contains a soul," and the largest, Emperor, a gigantic elephant who led ten teams of smaller elephants drawing ten gold chariots. In addition to her sharpshooting act, Annie played Mrs. Old One-Two to her husband Frank's role as Quaker Starchback in a comic pantomime, as the circus train took them to 187 cities in thirteen states until November, when the season ended.

In April 1885, Annie, who had taken the name Oakley from an Ohio town, showed up at Cincinnati's "premiere gun club." Before auditioning for Buffalo Bill Cody's Wild West Show in Louisville, she intended to break Doc Carver's and old Captain Bogardus's records—each had hit five thousand glass balls in a single day. Loading three sixteen-gauge Parker shotguns herself, standing fifteen yards from the traps, she shattered 4,772 balls in nine hours, a record she hardly spoke about afterwards.

At the Wild West Show's temporary encampment at the Louisville Baseball Park on Walnut Street, Annie Oakley was hired on the spot, given a ten-minute solo act she would keep for the next seventeen years. Introducing her as "Missie," a name that would stick, Buffalo Bill Cody gallantly escorted her down a colorful gauntlet of Wild West performers, Pawnee and Sioux Indians, Mexican *vaqueros*, cowboys with names like Bronco Bill, Bridle Bill, Coyote Bill, and the Cowboy Kid, stable hands, cooks, managers, and crew of all kinds, each one shaking her hand, welcoming her.

Ladies and gentlemen: The Honorable William F. Cody and Nathan Salsbury present the feature attraction, unique and unparalleled, the foremost woman marksman in the world, in an exhibition of skill with the rifle, shotgun, and pistol—the little girl of the Western plains—Miss Annie Oakley!

*—*FRANK RICHMOND, *from the grandstand*

Buffalo Bill's Wild West Show
Buffalo, New York
June 12, 1885

His ordeal over, Sitting Bull watched little *Watanya Cicilia* run down the grandstand gangway into the arena, blowing kisses, waving, bowing in all directions. She wore a tan sombrero with a six-pointed star on its rolled brim, a loose brown embroidered shirt with a starched white collar, a brown pleated skirt with blue ribbon trim, leggings with pearl buttons, low-heeled black shoes. She ran, light as a deer, into the center of the arena, to a small table covered with a silk cloth, piled high with twelve-gauge, double-barreled Lancaster, Francotte, Scott and Parker shotguns, and .22-caliber Marlin rifles. Yards away, her husband, acting as her assistant, began loading traps, releasing the hardfired clay pigeons, singly, doubly, triply, then four at a time. She shattered them faultlessly and fast, never missing, without a second's hesitation. Ambidextrous, she fired a gold-plated, pearl-handled Smith and Wesson .44-caliber pistol with her left then right hand, shattered glass balls filled with red, white, and blue feathers, threw glass balls high in the air herself, took aim, shattering two and three at once. Leaning backward across a chair, she fired at targets upside down, never missing, then moved on to the buck knife trick—turning her back to the target, sighting it in the gleam of the buck knife's blade, taking dead aim. She set a gun down in the dirt, ten feet from the table, ran to the other side, signaled her assistant to release a clay bird, ran, jumped high over the table, picked the gun up from the dirt, aimed, and broke the bird to pieces before it hit the ground. He watched her end the performance with her most difficult trick, a trick lasting only ten seconds using one rifle, five shotguns, and eleven glass balls. First tossing her long hair over one shoulder, she laid the five shotguns neatly on the small table, picked up the first and held it upside down. Her assistant threw the first of eleven glass balls into the air, she shot it holding her rifle upside down, dropped the rifle, picked up the first of five shotguns, broke two more balls in a second, exchanging shotguns five times until all eleven glass orbs were shattered, in less than ten seconds. Leaving the fifth shotgun still smoking on the table beside the others, she sprinted across the arena, and with a final wave to her thousands of fans and a fey upward kick of one heel, vanished behind the white canvas curtain.

"I feel now and then," Annie Oakley once said in an interview, "as if I could not miss."

Sitting Bull is one of the finest looking
Indians who ever committed murder.
—The Detroit Evening Journal

Americans thrilled to the outrage of the ferocious Hunkpapa Sioux chief butchering, then taking the scalp of General Custer at the Little Bighorn River, a place better known to the Sioux and Cheyenne as Greasy Grass Creek. Americans, especially Easterners, liked being terrified of Indians—red fiends, wily devils, bloodthirsty redskins, heathen savages who did unspeakable, un-Christian things.

At his first appearance in the Wild West Show on June 12, in Buffalo, New York, Sitting Bull was announced as the war chief of the Fighting Sioux. Wearing a headdress of forty large eagle feathers, a beaded buckskin tunic, medicine bag at his side, a crucifix around his neck, and holding a bow-and-arrow sack as well as a long peace pipe trimmed in ribbons, he was jolted around and around the dusty arena in a open buggy by the Wild West's business manager, Major John Burke. The "murderer of Custer" was hooted at, jeered, and heckled by a crowd of nearly ten thousand people, and for this he was to be paid a $125 bonus and $50 a week for the next four months, the duration of the season. In his contract, he had asked for "sole right to sell his own photographs and autographs."

Back at Standing Rock, when he was first invited to join Buffalo Bill's Wild West Show, he had refused. But when he was told *Watanya Cicilia* would be in the show and that he could see her every day, he agreed to come, bringing along, kept safe in a tin box, the signed photograph she had given him in Saint Paul. Eight

Sioux warriors from the Little Bighorn battle came on the Wild West tour with him; most of the money he made, he gave away to the crowds of urchin boys who followed him around the back lots. Downcast during much of his time with the Wild West Show, he would come and sit with his daughter in her tent, where she might read aloud from her favorite book, the New Testament. Her firm, sweet voice soothed him, and he would listen, smoking the pipe he had made back at his cabin near Grand River. As they toured Detroit, Saginaw, Grand Rapids, Boston, Canada, he told her stories about his childhood, the truth about how his people were treated by whites both in war and on the reservations; she listened, believed him, and one day instructed him in how to legibly sign his name. Often they sat quietly, Annie crocheting or sewing fringe on one of her costumes, Sitting Bull calmed by this daughter whose heart was so good that even other Indians traveling with the Wild West Show sought out her company, for advice, the comfort of her kindness. They were always welcome, she told them. One afternoon, during a violent downpour, when Sitting Bull's legs were particularly paining him—he had a bad limp from an old battle wound—she knelt on the carpet inside her kerosene-lit tent, rubbing his feet and calves with alcohol and liniment. They talked of God, more often of the woods and prairies—they had more in common than anyone guessed, and Frank, in his turn, tried to learn a little of the Sioux language. When he asked about the scars down each of the old man's arms, Sitting Bull only said that he had made a red blanket to cover his people.

A Sedentary Taurus: "as mild-mannered a man as ever cut a throat or scalped a helpless woman."
—The Evening Leader, *Grand Rapids, 1885*

They are faces of thoughtful men that are worn by these Indian chieftains. Their leader, Sitting Bull, has especially strong lines in his countenance, which is something of a reminder of the features of Daniel Webster.
—Detroit Evening Journal, *1885*

She watched his "grand" entry into the arena, seated upright in full headdress and ceremonial buckskin, his face stolid, expressionless. He sat in the buggy driven by Manager James Burke, looking straight ahead like a condemned man as the crowd of over ten thousand, silent at first, began booing and jeering. In a few minutes she would trip out into the arena, waving, tipping her hat with its six-pointed star, perform her series of dazzling sharpshooting tricks, hitting stone hard, Ligowsky red clay pigeons, glass balls filled with colored feathers, shooting backward, sometimes, though not today, at a full gallop on her paint pony, then bowing prettily and skipping out with a little kick of her heel—the star female sharpshooter in Buffalo Bill's Wild West Show, "The Rifle Queen," "The Peerless Lady Wing-Shot," "The Western Girl," and "Little Sure Shot." Well fed, well paid, a star.

And here was an old man with smallpox scars and battle scars, being heckled and spat at. Crowds of those same people would seek him out afterwards, stare at him, the bolder ones asking for his autograph, his photo, reaching out to touch him as if he were the bogeyman and they were acting on a dare. This was a world far from the gentle teachings of her Quaker mother, farther still from the green sanctuary of the Ohio woods she'd grown up in, hunting small game, ruffed grouse and rabbit, shot clean through the head so the shot wouldn't ruin the meat—the way her father had shown her—feeding her family, paying off her mother's small mortgage. This world was bluster, money, noise, greed, and profit. Frank protected her from most of its roughness, but she saw the toll it took on Sitting Bull, earning money from lies, money he could not seem to ever hold on to but gave away to every hungry child he saw. What was left, he sent home to his family. "The white man knows how to make everything," he said to her once, "but he does not know how to distribute it."

The wigwam is a better place for the red man. He is sick of the houses, and the noises, and the multitudes of men. Sitting Bull longs for his wives and his children. When he goes out the white men gather around him. They stare at him. They point fingers at

him. He likes to be alone among his people. Traveling is interest-
ing and it pleases Sitting Bull, but the forest is better and his fam-
ily pleases him more.

—St. Louis Sunday Sayings, 1885

Dressed in the same clothing he had arrived in—worn striped
pants and a calico shirt, not the chief's war bonnet and traditional
Sioux dress they had paraded him around in—Sitting Bull stopped
for a last visit in *Watanya Cicilia*'s tent, sat watching her embroi-
der. He gave her his council stick, his *chanupa*—sacred pipe—his
bow and sack of arrows, all to the daughter who had taught him
how to spell his name, how to write his name, touch pen to paper,
who had been a comfort to him in the white man's world.

He was returned to South Dakota, to the Standing Rock reservation, to his mud plaster and log cabin beside the Grand River, to
acreage he had been "given" but refused to plough. He came home
with a little money in his pocket and two gifts from his other friend,
Buffalo Bill Cody—a large, white sombrero and a white "trick"
horse that was trained, whenever it heard the sound of gunfire, to
sit down on its haunches and wave its front legs in the air.

THE BATTLE OF THE LITTLE BIG HORN

The Awful Reality of Furious Conflict and Massacre in Savage Warfare
Presented with Perfect Historical Accuracy of Detail
Introducing 800 Indian Chiefs, Braves and Warriors, Soldiers,
Scouts and Horses
With Every Accessory of Arms, Accoutrement and Savage Decoration,
Whose Inconceivably Overpowering Apotheosis of Mortal Combat
Is the Illustrious Tableau of
CUSTER'S LAST STAND AND HEROIC FALL

The World Will Never See Its Like Again!
Everything Presented is Realism Itself

—handbill, 1886

Madison Square Garden
New York
Friday, November 29, 1886

My dear Sister,

I had the strangest experience yesterday and thought to write to you about it. The widow of General George Armstrong Custer, along with Harriet Beecher Stowe, General William Tecumseh Sherman, General Philip Sheridan, and other celebrities, attended the opening of our new Wild West Show, a popular extravaganza called "The Drama of Western Civilization." Mrs. Custer so admired my performance along with approving the reenactment of her husband's valiant fight at the Little Bighorn (beginning with that spritely Irish marching song of the Seventh Cavalry, "Garryowen") that she invited me to sit with her in her box after my performance, where she rather imperiously invited me to her apartment for tea the next afternoon. I did not dare turn down her invitation and so proceeded to spend two of the strangest hours of my life.

Mrs. Custer, "Libby," lives in a Greenwich Village flat near Washington Square, and some ten years after her husband's death at the Little Bighorn, refuses to wear anything but black. She insists she will never remove her widow's mourning nor ever remarry. Like me, she has no children. Like me, she is as devoted to "Autie," her husband, as I am to Frank, with the exception that her husband is stone dead and her devotion akin to a nervous disorder—truly, it seems as if she is obstinately fixed on keeping him "alive" by a constant regilding of his questionable reputation. She has published one book, *"Boots and Saddles," or Life in Dakota with General Custer*, and is nearly finished with another, *Tenting on the Plains*, a book concerning her experiences as an army officer's wife. Much as I nearly envy her literary accomplishment—as you know, without Frank's tutoring, I would be dumb as a stick—I fear she overstrives in her writings to exonerate her dead husband from all blame in the loss of the Seventh Cavalry at the Little Bighorn, a battle I have heard described quite differently by Chief Sitting Bull.

As for Mrs. Custer herself, she is reserved but direct, with deep blue, haunted-looking eyes and brown hair spun into a thin lasso at the back of her head. Over tea, she told me she had grown up as Elizabeth Bacon, the daughter of a judge, only one hundred miles from our own Darke County, and that "Autie" too was born and raised in Ohio. She related a number of poignant tales about her life on the plains with her adored "Autie," how at night they read aloud to one another from favored books like *The Life of Daniel Webster* or *Campaigns of Napoleon*. She claims he always took care of the Indian people he met on the reservations, concerned for their illnesses and deprivations. And like a Pied Piper, he attracted pets wild and tame—hunting dogs, badgers, raccoons, a porcupine, a prairie dog, once a broken-winged turkey. Even antelope, normally elusive creatures, sought him out, a thing which astonished the Indians who witnessed antelope rubbing their heads on him and trotting after him. There was a field mouse at Fort Lincoln that took up residence in her husband's empty inkwell and loved to scamper up his shoulders and hide itself in his thick gold curls—she couldn't stand the mouse, so to please her, he set it free one morning, put it outside their home, only to find it, that evening, curled up in its usual spot in the inkwell. He had a magnetism towards animals, a way with them, and was impatient to the point of recklessness with any person or thing interfering with his own heroic interpretation of himself (my own thoughts here . . .)

I can hardly explain how strange it was to spend an afternoon with the woman so famously widowed by my friend and adopted "father," Sitting Bull, whose own people's victory that day came at the cost of her husband's terrible defeat. After her tender descriptions of General Custer, her personal recollections, I find the harsh portrait painted by his critics softening or at least becoming more doubtful in its accuracy. The same thing happened when I befriended Sitting Bull and other Indians in our Wild West Show—this fear of Indians as savage, bloodthirsty fiends is largely a fiction. It is more often they who have been, as a race, abused and sorely mistreated.

I got on with Mrs. Custer as I am able to do with most people, but when she ventured several disparaging and frankly ignorant remarks regarding Sitting Bull, I spoke my dissent, and from then a cooler tone arose between us which I am afraid never recovered its former warmth. Dearest sister, I am discovering that it is truly a mistake—it may even be a moral wrong, in fact—to judge. Truth is too complex, too contradictory, too mercurial, to be one-sided, though it is human nature to prefer the reassurance and ease of firm judgment. Judgment helps us to justify our less savory actions.

At any rate, for two hours or more, Mrs. Custer sighed like a moonstruck girl over her "Autie," at one point pulling a bit of his hair from a gold locket around her neck, a vital springing reddish-gold curl, even kissing it as she told me how she rode with him everywhere, even camping in a tent near him during his Civil War campaigns, dressed in a military uniform she designed for herself. No army wife ever proved as devoted (or obsessed!) as she. I hope I do not bore you to tears with this overlong account of my tea with Mrs. Custer, but in closing, there were two especially odd things she revealed during our conversation (a mostly one-sided affair—beyond a few cursory questions about my sharp-shooting abilities, she had very little interest in me, so I answered her questions as I do everyone's, saying that my favorite guns are the Parker, the Francotte, the Lancaster, and the Scott, all twelve bore—). She confided that General Custer had been convinced he had lived other lifetimes as a soldier, as he seemed to know it all so well beforehand, and that she herself absolutely believed in the healing properties of horse dung—something she had learned from the Santee wife of a trader she had met out at Fort Abraham. No one in New York City would believe her, she said, but she had seen for herself proof of its curative properties. Well, I have lived among horses and cattle for years now, the smell of horseflesh and manure always in my nostrils, even on my skin, but I cannot say I have ever known of that animal's dung to remedy or improve a thing.

Your loving sister,
Annie

*"Staten Island Trembles Beneath the Tread of Painted Warriors
on the War-Path"*
*"Just Like Real Fighting, Indians Fall From Horses, and Look
Like Dead Men!"*
— New York Herald *headlines, 1886*

Over the whole earth they are coming,
The buffalo are coming. . . .
The buffalo are coming.
— Ghost Dance song

On January 1, the Moon of Strong Cold, 1889, part of the state of Nevada fell under the darkness of a solar eclipse, and a Paiute there named Wovoka had a vision. In the spring, he said, Jesus Christ would return to the earth along with all Indians killed by whites. Great herds of buffalo and wild horses would return. All dead ancestors would return to live upon the earth again. The sacred ways of life would return, and all white people would be buried under new soil upon which fresh sweet grass would grow. Wovoka the messiah talked of this and taught a Ghost Dance, and instructed the people to make and to wear special Ghost Dance shirts through which the bullets of white men could not pass.

This Ghost Dance spread eastward from Nevada like sparks from a prairie fire, and by October, in the Drying Grass Moon, Sitting Bull was listening to a Minniconjou named Kicking Bear and to his own brother-in-law, Short Bull, tell of their pilgrimage to see this new messiah, of this new religion of the Ghost Dance, which brought hope to Indians imprisoned on reservations, starving and dying of measles, whooping cough, smallpox. At Rosebud and Pine Ridge and other Sioux reservations, the people, mostly the women and the old, danced until they fainted, the women dancing so that their dead husbands, their warriors, might come home to them. Sitting Bull doubted the vision, the idea of the dead returning to life, he worried about retaliation from soldiers, but he agreed to let Kicking Bear teach the people at Standing Rock this Ghost Dance. If they wore Ghost Dance shirts with painted-on symbols of turtle, magpie, crow, eagle, stars, and sun, Kicking Bear said, they could not be harmed by soldiers' bullets.

By November, in the Moon of Falling Leaves, the Ghost Dance had swept through Standing Rock. No children came to the schoolrooms, trade shops lay empty, no one farmed or harvested. In their white painted buckskin shirts and dresses, men, women, and children danced in the falling snow from dawn into the night, dancing for the return of their dead and of the buffalo, "Uncle" and all of his wealth, horn, hide, fat, meat, their way of life based on his.

The military blamed Sitting Bull for what they feared was a new and dangerous Indian uprising. His arrest was quietly ordered, but to avoid outright rebellion, General Nelson "Bear Coat" Miles asked Buffalo Bill Cody to come to Standing Rock and quietly persuade Sitting Bull to go with them, after which he could be arrested without incident. Unaware of the plan to imprison his old friend, Buffalo Bill rode his horse onto reservation land, his saddle bags stuffed with the candy Sitting Bull had come to enjoy during his time with the Wild West. Distrustful of Cody's ability to peacefully lead Sitting Bull to his arrest, Standing Rock's Indian agent, James McLaughlin, ordered Cody off the reservation.

At dawn on December 15, in the Moon of Popping Trees, forty-three Indian policemen surrounded Sitting Bull's wooden cabin on the Grand River. When they entered, they found him asleep on the floor, wrapped in a buffalo robe.

He stood up and came with them, asking only that his white horse, the one given to him by Buffalo Bill, be saddled for him to ride. By then over one hundred Ghost Dancers had shown up to protest the arrest of their leader, and in a moment of confused panic, Sitting Bull was shot down, just as he had forseen. His son, Crow Foot, and his adopted Assiniboin brother, Jumping

Bull, were also murdered. At the first sound of gunfire, the white horse sat down as it had been trained to do and began to wave its front legs. Everyone fell silent, staring at the strange apparition of a Ghost Dancing horse. Some present later claimed to have seen the spirit of Sitting Bull enter the dancing horse from Buffalo Bill's Wild West Show.

Sitting Bull had seen Custer's men, like grasshoppers, falling from the sky, and this also was true: five years before his murder, a meadowlark had alighted beside Sitting Bull and revealed to him "Your own people, the Lakota, will kill you."

> The heathen are those people who worship idols, or who know
> Not the true God.
> All mankind are brethren, descendants of common parents.
> When our friends die, they will never return to us;
> But we must soon follow them.

—NOAH WEBSTER, *The Elementary Spelling Book*, 1857

December 25, 1889
London, England

Merry Christmas, dearest Mother,

Frank and I have gone from living with our Wild West family in an old, draughty castle in Banfelt, Alsace, near Strassburg (with the Indians colorfully camped out in teepees in the castle's "*orangerie*") to staying with friends in London. England, to me, is nearest like home, and Frank and I have many invitations to shooting matches and bird hunting we are delighted to accept while we are here.

When our show toured in Germany—we performed in Magdeburg, Braunschweig, Leipzig, Cologne, Frankfurt, and Berlin—we found the German military to be fanatically obsessed with our logistics. Each day German officers came and took notes on the loading and unloading of our railway cars, the horses and gear, how we broke camp. They showed a particular fascination for our kitchens, food storage, preparation, manner of serving, and general diet. Every rope, bundle, and kit was meticulously inspected, noted, and mapped out.

I do have some fine, hand-embroidered table linens from Strassburg to bring back for you, along with souvenirs I've collected from our travels in Paris, Venice, Rome.

I am sorry to hear you were so distressed by the Buenos Aires newspaper's report of my death. That you cried for two days! At least I have had the rare and doubtful pleasure of reading a number of my obituaries. Apparently I was pretty well-liked and in some ways admired! The Colonel (Bill Cody) was home in North Platte when he heard the news of my death, and this came just after our old friend Sitting Bull was so horribly *murdered* outside his cabin at Standing Rock—I can tell you that had he been a white man, someone would already have been hung for his murder! Frank answered the colonel's frantic telegraph by sending one back saying Missie had just taken her fill of a lovely Christmas dinner and was in perfect health.

Many of the Indians in our show have gone back across the ocean, gloomy and homesick and drawn by rumors of unrest, trouble, and something called the Ghost Dance religion on their reservations. Colonel Cody, always kind to them and considerate to their needs, offered them the chance to go home to their land and their families. They have been traveling foreign lands for over eighteen months. Ten died of influenza in Barcelona and one in Italy of Roman fever. I have spent much time with the Indian people and have a heart for them and for their many troubles. As you know, Sitting Bull adopted me as his daughter. He called me *Watanya Cicilia*, which in the Sioux language means "Little Sure Shot." He was a kindly, very wise old gentleman, much misunderstood and much wronged. How many times when he was on tour with us did he come and sit with me in my tent—I could always manage to lift him out of his low spirits. He would confide in me about the way his people were being cheated on the reservation, their sugar allotment being half sand, their cattle counted twice, their land stolen by a string of false and broken contracts. "How is it," he once said to me, "that white people are so greedy, so stingy? The way the whites treat their own people makes me fear for how they will treat my own." I watched him give all his money away to the newsboys, though he couldn't read, and to the bootblacks, though he himself wore only moccasins. He gave Crackerjack and candy, all his coins, to the urchins who constantly followed him around the back lots of the show. He truly hated to see poverty, to see children go hungry, and did not understand the ways of a people who would not care for their own.

I know you never met this great Sioux chief, Mother, but he was one of the finest gentlemen I have ever known. After he returned to Standing Rock, I wrote to him, but never heard back. Perhaps my letters never reached him or there was no one to read them to him. . . . I cherish those things he gave me before he left us, they are more precious to me than the many medals I have collected, the kings and queens and castles I have known.

> *We elect men to make our laws for us.*
> *The skin of the Indian is of a tawny color.*
> *We are sorry when a good man dies.*
>
> —NOAH WEBSTER, *The Elementary Spelling Book*, 1857

What Annie Oakley did not trouble her mother or even her husband, Frank Butler, about was a dream she woke from on the night of December 15, a dream so vivid it caused her to sit up in bed and feel on her chest an oppression of dread and grief. In the dream, she was taking part in a shooting exhibition during a blinding snowstorm. As the stream of white pigeons was released and flew upwards, she fired and fired, missing every bird but one, which plummeted to the snowy earth at her feet, fresh blood reddening its feathers.

On December 15th, Sitting Bull, shot by Indian police, once in the head, twice in his chest, died on the ground in front of his cabin. His spirit traveled across the ocean to *Watanya Cicilia*, dreaming beside her husband on a featherbed in a London hotel. She told no one. Some things, as he had taught her, are best held sacred until the end.

A blade of grass is a single stalk.

A great part of history is an account
Of men's crimes and wickedness.

—Noah Webster, *The Elementary Spelling Book*, 1857

2276 E. Third Street
Greenville, Ohio
October 4, 1926

Dear Chelsie and Margaret,

I am glad the pictures arrived safely. I still have the "pipe" made and smoked for many years by Sitting Bull, his council stick cut on one end, while he used the other end for stirring his Pipe of Peace, as the "Braves" listened quietly to their "War Chief." If you would rather have the Pipe with the council stick than the big "Bow" which I sent you I think it would be much neater for you to keep than the "Bow." The museum here has had the "Arrow sack" and Arrows that go with it for many years, if you will exchange, I will send you the Pipe and council stick if you will send me the Bow at once and I will turn it over to them. You need not hesitate to exchange, it would be much better on both sides.

Please direct to above address, protect with corrugated paper, tied on flat board, covered with thick paper.

Love to Every one,
Aunt Annie

October 16, 1926
Dear Chelsie,
I am at last sending the pipe. I have been waiting for the big
bow so as to send the pipe in the same box. But as it has not
come yet, I am sending the pipe anyway. I am sending it for
twenty-five dollars and request a return receipt.
No one can say it is not the genuine article. The enclosed clipping
of Sitting Bull shows the pipe and council stick in his hands.
Lovingly,
Your Aunt Annie Oakley

Fancy sometimes helps us out in this big round world.

—ANNIE OAKLEY

Ten days after this last, scrawled letter, Phoebe Ann Moses,
Annie Oakley, *Watanya Cicilia*, Missie, ran backward and barefoot through the bowered archway of childhood in the Ohio
woodlands of beech, shagbark hickory, and hazelnut trees, running over hills studded with black-eyed Susans and gold tick-
seed, wearing an indigo-dyed dress hemmed in burrs and
stick-tights, chasing bumblebees and butterflies, scrambling high
into the dogwood trees, gathering blossoms to weave a queen's
crown with wild pink roses mixed in and all trailing down her
back, wandering among the blue iris, Indian pipe, and wake
robins, the Jacob's ladder, wild violets, and bluebells, the air alive
with the hum of bees, the turtledove's honied call, the drone of
the ruffed grouse and coy, piercing notes of the bobwhite, leaning back to rest a moment against a mossy fallen tree trunk,
breathing in the sweet damp of tall ferns, her father's old cap-
and-ball Kentucky rifle laid across her lap.
Then with a wave and a mischievous kick of her booted heel,
she passed for the last time through the arenas and courts of
kings, receiving the adulation of men, women and children alike,
before going on, in the company of those she most loved, to

"God's Great World," poorly described, but far freer than the lives of kings and queens, great soldiers, warriors, and chiefs.

At six years old, after my father died, I learned to make cornstalk traps in figure 4's, covered by brush and baited with corn for the quail. At seven, because of our family's troubles, I lifted down, without permission, my father's dusty old cap-and-ball rifle, along with its loaded powder horn, from over the hearth. I went out and learned the feeding places of the grouse, the hiding places of the quail. I loved sighting down the barrel, feeling the silky, oiled gun stock fit snug against the curve of my cheek. I was born with a more perfect vision than most, and a perfect trust in the natural, intuitive shot. I never liked shooting still game, always preferring the challenge of moving, flying creatures, of giving them and myself the dignity of chance. This earned me a quicker eye and surer aim. Hunting in cornrows, pastures, and deep in woods, among the walnut, hazelnut, beech, oak and butternut trees, even in winter, I brought home clean-shot rabbit, grouse, quail, pigeons, squirrels, fox, wild turkey, some for my family and most as dressed game to sell over at Frenchie La Motte's place and later at Charlie and G. Anthony Katzenberger's General Store. Being a staunch Quaker, my mother was opposed to the gun and against me, a girl, using it—but she was grateful for the food and the money, and in later years for earnings I mailed home from my fancy shooting exhibitions and from my years with the Wild West Show. I was always glad to give away most of what I had, for I had grown up hungry and without proper schooling, and wanted others to have a good start in this great battle called life. Most of my medals I had melted down, most of my money I gave away to family and to charity. I saw no point in hoarding. Frank and I, with no children of our own, "adopted" more than twenty young girls, putting them through school, giving them a strong start and glad to do so.

> *You are fools to make yourselves slaves to a piece of bacon fat, some hardtack and a little sugar and coffee.*
>
> —TATANKA YOTANKA

In 1891, the state of North Dakota paid a small sum to Sitting Bull's two widows, Seen By Her Nation and Four Robes, and took possession of his log cabin. Disassembling it log by log, the bullet-riddled cabin was sent by train to Chicago, reassembled, and became a popular part of the state's history exhibit in the 1892 World's Fair.

Buffalo Bill Cody made his way to Standing Rock and paid Sitting Bull's two widows fair money for his old trick horse. At the Chicago World's Fair, the white Ghost Dancing horse led the Wild West Show's Grand Procession, its rider bearing, proudly, invincibly, the American flag.

Oh, how grand God's beautiful earth seemed to me as
I glided swiftly through the woods!
                    —Phoebe Ann Moses

The old men
say
the earth
only
endures.

You spoke
truly.

You are right.

—Courtesy of the Bureau of American Ethnology Collection

ÉCORCHÉ:
FLAYED MAN

Florence, Italy
1798

1. *The Collector*

—wearing an oilcloth hat, overcoat, and soaking-wet boots, slogged through rain, a fish-shaped basket of gray willow sealed by a flap of leather across his shoulders. Shifting and reshifting his miserable weight, he dodged his way through an alley cobbled in the dark *pietra serena* of Florence onto Via Romana, a short distance from the museum's anatomy studio.

He had found her corpse, stays wrongly laced, skirt unfastened, hair undone, heeled against a wall beneath the shadowed portico of Ospedale di Santa Maria Nuova, and because he knew her, he had, at first, turned away. In the hospital's morgue, stripping off the familiar clothes, he grasped her damp, hip-length hair, still smelling of olive-wood smoke, in both his hands. Surprised by the quick hardening of his cock, he bent down, sucked each of her cold, rosy tan nipples, pressed one ear against her chest as if he might hear something, floated his hand between her chill white legs, dived his fingers into the black crevice that signified love. A despicable act suggested itself to him; instead, he opened the willow basket and, in an almost refined manner, laid her in it, tied down the leather flap. She was small, and this new weight of her, stony, slack, saddened him.

Better than anyone, the collector knew the brevity and meanness of her future—flesh sold to the museum's anatomy studio, limbs severed, torso flayed, select parts used for plaster and wax casts. When the dissectionists and artists were finished, he would shoulder her a second time, butcher's offal, to be tumbled into a communal pit for paupers, prostitutes, foreigners, criminals, beggars, a hellish tangle of the lost and rebuked. And in some perverse reciprocity, money he had given her for sex would be repaid him now by her corpse.

This grand book, the universe, is written in the language of mathematics, and its characters are triangles, circles, and other geometric figures, without which it is humanly impossible to understand a single word of it; without these, one wanders about in a dark labyrinth.

—GALILEO GALILEI

2. The Director

—noted unhappily that the museum's collector, Il Cinzio, had delivered a fresh cadaver to his dissection table along with a registered receipt, at the bottom of which was a line of ink, awaiting his peevish signature. The corpse, already turning a faint verdigris, had no further use for time or weather, while for him, warm temperatures, excessive rain, or lives wasted on debauchery and religion were archenemies of science.

A short, insatiable man, energized by intellectual vanity, at war with his own obsessions, ex-Abbot Felice Fontana of Rovereto, anatomist, physicist, chemist, former logician at the University of Pisa, now director of the Imperial and Royal Museum for Physics and Natural History, bit into the leathery skin of a dried fig dipped into a mix of wild thyme honey and bee pollen. The girl looked scarcely eighteen, unmarked, although the starry dots on her nipples, like nebulae, with faint blue rings around them, indicated an early stage of pregnancy. Her pudenda, slightly swollen, were anatomically marvelous. But suddenly he was sick of eating supper off the same scarred table he performed his bloody dissections on. Lately, he found he cared only for three things—his hives of Italian honeybees, the creation of a giant anatomical man of pine, and deciphering, before he died, the hexagonal codes of the universe. (To a lesser degree, he was interested in the subtle emotional pressures of architectural space, and had read just that morning an intriguing article about a certain Grand Ice Palace constructed half a century before in Saint Petersburg.)

Soon after being appointed court physician and museum director by Grand Duke Pietro Leopoldo, Felice Fontana had acted upon his own notions of liberty and confinement by flinging open sections of the museum to public scrutiny. By a maze of interconnecting rooms, he intended to expose what he considered to be the unrelievedly ugly, profane, secret interior of the human body. Beginning with a deceptively placid anteroom of wax skeletons, the visitor was shunted through increasingly morbid, gaudy exhibits of human musculature, tendons, sinews, nerves, and ligatures, the human body peeled back upon itself, layer by layer, until he entered, as if into a four-sided womb, the gynecological exhibit, then exited the labyrinth through a claustrophobic chamber of apocalyptic dioramas by Sicilian wax artist Gaetano Zumbo, entitled *Pestilence, Corruption of the Flesh, The Triumph of Time,* and *The Gallic Disease.* Lower classes, if cleanly dressed, were admitted to the museum's public exhibits from eight until ten o'clock in the morning. Ignorant riffraff, greedy and daft, they galloped straight to the gynecological and Zumbo "horror show" rooms to gawk at sex organs, nudity, gruesome depictions of disease and decay, the whole abyss of reproduction. Educated, nobler classes, arriving by one o'clock in the afternoon, shared the prurience of the lower classes but tempered their lust and morbidity by proceeding sedately through the labyrinth, pausing, as if genuinely intrigued, before skeletons and flayed men, lingering in front of endless cabinets of sense organs and cavities of thorax, abdomens, pelvises, gaping stomachs, each a repugnant rebuttal, in Fontana's view, to his Hexagonic Ideal.

The sweetness of the dried fig, the crunch from its seeds, tiny and pale as the white spray of dots on the dead girl's nipples, dissolved on his tongue as he stared absently at her. Past her. A man who failed to appreciate his own achievements, Fontana was obstinately preoccupied with his most elusive legacy, a man-giant carved of pine, whose wooden internal organs and viscera could, by ingenious design, be lifted out and studied by future generations of medical students. To replace raw, malodorous meat with solid, clean-grained geometry, to establish a theology of order based on nature's universal code—his failure to do either of these haunted and nearly depressed him.

He lived alone in a compact, stylish villa near the museum, steps from the Palazzo Pitti, where he tended his clay-tile bee-hives, harvesting raw medicinal honey and a superior wax for the museum's anatomies. Unsuccessfully schooled for the priest-hood, and known to don ecclesiastical robes on certain cynical occasions, Fontana was unrelentingly hostile to Catholic doc-trine. Ultimately, he insisted, a man's art and end had nothing to do with his theology—only science, Reason herself, could award humanity the gift, or poison, of immortality.

Still, his most gifted anatomist, Clemente Susini (a wreck of a man who insisted on living in a state of perpetual genuflection), would no doubt find the arrival of this flawless corpse, this rare girl, fortunate.

> "*Anatomy is, so to speak, the foundation of natural theology.*"
> —Eighteenth-Century Encyclopédie

3. *The Anatomist*

—knelt before the female cadaver, letting all fifty-nine beads of the rosary slip, one by one, in decades of ten, through his fingers as he prayed, *Ave Maria, gratia plena, Dominus tecum* . . . each bead a human vertebra, the crucifix itself said to be taken from the breastbone of an uncanonized saint from Naples. Three of his sons had died of lung disease, and now his fourth boy, the youngest, Angiolo, had begun coughing blood.

Clemente Susini no longer remembered when it was he had begun seeing men and women inside out, without their drab cloaks of skin. He was intimate with the glittering casket of jewels con-cealed within, the gem-sheen of organs, the ivory of bone, ruby of blood and muscle, lapis lazuli of arteries and veins, the pale gold nettings of lymph, sealed inside envelopes of blankness, plainness. Each body a reliquary, packed with soft-cut *bijouterie*. Yet the French portraitist Mme Vigée-Lebrun, who had painted numerous portraits of Marie Antoinette, once visited the museum's anatomy studios, and upon her return to Paris wrote a letter addressed to Susini, stating that the visit had ruined her. Whenever she attempted to paint a nobleman or woman, a prince or princess, all she could see were veins, blood, organs, bones, flesh, and fat. Since Mme Vigée-Lebrun's letter of flirtatious complaint, the French queen had lost her head, and Susini knew exactly what the inside of the queen's head looked like—they were all the same—her executioner had the same stuff inside his skull as had the queen—a cryptic revolution lay in such divine democracy! Too bad, he supposed, that the portraitist could no longer see people from their embellished outsides, arranged and posed, wigged and powdered and draped beside lean greyhounds, silver bowls of sugared fruit, bolts of Chinese silk. Mme Vigée-Lebrun, nauseated by such "disgusting slop," became equally horrified whenever she remembered all this mess pulsed inside of her, too. At such times, her famous brush would halt in midair, and as often as not, she wrote to him, she would faint dead away. What did he suggest for a cure? Ridiculous, he had thought, burning her letter as answer, this spoilt, profane woman with her fashionable Parisian viscera.

> . . . *the tasks endured by the petitioner have been unspeakable, for, beside the continued handling of the dead bodies, he has found himself on many occasions without sufficient time to get something to eat in order to attend to his unceasing work.*
> —Petition on behalf of "Il Cinzio," trash Collector
> for the Imperial and Royal Museum

4. *The Collector*

—done with his raw bacon and bread, his goatskin flask drained of a red wine so burning and thin as to resemble vinegar, lay sprawled, snout-up and snoring, near the cypress-wooded edge of the mass grave. A man of impressive height and girth, of a near-legendary strength said to be gotten from carrying cadavers, he was a pariah—no one ate with him or spoke to him—even the cheapest women shunned him. After she had arrived from Milan, ill, hungry, not knowing who he was, the girl had let him pay her, had coughed and spat blood on his filthy shirt, the stain of it still there, a dark red poppy stem. Swaddled in his damp overcoat, his soaked boots loosed from his long, knobbed feet, he slept not two lengths from the earth-vat where she lay in rough bits, scattered like coarse seasoning, herbs of lymph and ligature, tendon and bone, strewn over the others, all turning to grave-soil, their wormy whiteness lending luster to the soldierly black cypress nearby.

Two nights later, upright but sluggish, his limbs heavy as iron-grained wood, the gray nutmeat in his head a roar of pain, Il Cinzio zigzagged his way down the cobbled streets, a new corpse spraddled across his back. Since tumbling her parts into the mass grave, he had eaten nothing, drunk nothing but cheap wine dregs, and now he staggered under this newest sack and slosh of bones and viscera cloaking his shoulders. Taking a shortcut through the Giardino di Boboli, stopping to rest beside the green Turkish-style *Kaffeehaus,* the hump on his back a vestigial rot-twin, Il Cinzio picked and stubbed his way down a steep gravel path to the back entrance of the museum. Turning down a familiar dark passage-way, passing the carpentry shop, the glaziery, he stopped short when he felt, thought he felt, a small shudder across his back, and in a fury flung the basket to the black-and-white-patterned floor, kicking at the leather and willow to make certain dead was dead. Looking up, he spied a thread of light coming from one of the studios, and dumping his hideous still-life on Felice Fontana's table, plunged down the hall in as straight a line as his anvil-limbed body would allow, toward the thin seam of light.

Clemente Susini, wearing a black frock coat, scoured with age, a shirt with a limp ruffle, and a filthy cravat, stood with Il Cinzio over the pale, recumbent figure, a bank of guttering beeswax tapers illuminating all three of them.

Lo spellato. She stared open-eyed into some mysterious distance, his whore, lips parted, chin tilted to one side, her expression rapturous. Her arms lay at her sides, the knee of her right leg raised, slightly bent and suggestively open. He recognized the pubic hair as hers. She looked vital, replete with the little death of sex, and for the second time, not in front of her sad corpse but before her flawless effigy, he felt his fool of a cock stiffen.

Do you remember bringing her to us? How beautiful she is . . . with his tapering white hands (anatomists, from their handling of the dead, were said to have the finest hands, hands that never aged; then why were his, Il Cinzio's, so besmirched, so misshapen?), Susini took hold of two white silk tabs on either side of the wax-smooth, ivory abdomen, and as if it were a common kettle lid, raised the shell of her stomach. Revealed: a still, parti-colored, livid cosmos of entrails, stomach, liver, duodenum, heart, kidneys, lungs, glands, and further down, pegged into the scarlet, narrow-necked basin of her pear-halved womb, curled on its side, of less size than a man's thumb, a seed-child, attached to its mother's body by an anguine cord of ochre, amber, and green.

Reluctantly, Susini settled the soft white armor of her stomach back in place, and with Il Cinzio's help set a rosewood-and-crystal case over her. She was entombed in glass, canonized but for her nakedness, a single wanton strand of pearls around her clean, full neck, a neck made from the honeycomb of bees. Il Cinzio recalled her live, yielding flesh, the real child, his perhaps, plugged into her womb, a rotting fig. Looking at the wax replica, he felt his own life ending, at an end, and desired nothing more.

No one is free who has not obtained the empire of himself.
—PYTHAGORAS

5. The Director

—felt happiest these days eating honeycomb, its tiny hexagons fragrant with lavender and wild thyme, settled among his books, reading the Swiss polymath Albrecht von Haller's anatomical atlas, *Icones anatomicae*, reflecting on von Haller's theory that anatomy and physiology were linked, thus forming a *living* anatomy . . . *anatomia animate*. Poring over von Haller's accounts of dissections using injection and extirpation, Fontana concurred with his "theory of irritability," based upon human and animal experimentation. Irritability had been proven to be a property of muscle fiber, and sensibility, a property of nervous fiber. Muscle fiber demonstrated distinct irritability by contracting under the stimulus of pain, while nervous fiber, under the same stimulus, demonstrated sensibility (feeling). The pulsating heart was the most irritable organ of the body, and all organs—thus the totality of what was called human—operated independently of transcendental ideal or religious soul. Life: a fixed détente between anarchy and order, vitalism and entropy. This idea satisfied him.

It is sown a natural body, it is raised a spiritual body.
—SAINT PAUL

6. The Anatomist

—made his way through dull, lashing rain to his tiny neighborhood church, Santa Margherita de' Cerchi. Mass after mass, he shamelessly bargained with the Virgin—if she spared his only living son, Angiolo, he would dedicate his finest works to her. He had lost count of how many wax infant Jesus figures he had fashioned for the churches of Florence, he rarely bothered signing them, but the wax queen, *regina cera*, was his praise song to the Virgin, an alchemical remixing of the substance of a street prostitute into pure effigy, like the mystery of incarnation itself. And the bud of life he had found, cutting into the dead girl's belly, was it not like the doomed, mild infant he'd been faithfully creating and re-creating, the child of God, the child of sin, the same?

7. The Collector

—before his death, had loathed Paolo Mascagni, the young artist from Pisa, who, auditioning for the coveted but unpaid position of apprentice anatomist, startled everyone by unveiling, with an arrogant flourish, a life-sized wax figure of Il Cinzio, the Collector, whose body had been found in the public cemetery, lost to drink, foul weather, and the brute, swampy errors of his life. Mascagni, hoping to gain favor with Felice Fontana, had crafted from the giant, well-muscled cadaver a vertical gentleman of wit, rakish, one arm raised as if to tip an invisible hat, a skinless dandy, one leg thrust out in midstride, heading nowhere. Paolo Mascagni of Pisa was grudgingly awarded the position he sought, and within days was given his first assignment. Using one of the museum's newest microscopes from Paris, he was ordered by Fontana as a curb to his pride to dissect and reproduce in colored wax the speckled stomach of *Helix aspersa*, the common land snail.

8. *The Director*

—collapsed in the street outside his villa on an unusually hot spring morning. He would die, hours later, of a brain hemorrhage, cradled in the sycophantic embrace of Paolo Mascagni, who would briefly and disgracefully succeed him as director. In the final moments of his life, Felice Fontana's thready filaments of thought were not of his colossal, unfinished mistake, the man of wood; instead, he considered what a buffoonish figure Napoléon Bonaparte, after conquering Florence, had turned out to be . . . *le petit corporal*, bandy-legged, dwarfish, reeking of black licorice, strutting in pompously high, mud-caked boots through Fontana's labyrinth of wax specimens, showing only the most puerile interest in Susini's naked Venus, making crude jokes about her glued-on pubic hair, before becoming fascinated by the soft darts and limp arrows of flayed penises aimed uselessly at her recumbent figure from the west side of the room. Napoléon, his saffron-colored, gloved hands clasped behind his thick back, leaned close to examine the largest penis, a sluglike flaccid stalk that some wag had tied a violet-striped grosgrain bow around the neck of. Why, he asked, straightening up, does that one wear a war decoration? The emperor would redeem himself only slightly by ordering an entire set of full-figure anatomies to be sent to his military hospital in Paris, blatantly competing with the Austrian emperor whose sister he had married.

As Fontana reclined in his false heir's arms, his brain, that penultimate irritability, gave off dying impressions, like dreams. Leaking old, disorderly blood, it led him into Empress Anna Ivanovna's Ice Palace, built sixty-five years before, in Saint Petersburg. This niece of Peter the Great had hired an architect, Georg Kraft, to cut great blocks of ice, sprayed with water that then froze, acting as cement, to construct a castle fifty-two feet long, ringed by a balustrade, its roofline crowned by a series of statues. The windows were framed, the exterior walls tinted to resemble marble. Inside was a bedroom, with a bed of ice, an ice vanity, an ice fireplace with ice logs, a dining room with a clock whose inner workings were of ice, and beside the clock, an ice cabinet filled with ice dishes. At night, candles were lit and the palace glowed from the inside, while outside ice cannons were fired to amuse the people, and near the cannons were ice dolphins and ice elephants acting as fountains by day and torches by night. The elephant could cry out like a living creature because of a man hidden inside, equipped with a brass horn. Inside the palace, which endured three months, a wedding took place. The guests were jesters and cripples, and the couple, elderly Prince Galitzine, who had offended the empress, and his bride, a terrified Kalmuck girl, spent their wedding night shivering in their ice bed with its ice pillows and ice mattress. One year later, when the empress died, she would be lowered into her own chthonic palace of Russian dirt, watched over by an eastern orthodoxy of worms.

In its last, mordant parse of logic, Felice Fontana's dimming brain, the Distinguished Guest of itself, toured the empress's baroque castle of ice, marveling at its infinite crystalline structures of ice, which, like the honeycomb, were hexagonal. The ice crystals humming in his brain first turned into long-waisted bees making propolis, then into his own black-and-gold-striped Italian bees bearding during the rising of the Pleiades, when seven stars hung in the constellation of Taurus . . . and in a sudden, swift unspooling of all logic, Fontana watched floating remnants of geometry theorems reassemble into an ice hexagon, the hexagon an expression of Venus whose sacred number was six, the dual Triple Goddess, which then dissolved into Plato's doctrine of the transmigration of souls, which, among other things, stated that the souls of people most solitary and quiet during their span of days on earth were changed, as if by magic, into honeybees.

9. The Anatomist

—dizzy, out of breath, his hands and feet going numb from the effects of the mercury he had absorbed from his studio chemicals, ruined by dampness and odors, by overwork and a sickness of grief for his son, hovered near the center of the bridge, in no hurry to go home, gazing down into the rain-swollen river, mistaking it for the green-blue boiling wax he had used for her venous system. The Virgin had not seen fit to answer his prayers. Angiolo had died and he, Clemente Susini, was destroyed in health and hope, but that was not why his body would be found the next morning, beneath the bridge, drowned in a marsh of golden mud. Susini, dying of mercury poisoning, had merely leaned too far over the side of the wooden bridge to better see her blessed face, veiled by dark water, to better hear what enigmatic instruction she was giving him, and so lost his balance and tumbled—ingenious prayer!—into the cool answer of her arms.

Fairy Tale

Late at night, every night, when the long silent halls and rooms, the labyrinths of the Imperial Museum, were neither lit nor attended by living souls, an hour came when Il Cinzio, lifting his imaginary hat a little higher, raising his leg a little farther, stepped off of his white and gilt circular stand and made his way the short distance to Room XXVIII, to Display Cabinet No. 740, to her silken bed, where she lay naked, forever turning her eyes to gaze with overpowering sweetness upon him . . . and having once been a man of unusual strength, it did not take much for him to raise the crystal-and-rosewood cover, extend one flayed hand to help her to sit, to stand, to walk from place to place, from room to room, from garden to garden, and rule the world awhile with him.

Myth

Felice Fontana, ex-abbot, director of the Imperial and Royal Museum of Physics and Natural History, a reclusive scientist known on occasion to wear, in a gesture of sarcasm, his ecclesiastical robes, was buried in the church of Santa Croce, alongside the bodies of Michelangelo, Galileo, Rossini, and other famous Italians. The next day, when a solitary honeybee was discovered stumbling along the windowsill of the former director's anatomy studio, a young apprentice, recently arrived from Assisi, flung open the window so the honeybee could find its way, drifting on spring winds, toward the Giardino di Boboli, past the green *Kaffeehaus*, and vanishing into the Cistercian monks' herb garden where a plot of French lavender, having survived a late frost, was setting forth its first violet-spiked bloom.

Miracle

By the mid-nineteenth century, religious-art scholars agreed that no less than six of the forty-two wax infant Jesus figures existing throughout the city's churches had been falsely attributed to Clemente Susini. But one wax icon, bearing his signature, could be found in a shadowy niche of Santa Margherita de' Cerchi, an infant Jesus held in the Holy Mother's arms, said to sometimes turn his head slightly; and wherever the infant's mild blue gaze would alight, on whatever person kneeling, unaware, all illness would be cured. The Susini effect was commonest in male children, and although these miracles were formally repudiated by the Church, to those who were healed, the miracle of Susini's Jesus was cause for salvific, if unsanctioned, joy.

CAPTAIN BROWN AND THE ROYAL VICTORIA MILITARY HOSPITAL

Work on their horror of the same old thing. The horror of the same old thing is the greatest passion we have put into the human heart.

—C. S. Lewis, *The Screwtape Letters*

I

January 29, 1944

The war had not affected Captain Brown and his wife but for the deprivation of small luxuries. They had experienced no direct suffering. But tonight, taking the train from Southampton up the coast of southern England to Netley, Hants, Captain Brown could see that assumptions of safety, for him at least, had altered. What little could be glimpsed of Southampton, a port city and former seaside spa, was a gutted wasteland; he had been told its inhabitants slept out in surrounding fields at night, in fear of the Luftwaffe, their bombs.

Twelve minutes past nine, with his destination some miles away and the train compartment unheated, unlit, and, worse for him, without toilet facilities, Captain Brown could only hope that the cramping in his stomach would diminish and not worsen. Aside from his present staff, Captain Hayden, and Ensigns Breathwit and Poole, the compartment was empty. He looked out the window, not at the cold rise of hills or the ruins of Netley Abbey he knew were out there, but at his own reflection, patched and watery, a face exhausted by relentless travel, the two-week crossing on the *Queen Mary* from New York harbor to Gourock, Scotland, a ghost train to London, another from Euston and Waterloo stations to Southampton, and now this final leg to Netley, where he was to take command of a hospital he had never seen and prepare it to receive Allied casualties from a massive future operation in Normandy, France.

Captain Brown stared past his reflection, picturing the English countryside as he had almost sentimentally envisioned it for years. He was particularly interested in the medieval ruins of Netley Abbey, which he had read about while looking up the town of Netley in an encyclopedia, in preparation for his journey. Wondering if he would have time during this post to visit the Abbey, he felt the slim, maroon spine of the leather-bound volume of Shakespearean sonnets in his right hip pocket, a Christmas gift from his wife. Captain Brown was an unabashed Anglophile, and to relax from his grueling duties as a surgeon and hospital director, he took habitual refuge in reading English histories and literature, particularly the English poets, from Chaucer, Dryden, and Donne to Byron, Coleridge, and Keats, only sometimes favoring poets of the new century, like Wilfred Owen, W. H. Auden or T. S. Eliot, a native-born American like himself. He had discovered his passion for things English as a pre-med student at the University of Wisconsin, finding British poetry's exquisite language, emotional restraint, and passionate inquiry deeply consoling. A man of no discernible emotion—others saw him as taciturn, enigmatic, even a bit forbidding —Captain Brown had learned to reserve his feelings, to not invest in them beyond those hours when he would read his poets, and even then, it was as if he were only glimpsing the possibilities of his own heart, camouflaged, protected, within the lyrical meter and verse of English poetry.

A descendent of German immigrants with names like Brown and Plate, Barnsdorf, Hofmeister, and Duwe, farmers, teachers, and merchants who had settled in the rural village of Plum City, Wisconsin, Captain Brown had already risen beyond the modest expectations of his relatives. His impressive height, six foot three inches, and dark-featured handsomeness, in favoring him physically, had helped to propel him from a fate of farm labor or petty commerce into a promising career as a naval surgeon.

Initially assigned to hospitals in Haiti and Guam, then Florida and Philadelphia, he had now been given this post, which, judging by its secrecy and haste, had the markings of something major in the war.

He glanced at his watch; two hours to traverse six miles. He could have bicycled to his destination faster. Perhaps the dyspepsia in his stomach was the active, acidic realization that not only had he been entrusted by the Surgeon General of the Navy, Admiral McIntire, with this command, but that how well he managed to acquit himself would determine his future, whether he would swiftly climb ranks or be sent to some sleepy backwater post never to be heard from again. Either fate depended on his surviving this particular assignment, and there was doubt as to whether he would, given the German's relentless bombing campaign over Southampton's coastline. But Captain Brown was equally formed of ambitious resolve and disciplined capacities, and as his marriage had provided him security but little true happiness, all he had was his career to derive satisfaction from and to merit distinction because of. The slim, calf-skin volume, with its stamped gilt lettering, a wartime extravagance, curved to the shape of his hip, a rich pressure, as the train's brakes squealed, signaling a stop. In the seats opposite him, his companions stirred. In just a few moments, they would look to him, their commanding officer, for direction, instruction, morale. They were trained to entrust their lives to him. His bowels writhed and a cloudy, copperish taste crept into his mouth. Even as the train lurched clumsily forward, as if newly indecisive about halting, Captain Brown rose to his full height, his head grazing the roof of the train's compartment. It was important to be the first to stand, to silently rehearse the few words he would say as they began their mission in England together. Hardly Shakespeare's version of Henry V's speech before the Battle of Agincourt, hardly "We few, we happy few, we band of brothers—" but more along the lines of: "Here we are, gentlemen. Netley, Hants. Let us see what awaits us, and hope it is not too bad."

II

His first night spent on the property of the Royal Victoria Military Hospital, Captain Brown would neither sleep nor ever truly waken from his duties of the next seven months, not until he would be relieved of his mission in September and placed in a new post by Comnaveu in London. All he knew was that he was to assume command of an English hospital that had been declared an unmitigated architectural disaster by half the British Parliament in 1863. The Lady of the Lamp herself, Florence Nightingale, had condemned the vast stone folly as a meaner foe of England's soldiers than the whole of the enemy's combined artillery and force.

Captain Brown lay in all his clothes, save for his shoes, neatly set beneath the leather-upholstered, mahogany dining table that served as his bed, shivering beneath a rough, military-issue gray woolen blanket. They were housed that first night, not in the main building, but in a nearby Family Hospital, since its single room, besides the kitchen, was reliably heated, or so they had been told. As far as Captain Brown could tell, the heat was pure fiction. He lay listening to the wet, staggered snores of his companions, strewn about the room on hard sofas, and to Captain Hayden, twitching in dream, curlike, on the floor beside the nonfunctioning hearth. Because of his height, Captain Brown had elected to sleep, laid out like a Christmas calf, on the Chippendale-legged table, and now, though his stomach seemed to have settled, his neck ached sharply, as though a blunt axe had been taken to it. As his companions snored and groaned with cold under their lumped-up jackets and thin woolen blankets, Captain Brown sat up, slipped off the table's rounded edge—he could be surprisingly supple and agile for his height—and with his blanket shawled around him and shoes gripped in one hand, crept stocking-footed into the second room, a freezing, cupboard-sized kitchen.

From his years as a medical student, Captain Brown had trained himself to wake at least an hour before the world had any need of him and to study neither medical nor German language texts or, later, military texts, but to read poetry or history, sometimes both, and indeed there were rare periods when he was compelled to write poetry of his own, though he never showed it to anyone and never dared to think he had any real gift for it. His poetry, he knew, was all vicarious imitation. So though he had hardly slept, he was still up in the predawn darkness of southern England, tiptoeing into the kitchen and finding a place to sit at a small table near an uncurtained window through which he could see a black, shaggy bulwark of trees, cedars, on the other side of which, he assumed, was the main hospital. Just as there was no heat, there was no electricity, so in the day's first light, he attempted to read but found the print too small to make out. Even turning the thin pages, his surgeon's fingers felt thick and stiff with cold. He returned the book to his back pocket, rose, and quietly searched inside the cabinets for a teakettle, matches, something to warm him, but found nothing.

He then wished he had a bit of paper on which to pen a letter to his wife. Augusta had made him promise to write daily; he had never gone so far from her before, and not during wartime. If his hospital fell to the Germans, he wanted her to at least have the consolation of a few letters from him, wanted to give her at least this remnant of himself, a few pages of his turbulent, sloping, half-graceful script, proof he had been thinking of her.

Captain Brown did not love his wife. They had met in medical school while she was training (though she would never practice) as a nurse. They were from neighboring rural towns in Wisconsin, both from German farm families, and from the beginning, though he had felt none of the soul-stirring passion he had read about and listened to friends suffer willingly over, still, theirs was, initially at least, an affectionate, near-filial bond. From the beginning, she nettled him teasingly, his awkward height and a social temerity that looked like pride or, worse, arrogance, yet in later years, when he was a distinguished, decorated admiral, would be interpreted as innate dignity—and he liked to watch her, indulgently, as one would any fey, charming creature—her diminutive near-frailty appealed to him, along with her marcelled auburn hair, ivory skin and large gray eyes behind thick glasses. So a daily letter to

"Dearie" would hardly be a chore, it would be an anchor on himself, a gauge of what he was thinking, a tether to a less violent world, a habit to calm and batten down his morbidly anxious mind.

But there was no bit of paper on which to write to Augusta, just as there was no light to read from the book of verse his wife had slipped into his pocket, a surprise parting gift.

Perhaps a walk would warm, or at least distract him. He had a sudden desire to see his hospital, to view it from the outside at least, before the others woke, before the formalities of command and disciplines of wartime set in. A momentarily free man, he would walk the grounds, view the hospital from its exterior, gain his own first, private impressions.

Slipping on and tying his shoes, buttoning up his jacket, snugging the rough blanket around his shoulders, Captain Brown ducked through the kitchen's back door and stepped outside. To his right rose an inky scrim of windswept trees behind which loomed his future nemesis or triumph, grand edifice or imperialist monstrosity, depending on one's politics—the Royal Victoria Military Hospital.

Given other choices or circumstances, Captain Brown might have been a professor, a scholar; his saturnine temperament, attuned as it was to beauty, might have led him to try his hand, more openly, at poetry. As a general surgeon in the United States Navy, as a military officer, he was admired and not a little envied for his meticulous preparation, his liberal use of libraries, encyclopedias, dictionaries, newspapers, journals, and quarterlies, relied upon, too, for his quick grasp of facts and his rather astonishing memory. So as he stepped out of his temporary quarters at the Family Hospital and busied himself with the comforting ritual of lighting the day's first cigarette, drawing its resiny warmth into his lungs, into his bloodstream, he was already familiar with the history of the hospital, hidden on the other side of the clenched row of cedars, planted both as privacy screen and aromatic windbreak. Much like his wife, or more precisely, the institution of marriage that included his wife, facts were essential to Captain Brown, serving as well-lit instruments of navigation to lead him from the dark, tangled wood of himself. He depended upon their solidity. As he struck out past the unheated cottage that was the Family Hospital, where his men squandered their fast-dwindling fortune of sleep, and headed for the road that should take him to the Royal Victoria's main entrance, he mentally reviewed, as if he were a professor preparing a lecture, what he had thus far learned of his new post's history.

The hospital had been commissioned by Queen Victoria following the Crimean War, a horrific debacle in which eight out of ten of the queen's soldiers died not of combat wounds but of diseases exacerbated by filthy, unhygienic conditions, a disgrace exposed by that second iconic Victorian female, Florence Nightingale. In response, the queen commanded that a suitable place be found on which to build a hospital of the grandest possible scale and scope to tend all soldiers wounded in England's cause. A government surveyor and architect, E. O. Mennie, was hired, and a site selected at Netley, across from the Isle of Wight, twelve miles up the coast from the port town of Southampton. Begun in 1856, the hospital took seven years and half a million pounds to finish. Plagued by controversy and bitter debate (including the persistent accusation that architectural blueprints had been mixed, and that the building that arose in Netley had been intended for a hospital in India), the Royal Victoria would be the largest military hospital in the world, over one quarter mile in length, made of red brick, the same Hampshire clay the hospital stood upon, faced with Portland stone and plinths of Welsh granite laid along the foundation. There were dozens of pillared porticoes, cupolas, spires, turrets, and an enormous verdigris dome set above the chapel and granite-pillared main entrance. Inside, 135 wards were intended to care for over one thousand wounded men. The Royal Army's Medical School took up residence in the hospital, and a separate villa-like building, D Block, became the British military's first lunatic asylum. Included on the two-hundred-acre estate was a horse stable, tennis and badminton courts, a swimming pool supplied with seawater by a windmill pump, a bakery, and a six-hole golf course. The Royal Victoria was the most ambitious, ill-conceived, impractical hospital ever built, an Italianate behemoth, its seven-year construction tenderly watched over by the queen.

That was the whole extent of Captain Brown's knowledge, culled from an encyclopedia. He strode along a path running parallel to Southampton Water, its placid shore less than two hundred yards to his right, the cigarette livening him, the rust-colored blanket loosening around his shoulders. He found the entrance, opposite a wooden pier stretched out over gunmetal water, a long, elm-lined avenue, stately, and at this hour, deserted. Only the crunch of his shoes on the pale red, graveled road broke the wintry silence. The air smelled of ice, of decaying leaves and loam. At the end of the avenue, he stepped out in front the hospital, still distant and mantled by an acre or more of rolling, half-dead, yellow-white lawn. The sun sent a weak, ascendant gleam of light across the eastern face of the hospital, further brightening the white stone facing. Captain Brown stood rooted, stunned; he may have even gasped, a dormant bit of farm boy in the sound he made, an exclamation made of half-wonder and half-fright, upon beholding what could only be called architectural splendor. No engraving, no photograph could convey the magnitude and heaviness of the place, the somber, excessive majesty of the building before him.

Gustie,

You cannot imagine the size of the hospital they have put me, your weary boy, in charge of. In one look a man cannot take it all in . . . you have to begin either to the right or to the left and swing your gaze all the way round to the other side. It is a surgical palace, a medical Versailles, and the grounds surrounding it, over two hundred acres, are secluded, vast, and at this hour, dawn, eerily, burningly silent. I cannot describe it other than to say this hospital inspires a feeling of involuntary reverence, much like one must feel in the great cathedrals and palaces of Europe,

*places I intend to take you to one day. There is pride, too, in
looking upon this vast edifice, and not a little fear. To say I feel
as if I am dreaming is no small exaggeration . . .*

This imaginary, effusive letter to his wife trailed off as he stood
overpowered before such an imposing formality. The sky, rapidly
brightening, reminded him he had better get back to the others
before they woke. Still, the hospital's grandiosity staggered him,
held him to the spot a few more moments, struggling to describe
to his wife, to himself, what he was feeling. A medical version of
Oxford or Cambridge? Versailles? Was he to be king or doctor?
Insecurity shook him, and self-doubt, formed half of fear, assailed
him with near physical force as he continued gazing across the
pale, dead sweep of lawn to the imposing front of this building.
He was still there, looking, when a small, distinct movement
caught his eye—it came from one of the hundreds of arched windows, a third-story window near the central verdigris dome, a
human figure, gazing out at him. He gazed back for a long,
strange, suspended moment, before the figure seemed to step
away, vanish back into the massive interior of the building. A
nurse or patient, restless and eager for release? A chill settled into
his back and shoulder blades as Captain Brown turned to make
his way back down the somber, shaded avenue.

Then, as neatly as drawing a window covering shut, his famous self-discipline already at work, he slid a partition across
this first, private part of his day and entered the second, public
part, where he would take charge, unerringly, precisely, and, un-
fortunately for his subordinates, humorlessly. With the regulated
order of a Greek theater of memory, his mind began to file, com-
partmentalize, and outline, shifting into a mechanistic clock-
work, imposing discipline and coherence all around him. It
would not be until much later that night, in his own quarters,
lying down on his uneven slab of a bed, that he would slide the
partition back and gaze into this first part of his day, reflecting
upon the single enduring sensation he had felt upon seeing the

Royal Victoria Military Hospital for the first time: an almost supernatural sensation that here was a piece of architecture that seemed to precisely reflect, to mirror, his own nature. Years before, he had, while sleeping, dreamed of just such a counterpart in stone and glass and metal. It was like coming upon an architectural version of himself, he recognized it immediately, his double in stone. The building, too, seemed to recognize him, welcome him . . . and the figure in the third-floor window, an aspect of himself? The strange hubris, the possible insanity of such a thought imposed a vital secrecy upon him, yet it would influence a number of decisions and actions, affecting his fate and the fate of others, in the months to come.

But now, as a wintry sun, white as champagne, began to wanly gild the upper, thorned reaches of the cypress trees, as the first birdsong, sweetly tentative, broke the freezing air around him, he rounded the corner, striding rapidly, making his way up the path to the Family Hospital, grateful that the hollow rumbling of his stomach was hunger this time, and not the previous unpleasant sickness.

III

Following a lamentable breakfast of weak, unsweetened tea, hard bread, and a gray, soupy porridge, Captain Brown and his advance party were given a tour of the hospital and its two hundred acres by an army colonel who had picked them up in his jeep. The colonel, truculent in his impatience to be gone from a place he loathed and cursed, recklessly sped his passengers, by turns silent, somber, appalled, and awed, beneath a brittle, achromous sky, around the vast premises, pointing out the lunatic or "shell-shock" asylum, Block D, the empty horse stables and paddock, unused golf course, dry swimming pool, closed-down bakery, inoperative fire station, an isolated place designed for self-sufficiency, with every amenity, but now amenities were nonexistent, isolation broken by German air assaults and self-sufficiency a distant notion of the past. The Royal Victoria, the captain thought, half-listening to the colonel's litany of complaints, seemed to be as much a casualty as the wounded it had been built to take in. War brought plagues of deprivation, and from his vantage point, from all he could see and was being told, this hospital, for all its grand, classical exterior and parklike setting, showed a shocking lack of medicine and supplies— antiquated surgical theaters and storerooms, mechanically defective surgical instruments, only thirteen units of plasma, no syrettes or syringes of morphine, penicillin, codeine, or sulfa compound, no bandages, suture material, X-ray machines or film, anesthetic apparatus, blankets, linens, surgical beds, material for casts and spicas, insufficient tubing, glassware, and needles, not to mention barely operative hydraulic lifts, unreliable steam heat in the corridors, broken plumbing, foul water. Not only were there next to no supplies, there were no typewriters and not paper or ink enough to write down a list of all that was missing, adding further insult to a barbarous irony—that they were here to repair soldiers to reenter battle, be reinjured, blown apart, killed.

Driving past the hospital's rear entrance where a rail line, currently in disuse, had run medical transport trains from Southampton directly up to the hospital's back doors, the colonel parked near the massive front entrance. Through a pair of great wooden doors that opened inward, they entered the shadowed gloom of the Royal Victoria Military Hospital.

To the left of the enormous high-ceilinged entry hall was a two-room museum dismissed by the army colonel as a queer little job full of skulls and dead birds. They climbed four flights of shallow granite steps, each edged with a lip of white marble, stopping to tour each of the floors. Like an unvisited mausoleum half-submerged in dead leaves and rubbish, the hospital's interior was echoing and icy, suggesting no hospital atmosphere the captain had ever known. No matter how many patients or medical staff might fill its wards, corridors, operating theaters, galleys, mess halls, storerooms, boiler rooms, barracks, and wards, he was certain it would always feel ghostly and hollow. In contrast to the weighted, palatial formality of the exterior, the maze of the hospital's interior felt tenebrous, Stygian, and bleak, yet, to the captain, it also appeared strangely authoritative, even grand, in its disastrous proportions, its miscarried ambitions. For the next several hours, they walked its stone-floored corridors, infinite-seeming in perspective, glassed along the water side, two hundred floor-to-ceiling windows on each floor needing to be covered with blackout shutters at twilight, unshuttered again each dawn. From one corridor's end to the other, there was only a telescoping darkness, glacial, minatory, lifeless. The colonel took some delight in telling them how the Army Postal Service had taken first to bicycling, then to driving jeeps down the corridors, just to get things done faster, the mail delivered, and have a bit of a lark as well. Captain Brown imagined it, the surreal sight of a bicycle, its chrome bell ting-tinging, or a modern, American-made jeep honking, motoring irreverently down the dark corridors. The wards were preposterously small, badly ventilated; most had only a mean, northern exposure to light. The plumbing system consisted of an open metal sleeve running around the walls of each ward, carrying water and waste to floor drains. Small fireplaces stood at one end of each room, heat provided by cumbersome bricks of compressed coal dust and oil, most smoldering before going out completely. A constant shortage resulted in the sparing use of even these.

Startled to find several of the unheated second-floor wards still filled with British soldiers, men who lay flat as cards under tight-cornered, rough plaid blankets, gas masks dangling from the end of every bed, quiet men staring upward at white ceilings, screens on which they could replay the bloodsoaked nightmares that had brought them here, Captain Brown stopped to speak to a few of the men, finding them polite, mild fellows, unshaven, unwashed, their bed linen, if they had it at all, soiled. When he asked if they wanted anything, most said no, though several did ask for a glass of water, please, or a cigarette. Their gentle resignation hung in the air, plaintive, disturbing.

After the army colonel took abrupt leave, the party quickly agreed there was a critical lack of supplies, shortages grave enough to make them wonder how they could possibly get this hospital up and running in three to four months' time. Faced with transforming a collapsed palace into a functioning medical facility, Captain Brown's staff would later privately agree that were it up to them and not to Captain Brown and the secretary of the United States Navy, they would unanimously declare the Royal Victoria Military Hospital an uninhabitable, hellish relic, unfit for operations, a medical hazard unfurled with fraudulent majesty along the Southampton coast, and instead recommend erecting dozens of temporary Quonset huts on the hospital grounds, modern, efficient, American-designed hospital facilities. Captain Brown, they agreed, had been given a Sisyphean task, and the cynical haste with which the army colonel had briefed them, then taken off for London and a fresh assignment, told them everything.

With the rest of his staff scheduled to arrive by train from London within the next week, Captain Brown found himself dreading the thought of the fifty doctors, ninety-eight nurses, twelve hospital corps officers serving as technicians, four hundred hospital corpsmen and nearly two hundred maintenance men who would gather before him, ranked and uniformed, awaiting his leadership in the face of such a challenge.

But for now, his advance party was in need of a chance to step outside, relax a bit, have a smoke. After stowing their gear in the officers' quarters, a grim warren of unheated rooms tucked away in one wing of the second floor, the walls incongruously wallpapered with overblown pink cabbage roses floating against a murky taupe background, Captain Brown dismissed Captain Hayden, his executive officer, and Ensigns Breathwit and Poole, first ordering Hayden to locate a blueprint of the hospital and inquire as to the availability of bicycles.

Ensign Poole set the captain's bags down in his room, saluted, and left. If he'd wanted, Captain Brown could have lived offsite in a pleasant-looking, thatched six-room cottage called the Coppice—he'd seen it—but he dreaded the solitude and distance and chose to stay in a low-ceilinged garret no larger or more lavish than those of his immediate staff. He hadn't the heart to settle into it just yet and simply left his bags where Poole had placed them, closed the door, and set off to look around on his own. He could not dispel the peculiar, almost gravitational allegiance he felt for this hospital, constructed with such cruel disregard for its patients, cavalier in its dismissal of basic needs, surreal in its vast, hostile proportions. It would be his, the Royal Victoria, during a historic time, and he had one afternoon, this afternoon, to get both his bearings and the strength to rise to a task strewn with a thousand leviathan difficulties.

IV

He was not in any of the places one might have expected to find him, interviewing patients, investigating supply rooms, or talking with those who might have advised and perhaps aided him. He appeared to be refusing, in any predictable, straightforward fashion, to take charge. With a loping, half-somnambulist's gait, he found his way back to the hospital's main entrance and stood inside its great hall, an aggressive, improvident space suggestive, with its vaulting airiness and height, of a railway station. He stood before the hall's main attraction, a zoological display, apparent centerpiece of the hospital's small Museum of Natural History—the bleached, cavernous skeleton of an Asian elephant. The dominance of the pachyderm, its bowled eye sockets holding dead pools of air . . . he stretched out his hand to feel the cool bone skate of its head. The point of an elephant taking up the entryway of a military hospital eluded him, still he marveled at it.

Such a display alluded to the hospital's Victorian origins, the previous century's mania for collection and preservation, for specimen mounting and the patient cataloging of specimens— for the ringside theatrics of natural science. Admittedly, it thrilled him. As a boy, he had loved roaming, hunting in the deep woods behind his family's modest farm, trapping and skinning, collecting and ordering. He understood the mind's pride, filleting, pinning down life. Understood taking apart, reassembling and labeling. To understand was to control, to keep the terror of human insignificance at bay. It was routine to self-importance, this ability to kill and to rebuild, to catalog and stop any motion too directly pointing out human limitation and death.

He stepped away to peer closely at another exhibit, this one arrowing upward along the staircase wall, struggling upward in an eternally fixed fleet—the preserved bodies of crocodiles. Above them, forming an erratic, spiky border, were a dozen or more racks of antlers, antelope and deer, along with the dun hides of medium-sized animals, spread and pinned, coarse-bristled cartographies.

He bent his own large frame to look beneath the open stone staircase; on the wall beneath the staircase, carefully mounted, preserved in cement, a swarm of stuffed fish, made their way into oblivion.

The door to the museum, when he tried it, was unlocked. Inside, he found a half-lit dinginess overrun with manic clutter. He moved cautiously among glass cabinets, tables with gigantic bell jars filmed in dust, containing owls, yellowhammers, ravens, kestrels and magpies, their talons wire-curved to mossy branches, shelves holding the skeletons of badger, fox, shrew, mole, rodent, squirrel. He stood awhile in front of a glittering seam of glass specimen jars—each with a serpent spiraled in its own cold, topaz brine.

In the museum's second room he came upon a gigantic rack of elk antlers fashioned into a hat stand. From each of its bony tips hung a military hat from the Crimean War, hats tasseled, cockaded, feather-plumed, each hung as if suspended in air the color of old shellac, a crowd of souvenirs, war's haunted rummage. Hats tagged and labeled in brown, spidery ink, with an infantryman's or officer's name, or more often, simply the name of a battlefield or nursing barracks. Battle of Alma, Battle of Sevastopol, Battle of Balaklava, Selimiye Barracks, Scutari . . .

The poignancy of these hats made him think a moment of his mother, Anna Brown, buried in Plum City's German Lutheran cemetery in her red watered-silk dress, her favorite hat, made of white ermine, clasped in her still hands. He recalled her milliner's shop on Plum City's main and only street—of the concoctions she dreamed up, sewed, decorated and placed in her display window to be bought by farmers' and merchants' wives, most, like herself, of German descent and longing for some bit of finery, some feathered, mink-trimmed, satin-ribboned bit of beauty in their otherwise scrubbed, poverty-stalked lives. His mother would have admired the flair of these military hats just as much as he liked to muse on the heads that wore them. This memory of his deceased mother softened him just as the inevitable, accompanying thought of his still-living younger brother, Ervin, oppressed him. Captain Brown had been his mother's pride. He had brought her joy when nothing else could, and a harmony in one another's company had always existed between them. As his younger brother plummeted, descending into the same alcoholism that had claimed their father, as Ervin crawled, begging, from doorstep to doorstep, keeping always more ruinous company, so did Anna's oldest son, Clarence, ascend from achievement to achievement, rung by bright rung, allowing her to hold her head high, hatted or bare. Even if she had one son following in the tragic footsteps of his father, she had another she could speak proudly of, sleep better at night because of. This lifelong burden of his mother's pride, added to his own expectations of himself, had buried Captain Brown alive.

He stood before a collection of nineteenth-century surgical instruments, cleverly paired with weapons whose inflicted injuries would have required the aid of such instruments—halves of a lance, for instance, which had passed through a soldier's body, placed beside the steel-toothed saw used to cut the lance in two. He went on to regard shelves of carefully labeled human skulls, a congregation of hollow spheres, the skulls of indigenous peoples from places like Java, New Zealand, Malay, Africa, each meticulously labeled and dated in a spidery, cursive hand, "Kaffir: Tambuki tribe," "Kaffir: Amulosali tribe," "Hottentot and Maori," "Tasmanians" and "San" Bushmen. One shelf held dried heads mummified to the color of dark tobacco and tar. "One of the best and largest collections of Asiatic and African skulls in the world," read the neatly printed sign above the rows of skulls. "From the catacombs of Fort Pitt, Kent, Sir James McGrigor, director, 1833."

He almost felt at home, moving past this lusterless, ghoulish seam of human skulls, outdated weaponry, war relics, and blunt, heavy surgical instruments. He found the antiquated ghastliness nearly preferable to what was occurring in Europe—mass, horrific slaughter, barbarism accelerated by technology—although, in truth, the second had evolved from the same perspective as the first. He pictured his own skull, shaken clean, a bony gourd, eyeless, tucked in among the others, labeled as himself, his skull's former inhabitant, the brain and all it knew, had studied, learned and dreamed—his brain! Him!—dissolved, gone into a mysterious substance not-him anymore, not as he had known himself.

Regardless of his unsmiling mien, Captain Brown was a romantic, his romanticism held in check by a weak strain of melancholic fatalism. Unlike his charismatic, feckless brother, he was not tempted by alcohol. His drink, his oblivion, was work, the call to duty. There was safety in duty, in the unwavering, uniformed chain of command; obedience shored him up against his own native tendency to lapse into permanent cerebral gloom. He was not unpleasantly afflicted with a poet's sentimental turn to loss, it perked him up, in a dour sort of way, to grieve for the state of things, to reflesh the pachyderm, return him to his Burmese jungle, or deflesh himself and in a monkish scourging, kill himself off. In the elephant's case, Captain Brown could easily trace the fate of the creature's skeleton backwards, see it hunted, shot, boiled, its bones prised apart, then labeled, crated, hoisted on the backs of newly conquered British subjects, buried down in some ship's hold, then floated, a nest of bones riding seawater to England, where the disassembled creature would next travel by rail, vibrating in the black fragrance of cedar boxes, only to be unpacked and reconstructed in the great hallway of the Royal Victoria Military Hospital, stuck through with iron pins and rods, stood upright, posed in midstride, facing no more danger than a four-foot-thick wall made of dull red Hampshire clay, on the other side of which, a short distance away, stood the lunatic asylum, a windowless, locked crate for those men whose soldiering had shocked them into a place of trembling and recurrent nightmare. This Burmese elephant, Captain Brown mused, was capacious enough to sit inside of and dine comfortably with five or six other men at a small, linen-cloaked table.

The museum's parting exhibit, displayed by the door, was a clumsily knit rose wool coverlet. According to the engraved brass plaque beside it, Queen Victoria had knitted the blanket with her own hands and given instruction that it was to be laid, an honor, over those British soldiers who had performed most valiantly in the field. The difficulty was, the most valiant soldier was also the one most likely to die from his wounds, however bravely incurred, so within a short time, the Queen's homely coverlet became associated with death, a sort of royal last rite, and no one begged for such funerary distinction. It was eventually determined that the Queen's pink-knit shroud might be better off in the nostalgic setting of a museum.

As he stepped into the foyer, Captain Brown encountered the museum's part-time curator, Nigel Wandle, just arrived from Southampton. The curator was a short-legged, moist-looking man with pewter-colored hair and plump, florid cheeks; his damp spaniel eyes were desperately kind. The two men enjoyed a brief chat, until, upon Nigel Wandle's inquiry, Captain Brown explained his position as the hospital's new American commander. This sent the curator into a bow of such deep obsequiousness it seemed he might never recover, though he did straighten up enough to inform Captain Brown he would be delighted to give him an immediate private tour of the museum.

But the captain, who had enjoyed his solitary hour, needed to move on. Thanking Mr. Wandle, he made his way up the stone staircase, past the crocodiles with their serrated, olive-colored hides and hooded, glassy stares. Had they been speared and collected during the Zulu Wars, had they once glided ominously beneath the deep moonlit waters of the Nile? He mused on these wall crocodiles until he attained the top of the stairs, where he began his own transformation into that creature of duty he had spent most of his first day here evading. As each step led him further from the museum, his personal life receded, his private imaginings would be compressed into a few obligatory though not unaffectionate lines to his wife before retiring, a few moments of reading poetry each morning upon waking. From now on, the main body and consciousness of Captain Brown, naval surgeon and commanding officer of the Royal Victoria Military Hospital, would be given over to authority, leadership, and the thorny, execrable irony of his mission: the dispatching of young men, patched up, splinted, medicated, back into the fields of battle, doomed actors in the improvisatory theater of war.

March 28, 29, 30, 1944
Gustie,

Springtime in southern England, even war-ravaged England, is a thing of great beauty—the almost painful greenness of trees and woodlands, the perfect mildness of air, cool morning rains followed by sparkling sun, the world advertising its fertility with such blossoming and fragrance that we are all heady with it, intoxicated as bees in a rose garden. I have set out by bicycle several times now, on Sundays, cycling through nearby villages, hamlets, down lanes bowered with clematis and honeysuckle, passing quaint thatched cottages, each with its climbing rose. The people are so hospitable one nearly forgets there is a war. At the hospital, everyone naps midday, falling asleep as if under a spell.

I am enjoying John Donne, whom I am reading now, having read and reread the Shakespeare sonnets you gave me. When I return home, I will read some of Donne to you and perhaps put you in more of a mind to like poetry, which you claim, unfairly, to abhor.

Dearie, I would like to get you a bicycle when I return. I know how you feel about exercise (superfluous motion, I believe you once called it), but everyone here gets around on one, and it is the mildest of efforts, cycling, the two wheels pleasantly carrying you so much farther than you could go on your two legs, and at a "round" speed.

Thanks to everyone's Herculean labors, the hospital is coming into decent shape, and our job becomes to maintain, rehearse and wait. I cannot tell you anything other than that we will soon be put to the test, and bicycle excursions, afternoon naps in an aspen grove among great pools of bluebells (which I did this past Sunday) will be distant dreams.

I know I've written to you some of the hospital's history, but I've not yet told you of our resident "Grey Ghost," as she is called. One of our orderlies claimed a "sighting" last night, and there are many tales of her appearance in the corridors and wards, mainly late at night, between 2:00 and 3:00 AM. Some claim she is Florence Nightingale, a few insist it is Queen Victoria, but most go with the theory that the specter is a British nurse who, during the last Great War, neglected a soldier who then died on her watch, and in abject guilt, she flung herself out a window and onto a parapet. Whoever she is, she adds to the atmosphere, the place is abuzz with talk of ghosts and things that go bump in the night. I have been restless of late, unable to sleep, so who knows, one night when I am up roaming, spectral myself, I may bump into Miss Grey Ghost and have a chat.

This is a three-day-long letter, Gustie, and my handwriting cramps to fit these last pages. My longest letter so far and a challenge to the censor! It is an indication of my sleeplessness and strange energy—the weight of what is to come, the worry of whether we are ready, not just in supplies and strategy, but in resolve. I pace in the old way you know, head bent, hands clasped behind my back. I would no doubt shock you could you see me, tired, losing weight, grimmer than usual. The food is dreadful— how I long for one of your Sunday suppers, deep-fried chicken, potatoes and gravy, string beans and apple torte. I am certain I look "peaked," though the real test has not begun. Even during air raid alerts, I pace the corridors. From 5:00 PM until 8:00 AM, the floor-to-ceiling windows are covered with blackout shutters, casting the hospital into a cryptlike darkness. I sometimes feel I am on a ship, the S.S. Royal Victoria, and we are becalmed, though not at sea, instead we are set against, dug into, the red clay of Hampshire.

Tomorrow is Sunday, and after chapel and inspection, I'll try to get to Netley Abbey—a small group has planned the excursion and kindly invited me along. There are not many days left when we will have such hours of leisure, any of us, so I will try to go, and you may be sure I will tell you about it.

You asked in your last letter about the British nurses. The younger ones are taking lessons from our navy girls, sprucing up, braving smiles and more cheerful attitudes. Our men have organized baseball teams, with quite a contest going, so it is not all as grim as you might imagine. The British girls are thoroughly taken by our "Yank" soldiers with their crisp khaki uniforms, appealing accents, and friendly ways. There are complaints, too, of "freshness," but that is to be expected, another reason I stiffen my demeanor, to keep everyone in line and in fear of their stern captain. Compared to everyone here, I feel ancient, an old codger, though I am not yet fifty.

I enclose a few dogtooth violets and yellow primrose I found beneath a copse of beech trees the other day, hidden there, a token of England. I hope you find a bit of fragrance left in them.

—Your old CJ

And he did feel old, a codger. He permitted himself to play no games of baseball, attend no picnics or dances or showings of films—he did not dare soften his demeanor, and the more gorgeous the spring days and perfumed the night air, the sterner he became—only softening privately, when he read his poets and wrote to Gustie, or picked violets and primroses for her in the woods. His letters, too, so much longer than he would have ever predicted, were a place of refuge.

His insomnia, the first he had ever suffered, was a baffling ailment he had assumed would pass. But it hadn't, it had been weeks now of the same thing: dropping off to sleep at 9:00, awakening between 2:00 and 3:00 AM with a drumming panic in his chest, a feeling of gasping for air, his only relief to sit, then stand, pace about the room, then the half-mile corridors, all three floors, walk himself into a blank white exhaustion. Like an abbess counting her rosary beads, he counted off the blacked-out floor-to-ceiling windows (600), wards (135), beds (1000), supplies (he lost count), encounters with the Grey Lady (0). Eventually he would tire and, stumbling with fatigue, make his way back to his room and sleep the one or two hours remaining until dawn.

He knew, from daily secret briefings and coded correspondence, what was bearing down on them. He knew what was to come, and that knowledge had him keyed up to a fevered vigilance. He feared relaxing because he feared failing. The country jaunts he described to his wife, mostly to reassure her of his safety, were increasingly spoiled by his exhaustion, the strain of responsibility. From what he could infer, the coming invasion into occupied France was to be the lynchpin of the Allied campaign, and here he was, in command of a cavernous, outdated hospital, charged with taking in the wounded, the dying, even prisoners of war. He would receive them all with the straight-forward system he had put into place, meticulous, efficient, disciplined. Still, he could not afford the complacency of assuming he was sufficiently prepared.

It seemed miraculous the hospital had not yet been bombed. From the air, it had to be a massive target, and during nightly air raids, bombs from low-flying Messerschmitts on their way to Southampton had, on occasion, fallen almost lazily around them, but none had made a direct hit. Perhaps the Nazis were waiting, diabolically, until they knew the wards were filled with Allied soldiers. The possibility of the hospital's being hit added to his vigilance, his inability to rest.

Halving over the white sheets of paper covered with his long, loping handwriting, a distinctive script with inadvertent splashes of white space where a line of lettering should have been, edging them into an envelope along with the fading woodland flowers, he lay down to sleep, or lie awake, anticipating the trip to Netley Abbey tomorrow, the one excursion beyond his regular Sunday afternoon bicycling he would allow himself. Military equipment and troops had been steadily pouring into Southampton's coastal areas, Spitfire factories and landing fields, oil depots and ammunition dumps, active shipyards and new training stations, the military presence suddenly so heavy, this would likely be his only chance to see the Abbey.

V

At six foot three inches, Captain Brown towered over most men. Height alone awarded him an advantage, invested him with social authority. He quite literally viewed the world from a loftier perspective than most people. He saw the tops of their heads, for example. He saw what was domestically neglected, the mousey veils and gray catkins of dust on the tops of shelves and iceboxes, the spider in its ceiling web, he saw what others could not, an innocent blindness lending them, from his own point of view, a naïve vulnerability. As a young man in Plum City, he had often been asked to fix or fetch things requiring a short ladder or steps, neither of which he needed. How easy for him to pluck a tower of floral-patterned hatboxes from a shelf in his mother's shop! He was slender, too, not lanky, but of such a sinuous, elastic height that movements others didn't think twice about became for him a series of kinetic navigations requiring a gradual inversion or folding up into himself. While his height commanded respect, it also set him at a societal distance. It didn't help that he was extravagantly good looking, not merely attractive as in evenly featured, well proportioned, or pleasantly formed. He had been a beautiful child who had grown into a handsome man, closely resembling his tall, beautiful mother, more so than his brother, who took after his father, Henry, in ways far more unfortunate and ultimately tragic than looks alone. Clarence had his mother's broad face, her high, chiseled cheekbones, long, rich mouth, and seductive, almond-shaped black eyes. He had Anna Brown's features, though given a strong masculine cast, and her thick, lustrous black hair and a light, fine-textured skin that browned easily. If his height gave automatic authority, his face provoked gazes of furtive or open admiration. His wife felt lucky to be the one nurse, among many who had harbored a passion for the young surgeon, he had chosen.

Even after they were married, she never let on how fully she adored him. Added to all this physical advantage was his resolve to rise up from Plum City, Wisconsin's immigrant German farms, churches and shops, including his own mother's millinery shop, and distinguish himself among men. He grasped early on that the way out of a mundane existence was education, and he chose to study not English history or poetry, but internal medicine, then surgery, to become one of the few men granted access to the interior cosmology of the human body. Pragmatically, too, he entered the navy. Fueling these choices was the endless desire to please his mother, to negate the twin humiliations of her drunken, absent husband and shiftless, alcoholic youngest son. To make his mother proud, or at least able to hold her head high among relatives, friends, and townspeople, became his impera- tive. When she died of pneumonia in the same bed she had given birth to him in, he was already ascending through the ranks of the navy, with college and medical degrees, and a respectable marriage. He had already served posts in Haiti, Guam, Florida, and most recently, Philadelphia; yet after she was gone, unknown to anyone, even his wife, he began to wrestle with the shadows and temptations born of her absence.

Within a year of Anna Brown's death, when he was in his mid- forties, Captain Brown began to exhibit a benign but repulsive skin condition. Moles, sable brown, velvety, began to float to the surface of his shoulders and back, muddy constellations scatter- ing across the wide, white-fleshed sky of his back. Imagination suggested to him that these were malignant thoughts, sins made manifest. The larger moles represent his greater sins, the smaller the lesser. An absurd thought since he had been reticent all of his life, uncommonly decent to the point of dullness among his peers and an elevated regard among his elders. Having been given so many natural gifts, he sought to be self-deprecating in compen- sation, and the fear of sin was in him, not because of theological faith, for he had none, but for dread of disappointing his mother any more than she had already been wounded by life. He per- ceived himself as her knight, her source of pride, and whether this was because he had only sensed that this was to be his part in her life or she had told him so directly when he was a child, it was, in any case, deeply true for him. This contract would last until her death, but even then, habit held him to its terms. Morally pristine, impeccable, and ultimately dull. Following his mother's death, he speculated over the dark blossoming of these moles. Was each a wicked thought, an evil impulse, an island of unexpressed cupidity, damped anger, or violence? His own body spoke an alien language. He knew no one else with such an affliction, and the fact of the moles surfacing within a year of his mother's death gave rise to a quiet but very real dread of himself. His superstitions, ideas, and actions, all his natural inclinations, tightly leashed, reined in by mother-love, were such that he had not been able to develop any deep love for his wife. Augusta was everything his mother was not: pale, red-haired, timorous yet alert to social status, emulous and eager for the ascent. It was a perpetual mystery to him why he had chosen her, aside from their common background and a mutual interest in medicine. He concluded that he had chosen his wife out of good sense, for qualities which would help to advance him. His ambition, not his heart, had selected her. His heart belonged all to his mother, the tall, black-haired, mysterious Anna who sang sad German songs, *lieder*, as she invented lavish, impractical confections, her hats. His beautiful mother, who lived only to believe he was born to greatness.

VI

Standing on the ferry's deck, Captain Brown attempted to concentrate on the inane prattlings of the Southampton guidebook, published in 1912, before this war or the previous one. The musty little green cloth book, written in turgid, sentimental prose, had been lent to him by Doris Heck, the British nurse sitting beside Captain Hayden, across the deck from him. It was as obvious as his own solitude that his executive officer and the pretty nurse were far less interested in the ancient history of the Southampton coast than they were in one another's company. Captain Brown could only hope they would not impose too much of their infatuation upon him and spoil his sightseeing trip.

Morning light, gold-etched, effulgent, gave a truer greenness to the mixed forest along the shoreline. As the ferryboat prepared to dock and lower its ramp for tourists like himself, curious to see the famous ruins of Netley Abbey, he paged doggedly on through the guidebook's version of the Abbey's history. In 1259, Cistercian monks had made the journey from Beaulieu to this remote, wild forest. Funded by Henry III, Netley Abbey was designed in the still-innovative gothic style of Abbot Suger, who, one hundred years before, had built the Abbey of Saint-Denis outside Paris. Vaulted ceilings, arched buttresses, and stained glass flooded the lofty space with *lux nova*, a transcendence of light, God's presence suggested and represented by the haunting astral blue of thirteenth-century stained glass. A century later, ships coming into Southampton's busy harbor brought bubonic plague, with fleas from ships' rats wiping out over one third of Europe's population. Netley, decimated, met with a second disaster, the Reformatory zeal of Henry VIII, who ordered Netley sold off. Passed from private owner to private owner, falling into neglect, it accrued the spectral luster of ghosts, siren rumors of hidden treasure. With Sir Horace Walpole's discovery of Netley in 1755, its life as an eighteenth-century gothic curiosity began. Aristocratic visitors to Southampton spa, after taking the sea and mineral waters, ferried over to Netley. An adolescent Jane Austen, on a day trip with her family, was said to have been sufficiently inspired by the decaying monastery to pen her gothic satire, *Northanger Abbey*.

Captain Brown's temples ached, perhaps from the sun's glare on the cramped print. Tucking the outdated guidebook into his jacket pocket, he followed the others, six in all, off the ferry's wooden ramp and onto the rough-pebbled shore. The famous abbey was only a short walk ahead.

He stood before it, disappointed. Perhaps Netley was better appreciated in moonlight or mist, some more somber, miasmic atmosphere than a cloudless, unsullied spring day. He imagined a party of eighteenth-century revelers traipsing about the mordant bulk of stones beneath the burnishing light of an autumn moon, the abbey cloaked and swathed in a shingled gloom of black-veined ivy, indifferent to the amorous gaiety of its visitors. Here he was, in broad mid-twentieth-century daylight along with an elderly Southampton couple, two female schoolteachers from the Isle of Wight and Captain Hayden with his rosy-cheeked nurse, the very cliché of springtime lovers, nestled against one another, her arm twined around his, whispering, the air around them a nimbus of sexual excitement. Beyond his headache, his guilt at leaving the hospital was spoiling his impression of the abbey as well. Although there was nothing left to do but recheck supplies, rehearse triage strategies, review lectures on chemical defense, drill and redrill for potential scenarios, confirm his staff's readiness for the invasion, scheduled, according to the most recent briefing, for the first week in June, still, the entire weight of the hospital's role in the invasion rested upon him, and to step away for something as indulgent as a day trip felt like a mistake. Some part of him had remained at the hospital, and the part that had made its way here found itself nettled by everything. Then again, had he stayed behind, all he would have done was repace corridors, order operating theaters and wards rescrubbed, though they could hardly gleam with any greater austerity.

Vanished, his lovebirds, into the overgrown, winding depths of the abbey's ruins. He could not even hear them, and the other two couples were at a distance, pale touches of color, picnicking on the daisy-whitened lawn. Left to himself, beginning to poke around a bit, Captain Brown accidentally dislodged a bit of tile with his shoe, picked it up, studied and felt with his fingers the small fleur-de-lis design engraved upon its hard surface, then carefully set it down again. He located the abbey's foundation stone, dedicated to Henry III, and again felt with his fingers, tracing over the cold, ancient letters "H: DI. GRA. REX ANGL.," "Henry, by the grace of God, king of England."

Still, a different sort of day, raging with storm-tossed clouds, some atmosphere to underscore the moodiness of the place, would have been preferable. The silence of Netley fell hard on his ears, vastly different from the vow of silence the Cistercian monks had imposed upon themselves centuries before, moving about in their white wool habits, tending cattle and sheep, nursing lepers who sought sanctuary. Captain Brown's silence burned with the drone of distant Allied planes, with the disjointed chatter of his own mind. Still, he'd decided, the place was remarkable, its message clear—whatever man builds, whatever monument to self or to God, is subject to decay and death, to time's scepter, death's scythe. . . . *And, like the baseless fabric of this vision, the cloud-capp'd towers, the gorgeous palaces, the solemn temples, the great globe itself, yea, all which it inherit shall dissolve; and, like this insubstantial pageant faded, leave not a rack behind.* . . . Melancholy seized him with its blue, ruminative weight. In the midst of war, it shocked his perspective to walk inside of a Catholic ruin, a place subject for over eight centuries to pestilence, death, and the vagaries of royal power, to silent fasting and amatory liaisons, exposed to the eyes and sensibilities of artists and sensation seekers, cheapened by gaudy trinkets and tinted postcards, gothic aesthetic, Victorian souvenir, a paste memento of British history—while not more than an hour away, by ferry, stood an eighteenth-century-style stony statement of nineteenth-century British hubris with its haunting waste of space and light, poor plumbing, and inconsistent heat, yet a space prepared now, he hoped, for the bloody aftermath of that most gothic of human horrors, war.

He found a grassy, secluded spot inside what he guessed might once have been Netley's refectory, and lay down, stretched full length, arms clasped beneath his head, eyes closed, ankles crossed. He remembered green and seeding summer fields behind the farm in Wisconsin, and woods where he had loved to disappear as a boy, hunt small prey, dream of mythic battles, noble knights' heroic deeds. He had been an impressionable boy, reading and rereading the books his mother had bought for him, *Ivanhoe*, *The Last of the Mohicans*, *Treasure Island*, *Robin Hood*, the tales of King Arthur's Court. He'd believed in them all. Aspired to bravery.

On the ferry back, he noted an oily smudge of vermilion lipstick on Captain Hayden's rumpled khaki shirt collar. He felt old and unlight; he had taken in too much of Netley's architectural homily on the futility of desire, ambition, even charitable labor, a message he would soon witness for himself, as the dying and wounded flooded like so much bloody flux into his hospital, lifted from ships and barges, ambulances and rail cars on stained and sagging canvas stretchers. The whole truth and vulnerability of his species would be before him, the swiftness with which one generation of young men could be mown down, falling like shadows back into earth's endless maw while the next harbored its false dreams of immortality and power. Fleeting, the love between Hayden and his pretty nurse; nothing sweet outlasted death, nothing was surer, more destined than loss. That truth had given Shakespeare his eloquence . . . the appalling lines he had memorized in the predawn hours—*like as the waves make towards the pebbled shore, so do our minutes hasten to their end; each changing place with that which goes before, in sequent toil all forwards do contend . . . and Time that gave doth now his gift confound . . . and nothing stands but for his scythe to mow . . .*

Later that night, failing again to sleep, Captain Brown would suddenly long for the distraction of war, for his full powers as a surgeon and military officer to be tested. His mind haunted him with grim, tormented musings, though in his next letter to his wife, his last before the invasion, he revealed none of the bleakness that had enveloped him that day at Netley Abbey.

Gustie,

We are well into the month of April. Yellow buttercups, bluebells, forget-me-nots, the white hawthorn, lilac, azaleas, and of course the rhododendron, bloom in cheerful, innocent mockery of the reason we are here. Everyone is restless with waiting to be put to use. The surgeons, nurses, and corpsmen have had enough of bridge and poker games, of chess and checkers, of Friday night cinemas, endless reruns of Abbott and Costello and Charlie Chaplin, of dances to Jimmy Dorsey and Guy Lombardo, of sing-a-longs—"Chattanooga Choo Choo," "Deep in the Heart of

Texas," and "I'll Be Seeing You," are real favorites—of passing around dog-eared paperbacks, old Reader's Digest and Life magazines, of picnics on the grounds, of baseball games and cookouts—the resort-like atmosphere, even the familiar American pastime sounds of "batter up, strike, ball, and safe by a mile!" are beginning to wear. There is too much leisure, and yet there are signs alerting us that we will soon be busy enough to tax the most energetic and skillful among us. Since late March there have been new, heavy restrictions on travel. A ten-mile "war belt" is in effect, and the skies and roads all around are thick with military transports, with plane squadrons flying overhead to Calais, with a near impasse of all roads due to trucks, tanks, supplies, and troop movements. On Southampton Water, pontoon bridges are being built, and from the shore we can see tankers, barges, LST's and LSI's Liberty ships, and an increasing number of barrage balloons. After dinner, at six o'clock, a lot of us listen to the BBC radio broadcast, which always begins with Big Ben striking the hour, followed by the opening bars of Beethoven's Fifth and that unflappable voice. . . . "This is the BBC in London . . ."

Yesterday, Sunday, I made the trip, while I still could, to Netley Abbey. It's a three-mile ferry ride from Southampton harbor to the shores of the former Abbey . . . the ruins are still pretty impressive, the roofless nave, walls cloaked in dark ivy, shaded by ancient beech, oak, yew, or English cedar, with birds, finches and sparrows mostly, flitting in and out of windows long empty of stained glass. The place offers a sobering beauty. One can hardly help meditating on time and decay. But do not let me depress you! On a lighter note, Captain Hayden, my assistant and executive officer, a very nice young fellow from Baltimore, has fallen hard for a certain English nurse; I don't think the beauty of Netley or its antique history impressed either one of them as they walked arm and arm, leaning close into one another and talking softly. They could have been anywhere for all their blindness to anything but each other. In the same spot on earth, Captain Hayden and I, yet what opposing impressions of the day!

Thank you for your latest package, which managed to get

through. I shared much of it with my staff, who particularly delighted in the honey and molasses coconut kisses, the decks of cards and cigarettes . . . the socks are perfect, as my old ones had developed ragged holes from all the miles of corridor I've walked, and the handkerchiefs will be used in all manner of useful ways beyond the usual nose-blowing. I appreciate your amusing take on current shortages, from tires to nylons to meat and butter . . . your portrait of Captain Archembeault's wife, Maude, complaining about her unacceptable lack of a girdle due to the rubber shortage made me smile. Do take care of yourself. I may not be able to write once our job begins in earnest.

—*As ever, your weary boy, Clarence*

VII

Captain Brown stood in the doorway of D Block's first-floor ward, trying not to envisage himself strapped down onto one of its iron beds, restrained, judged a coward, a raving lunatic, or a victim of syphilis, as most shell-shock victims were. He had seen the several padded cells, had read an attending physician's handwritten accounts of soldiers sent here during the Great War, including the poet Wilfred Owen, briefly a patient in this great chilly ward with its low, narrow beds, scoured walls, bleached floors, and barred windows, the air purged of chronology or hope. Order, cleanliness—an unvital emptiness—comprised the prescriptive arsenal against madness. Captain Brown had put off his visit to D Block until today because, unknown to anyone, he feared his own propensity to madness. He distrusted his own nature and curbed his tendency to brood, to be saturnine and dark spirited, with habit, routine, and a meticulous attention to detail. Much of the reason he believed he had been promoted and now found himself in a position of serious leadership was as a result of the draconian curatives he had devised for himself. Yet as he was given more responsibility he found that leadership increased his isolation, his sense of leading a secret life. As authority elevated him, loneliness formed in calcific layers around him.

Everyone was polite, deferential, their facial expressions and speech masked by codes as precise, rigid, and unforgiving as the rows of beds stretching unoccupied but for ghosts of previous occupants in the dreary, tallowy half light before him.

The Royal Victoria Military Hospital had built this villa-like structure apart from the main building, enclosing it on all four sides by a forbidding, natural enclosure of fir trees. A short distance from the soldiers' cemetery, D Block was England's first military ward for lunatics. Its stately, restrained exterior misled one, perhaps intentionally. Once inside, the architecture took a drastic turn toward its more chilling intent—to subdue and, in the common thought of the day, humiliate and punish soldiers weak, cowardly, traitorous enough to mentally break down. Today the ward was empty; the few remaining patients, five or six, to be transferred to Craiglockhart outside Edinburgh, were temporarily housed in a second-floor wing of the main hospital. D Block rang with a ghastly unquiet, with the rancorous, atonal chords of mental disturbance. *That's it,* thought the captain. *I've seen it, touched its surfaces. Done my duty. I need never return here.*

As he made his way down the gravel pathway to the main hospital, a path bordered by a mixed hedge of blackish-green, sharp-edged holly and bitter-scented hawthorn, he thought how remarkable it was to hear birds, mainly finches and warblers, piping from the nearby woods as though there were no war. Wherever it was left undisturbed, the natural world went on as before, just as the dead in the nearby soldiers' cemetery lay in their same postures, deep in Hampshire soil, dissolving, oblong traceries of bone imbedded in striations of red clay, the brutality above them of no further concern.

Around a bend in the pathway, past the unused tennis and badminton courts, their cracking ochre surfaces sprung with burdock and nettle, beyond the cemetery, still pristinely tended, beyond the early sweet cries of nightingales concealed in spired green fir and golden gorse, with the sky flaring into violet and cerise above him, Captain Brown, his gaunt form moving, giraffelike in its clean hide of pressed khaki, continued around the long, sinuous bend until the rear of the hospital came into view, severe, palatial, with its rectangular, arched windows, surreal in their glassy regularity, on and on, three formal queues of windows without pause or deviation in size or glaze, an impression of utter emptiness, until he paused in midstride, seeing a flicker of movement in one of the third-floor windows. He felt the same unsettled sensation he'd had that January dawn, his first day, when he'd come upon the front of the hospital's full, majestic visual force, and seen then, too, a figure standing upright, very still, staring down at him. Third floor, west wing. An unused ward, he recalled, a former lecture hall for the Royal Army Medical School; he had never gone up there beyond the first day's hasty tour through too many vast, unheated freezing corridors and sour-smelling rooms. He'd had no reason to. He stood gazing up, regarding the figure that just as calmly regarded him, and as he did so, the colors around him, the violet and fuchsia-bordered skies, the darkening forms of trees, the air itself, glowed newly, supernally bright. Motion stilled, too; sounds muted, ceased. This went on seconds or minutes but once again, as the first time, if indeed it was the same, the figure receded, melting backward from the window, its enigmatic presence replaced by the blank maddening uniformity of glass.

He wished he knew better the names of trees, shrubs, flowers. He thought this dully, in a sort of stupefaction, after the air regained its normal layers of sound, as colors gradually returned to their normal hues and gradations. A good poet would know these things, be able to name the minutest particulars of the natural world. If poems could be written about the interior of the human body, a landscape he knew intimately and could label perfectly, then he supposed fine poems could be penned about the spleen, the liver, the gall bladder, or lungs, though he wasn't the man or the poet to do it. Captain Brown felt unbalanced, almost giddy. Perhaps it was hunger, for he never ate enough, and under wartime rationing, there was never enough to eat. He quickened his pace, lengthened his already long stride. Gustie liked to say he looked like a protractor when he walked, with his long needlelike legs. And bad though British chow was, an abhorrent kidney and parsnip pie last night, he couldn't afford to miss it—he would need his strength in the days to come and his wits as well. For the hundredth time in the last few days, with all of them, he and his staff, stiffening into permanent readiness, all of them bored, anxious, the hospital fairly throbbing with this uncomfortable set of emotions—he wished, nearly prayed, for the invasion to begin—for casualties to pour in by rail, by ambulance, for the medical work they had all been shipped across the Atlantic for to finally begin. He wished, in short, though not as bluntly as this, not nearly as callously, for other men to be wounded, harmed, shattered, so that he could be, finally, of some earthly use.

As he entered the hospital through its rear entrance, his posture and facial expression automatically shifted, took on the taciturn gravity associated with command, his command, though as he did so, he also made a note to ask the museum's curator, Nigel Wandle, something of an odd specimen himself, if there were any books on local flora and fauna he could borrow, so that he might study taxonomies, seasonal blooming, the Latinate names of things. It would be a wholesome distraction. Deliberately he put any further thought of the mysterious third-floor figure out of his head.

VIII

Supplies and operative equipment were secured, wards, shock rooms, and surgical theaters had been repaired, scrubbed, sterilized, resterilized. A triage system had been overrehearsed, as had contingency plans. Among the surgeons, nurses, and corpsmen, the mix of apprehension, impatience, readiness, and a gaiety that had soured into a chafing ennui infected the hospital's atmosphere. Romances, friendships, enmities were all in full, complex expression, barely tamped down by military discipline and medical professionalism.

Late from his walk, Captain Brown managed to sit down to a decent plate of the night's offerings, boiled meat (three-legged jackass, Captain Hayden joked), lumpy mashed potatoes drowned in starchy gravy, two squares of dry lemon cake, and black tea—always plenty of that; his blood by now had to be half tea—he sat at his customary spot at the officer's table across from Captain Hayden, the closest person he had to a friend, and casually mentioned D Block, that he had wandered over there. He did not mention the figure in the third-floor window.

"What is the name of that spectacular blooming tree, Captain Hayden, the one out back? There was another just like it over by D Block."

Captain Hayden had no idea and didn't care, but figured his pretty British girlfriend did. She was an avid gardener like her mother, and in peaceful times, the two of them had won regional awards for their old-fashioned French roses. He would ask Doris.

"The curator might know as well," added Captain Brown, "he seems to be an authority on pretty much anything local. He's been extremely accommodating."

Hayden snorted. "Accommodating? That's one way of putting it."

"What do you mean?"

"You know his story, has he told you? Probably not. Doris told me the other day, she knows his family."

Forcing down a second serving of the tasteless heel of meat, he heard Hayden's story, first told to him by his British girlfriend, about the mild, bespectacled little curator with his frayed, elbow-patched brown cardigan and pink-pudding jowls, who spoke so breathlessly, a touch of soprano in his tone, his spaniel's damp eyes gleaming behind thick, smudged lenses. According to Doris, Nigel Wandle had been a transvestite nightclub performer in Paris when the war broke out.

"After the Nazis took Paris, a lot of German officers used to go to this high-end club where Wandle performed . . . he had his own solo act . . . so he says. He was befriended by one of the Jerries, a high-ranking officer, and they had a relationship. He actually moved in with him, and they lived together for some months. Meanwhile our queer little curator was in the French Resistance, running messages, sabotaging railway lines, factories, convoys, things like that, all while living with the German officer who had no idea. Eventually, Wandle felt so guilty about the whole thing he moved out."

"What happened to the officer?"

"Ordered to the Russian front. Killed."

"How did Nigel get here?"

"He's from Hound, nearby, same as Doris. He came home, cleaned up his act. He volunteers here, though God knows what else he does with his mincing little ass. Sorry, the guy gives me the heebie-jeebies."

Captain Brown tried to imagine Nigel Wandle tarted up in a wig and makeup, belting out torch songs in a swanky Parisian nightclub, but it was a pretty far stretch. He wondered what else he didn't know about the people around him. Even someone as regular in appearance, as straight-shot, as Captain Hayden, really, who knew?

"Don't get me wrong, he's nice enough, but ever since Doris gave me the skinny on him, I can't stand to be too close, or even in the same room. Gives me the creeps. If he ever flirts with my ass, I'll clock him. You ever know anybody like that?"

"No, I haven't."

"Think of it. A fairy Englishman impersonating a Parisian dame in a nightclub, working for the French Resistance, in love with a Kraut officer, you-know-whatting the enemy, it's completely nutso. Makes you wonder what other stories are out there. It's a crazy world. Well, I'd better shove off. I'm supposed to help Doris set up a rerun of that Charlie Chaplin movie. Will you join us later, captain?"

"I've seen that movie twice now, and don't care to see it again. I think I'll turn in; thanks though. I expect I need to rest up for the days ahead."

"We're ready for it, sir. Eager. Every one of us."

"I know it, Captain Hayden. All of you are more than ready.

I may write a note to my wife before hitting the sack . . . no telling when I'll have another chance."

This was an unfortunate comment for Captain Hayden to hear. Back home, he was engaged to be married, and his letters, dashed off and frequent at first, had slowed down to the kind of silence he hoped his fiancée would attribute to war censorship. He needed to see how far this thing with Doris went before making any decisions. She was a swell gal, and he was definitely sweet on her, but wartime romances were notoriously short-lived. He was hedging his bets, and bad as that sounded, he knew plenty of other fellows in the same boat.

As for Captain Brown, as long as the inevitable romances stayed within decent bounds—which meant out of his earshot and not a detriment to the high standards he demanded—he was tolerant of the wartime relaxation of normal social mores. The "Yanks" were handsome, young, and fit, and, English nurses, even some of the American ones, the Waves, were more daring than in peacetime—and besides, it was spring, and there was an ocean between the men and their wives and girlfriends back home. War and death were aphrodisiacs, and keeping military morale high was an unspoken justification for lapsed behaviors and betrayals. No one said anything, but everyone accepted it.

After brushing his teeth with baking soda, he stripped down for the night, noting again the considerable weight he had dropped since coming here. Four months of walking long corridors, plus unfamiliar foods and his own nerves, had blunted his appetite. He went to bed early, bone weary, not even bothering to squeeze off a note to Gustie—his promise to write her every day broken weeks ago due to overwork and the monotony of his experience. There was little of interest to report, and most nights his own fatigue toppled him. There was also a shortage of writing paper, pens, and envelopes, and increasingly he had to monitor what he talked about, so there were plenty of reasons his letters had fallen from six a week to scarcely one, though hers continued to arrive as if off an assembly line, square, cream envelopes with violet-scented paper inside, her script, half-round, girlish, and trailing off the page at a steep downward slant, her repetitive endearments, her litany of complaints (butter and sugar shortages, the ban on leather shoes, no more than six pairs) and homely bits of news (she was reading Betty Smith's *A Tree Grows in Brooklyn*, wanted to reread Lloyd Douglas's *The Robe*), and the usual updates about her bridge-playing friends. He could hardly admit to himself that he found her letters tedious, shallow. As various distances between them widened, he missed her less, found less to say, it grew harder to convey what he was thinking and experiencing. If he survived this war, he wondered how he would manage to take up the heavy yoke of marriage he shared with her.

Undressed, he glanced in the speckled, tarnished glass over his bureau and found the lean, grim-faced man looking back at him as odd a figure as moist-eyed Nigel Wandle crooning onstage, a flaming Parisian chanteuse, as mysterious as the dark figure in the third-floor window, looking down at him.

IX

Secretly briefed, Captain Brown knew before anyone else at the Royal Victoria Military Hospital, now known as U.S. Naval Base Hospital No. 12, the exact hour the invasion began. The others were made aware, unofficially, viscerally, by a thickening drone in the mild, chalky English sky above them, by the false darkness and herringbone shadow patterns crossing over them, wave upon wave of fighter planes in formation, heading for the Normandy coastline. They knew by the buzz and high-pitched whine of individual engines, by the aggressive, hive-ish sound of bomber squadrons passing low overhead, each plane with its fragile human crew, men who may or may not have glanced down at the hospital's rooftop, at the ponderous grandeur and stony pomp, an ill-equipped, ill-conceived monument to sacrifice—a war memorial—the newest subjects of its tribute not yet dead. How many pilots, American, British, or Canadian, taking off from Southampton airfields toward the French coast, bothered to glance down and see a place they might soon return to, tagged, blanketed, on stretchers, if they were ever found at all?

Captain Brown ordered his full staff, close to seven hundred —doctors, nurses, corpsmen, technicians, and maintenance crews— to assemble on the hospital's front lawn so that he could formally announce what they already knew, that within an unknown number of hours or days, the first Allied wounded would be brought in from evacuation and field hospitals by boat, rail, and Red Cross ambulance. They stood at attention before him, uniformed, ranked, and solemn, as fighter planes unfurled like dark, streaming flags and shook the air above their heads, rendering their commanding officer's words occasionally inaudible. They stood in tight-seamed, ranked rows, in crisp lines of navy and white. After months of meticulous scrubbing, repairing, unpacking, sterilizing, rehearsing triage procedures, preparing each ward and each surgical theater, counting and recounting supplies of whole blood, plasma, sterile alcohol, sulfonamide tablets and sulfonamide powder, penicillin, morphine, medicinal whiskey, codeine, bandages, orthopedic equipment, cotton, plaster of Paris, sheet wadding, crinoline . . . the work they had come across the ocean to do was about to begin, and not one of them could foresee, though all guessed, at its magnitude. As if in meteorological empathy, the morning turned cold, blustery, gray, more February than June, and Captain Brown did not keep his staff outside any longer than necessary, as he watched their dark blue and white uniforms be molded flat against them by the wind, their faces grow pinched and chapped. Even as they saluted their captain and turned to file indoors, a deluge of rain opened over them, so that this first official day of the invasion, June 6th, and all the next, the 7th, were spent indoors, hemmed in by a hostile onslaught of howling wind and drumming rain, muffling the sound of bombers scudding in low, tight formation over the hospital and its grounds. Eventually these ceased, as did the rain, and there was only a deadening quiet from both the waterfront and the skies, while in the far distance, the distant roar of cannon fire could be heard from France.

The hours dragged with exceeding slowness, slowed, too, by anticipation and mild dread. Everyone smoked more, coughed, paced, overate or couldn't eat, tried to read, tried to sleep, worried whether they would be up to the task. It was as if a great drama, rehearsed beyond perfection, had begun to fray in its untested certainty, and there was only this lulling, half-atrophied suspension of time before the opening of the curtain, before the first actor's entrance and the first spoken line. The curtain did draw back, at last, with the heavy, ominous sound of the first train, the squeal of its brakes as it slowed then halted outside the back of the hospital, and with the lifting of the first soldier down from the first compartment, blanketed on a canvas litter, unconscious, bearing a four-by-six-inch tag—identification, diagnosis, medication—his helmet cached between his knees, field bandages soaked in a brown-red gloss, crusted with the gritty, kelp-smelling sand of Normandy beach. The trains, great red crosses on their muddy green sides, ground forward, stopping beneath the glassed roof, hospital cars backed up as far as one could see, and Red Cross ambulances, streaming in from Southampton Water's dockside, pulling in casualties from hundreds of landing craft, tankers, LSTs, hospital ships. The numbers defied counting, though of course there were those present to count, to carry out the first rule of order laid down by Captain Brown—to record each casualty. The commanding officer seemed to be everywhere at once, unhurried, a tall sober figure available at any hour to consult, to give orders, to orchestrate and conduct this vast, teeming, groaning epic of suffering.

Captain Brown found himself living fully inside the nightmare that had kept him awake for weeks now. If he had passed troubling hours doubting his ability to lead, fearing this day, he now understood his superiors had shown some wisdom in selecting him. They knew he would be capable of overseeing, without visible emotion, the care of thousands upon thousands of men, carried in by water, rail, and roadway, dumped like bloody, glistening roe into the stone maw of Base Hospital No. 12. As he watched them, his nurses, doctors, technicians, and hospital corpsmen, he remembered how, only days earlier, they had been occupied writing letters home, playing baseball, cycling into nearby villages on weekends, watching film reruns, dancing, falling in love, and he saw that all of them here, now, were called to some loftier purpose, shorn of selfishness and functioning like one vast, great, succoring organism of mercy. They stabilized blood pressure, hooked up saline and plasma infusions, debrided wounds, bandaged, cut, sutured, operated, amputated, trans-fused blood, gave morphine, penicillin, sulfa, bathed, cleaned, put into clean beds, refused rest for themselves. Their com-manding officer understood everything could go on with or with-out him now because it was in the nature of the event and of these medical workers and the soldiers they attended to act with automatic, selfless skill. That was how he ennobled the horrors he saw. From the unending streams of wounded, he could not gauge the scale of the invasion, nor could he predict how the battle was going or in whose favor. Eventually he would learn, but for now it was all he had in him to stride with mechanical ra-pidity from one operating theater to the next, from the trauma room to the orthopedic room and out to the receiving platforms, to speak to the wounded, laid out in rows, blanketed on litters, waiting with the eerie vacancy of shock to be taken inside. For now it was enough to see that all was occurring as it should, that supplies were holding up, and that his staff had managed to eat the sandwiches brought to them, to drink the tea intended to keep them alert.

All this went on for a great many days and nights before the ships, trains, and dockside ambulances began arriving with fewer wounded, with less regularity. Each soldier's story was nearly identical—picked up from the field by a medic, given morphine, carried to an emergency station, given plasma, taken by ambulance to a field station, X-rayed, treated further, then put on an LST or other landing craft to be taken by train or am-bulance to the hospital at Netley. This went on with morbid reg-ularity until there began to be lulls of twenty minutes, then an hour, then two. And when the skies cleared of war planes and returned to its natural stillness and cloud-washed blue, only then, because of the sustained and almost terrible quiet, did they know the beach assault, this first phase of the invasion, Operation Overlord or D-Day, was over.

Inside the hospital, work continued. Jokes could be overheard, the staff took cigarette breaks and catnaps. Red Cross aides wrote letters home for the soldiers, rolled book trolleys up and down the corridors and into wards. The paratrooper who had broken his leg during the first airborne assault was hobbling up and down the ward on crutches, singing first "Oh, What a Beautiful Morning," then "June Is Busting Out All Over" from the musical *Oklahoma*. The infantryman stringing cable along the Normandy beachhead when an eighty-eight-millimeter shell exploded over him was recovering after a two-inch piece of steel shrapnel had been removed from his left lung. Several cases of rare gas bacillus had been successfully treated. And on it went, in the hundreds, surgeries, suturings, amputations, plaster castings, bullet and shrapnel removals. The first Sunday after D-Day, there was a service in the main chapel and another in the smaller Catholic chapel. All those who could crowded solemnly into both churches, every pew filled, every standing spot taken.

Early Monday morning, when Captain Hayden searched for Captain Brown to inform him of the wounded French sniper just brought in on the last transport, to ask him what to do with her, he located the captain seated on an empty plasma box in one corner of the main supply room, head slumped to one side, dead asleep. As he stood above his superior, requesting permission to put the young woman, a resistance fighter, into a room following treatment, he couldn't be sure whether the captain was fully awake, wasn't just talking in his sleep, when he answered, "Yes, I'll go see her directly." He thanked Captain Brown, already gone back to sleep, and returned to the ambulance, requesting that the unconscious woman be taken first to the surgical examining room and eventually to a private room, away from the others, on the second floor.

X

It was a muggy, opaque day, the white sky rippling with midges like a country pond, bright with swallowtail butterflies, quiet except for the iridescent, occasional whir of dragonflies. In the skies, on the roads and rails, the war had receded but for the infrequent arrival of mostly empty train transports, some arriving to carry soldiers to other hospitals for long-term care, others to deliver them back to the front.

Stiff from spending half the night asleep on one of the empty plasma crates in the first ward's main supply room, Captain Brown stood and gingerly massaged the hard knot on the left side of his neck, hoping to stave off the headache just beginning to rise up from it. He was thankful he had so far avoided catching the summer cold making the rounds of the hospital, with its minor fever, sore throat, and dry cough. Stepping outside to savor his first cigarette of the day, he considered the new deference being paid to him by his staff. Since the invasion, his reputation as commander of operations at Base Hospital No. 12 had increased to the point of near worship. Yet with this temporary celebrity his sense of isolation had increased and with it, his loneliness. He hadn't done much, certainly nothing requiring courage. He had not even taken part in a surgery. He had acted as an administrator and was, if nothing else, a man of duty.

Still, he felt a moment's contentment, walking down the gardener's path he'd discovered days earlier, a narrow dirt trail leading into a small orchard of pear trees. Finding a seat on a low stone wall—the stones rounded, light pink and mottled with white lichen—he thought how even the dead, old or new, must be tempted to stir bones and memory in such a clemency of climate. He thought, too, of the letter he had managed to scrawl off to his wife the previous night—a telegraphic, dashed and dotted sort of missive, to let her know he was well, his work had been noted, praised by higher-ups (last week's visit from Admiral Stark, commander of the United States Naval Forces in Europe, with his subsequent letter of commendation, this, he knew, would please her). The thought of this letter led naturally back to his quarters, his stuffy little garret, to the uniform he'd worn yesterday, in the upper-left pocket of which, neatly tucked, he'd placed the letter, ready to be posted, and from there to the realization that this same uniform had been picked up that morning for laundering (officers were again getting their uniforms regularly cleaned and pressed), causing him to realize, with a small jolt, that if he had left the letter in his uniform pocket, with the uniform now on its way down to the laundry areas in the basement, then his letter to Augusta, the first in weeks, was in imminent danger of being washed to bits.

Which is how he found himself, gone from sitting peacefully on a sun-heated stone wall in an orchard of green ripening pears, to ducking his head to avoid the overhead water pipes and heating ducts as he stepped into the entrance of the cavernous, steamy laundry rooms—one kink of bowel in the great interior of the Royal Victoria he had thus far been spared visiting. He explained his dilemma to the woman, Mary, who came forward to help him, and as she cheerfully went off in search of his uniform, yes, she thought she remembered it being brought in with the others earlier that morning, he stood idly waiting, which is when he first saw another uniform, homemade looking, soaked with blood, laid out on a wood table as if someone had been examining it, perhaps with curiosity, as it was a uniform quite different from all the others that had made their way down here. He walked over and gazed down at it. Pants, a short jacket. It looked like a child's, so small a boy could wear it, and the incongruity of the tiny size with the amount of blood dried upon it clashed in his aching head—he nearly felt as if he were hallucinating, his long, pale, clean fingers barely touching, with revulsion, the blood-stiffened edge of this dreadful garment. When the woman, Mary, came up behind him, he was holding the tricolor armband, blue, white, and red, its black letters FFI below the black double cross.

"Here it is, sir, just as you said. Good thing you came down just now. It was going in the next load."

When he didn't reply or turn to take his letter, she followed his point of attention, though not before observing that the poor man, tall and thin as a scarecrow, an officer from his bearing, looked dead on his feet.

"Tiny, isn't it. Speck of a thing. French woman, sir, that's what we've heard. Not sure it can be salvaged, but we'll do our best. Child-sized, almost. My youngest, Meaghan, at ten, could likely wear it."

"Yes." He turned almost sleepily, putting down the armband and taking the letter while looking down at her. "Yes, it is very small."

The drying map of the French woman's blood haunted him, though he had seen enough blood in the last weeks to fill a small lake. Still, this blood, this tiny, homely uniform, devoid of decoration, moved him. He determined that after the day's normal business, after correspondence, patient rounds, sick calls, and consultations, when he had a free moment, if he had a free moment, he would find this woman and meet her.

But the morning, which had begun with losing then retrieving the letter to his wife, refused to take on any normalcy of pace or routine. No sooner had he come up the ancient lift from the laundry room and given one of his junior staff members the letter to be posted, than he was handed a large manila envelope with his name on it, and stamped in red *Top Secret*. Going into his small office, closing the door for privacy, he sat down at his desk to open the envelope and read its contents. The first order was clear—an incoming shipment of one hundred and fifty German prisoners was to be temporarily housed at his hospital. This was not a problem; he would simply put them in the POW camp with the others, bringing the total number now to what, a little over four hundred?—but the second order was specifically for him. Among the incoming shipment of prisoners was a commanding SS officer with the second SS Panzer Division "Das Reich", captured just outside Falaise. He was to be taken under guard to D Block and, under the personal direction of the hospital's commanding officer, be subjected to psychological inquiry. He read the second order again, slid both back into the envelope, laid it on his desk, and stared out the window, the pleasant view obscured, darkened by his thoughts. He was no psychologist, he was a general surgeon, but with his usual preparatory zeal, he had consulted with American and British psychologists, read current articles in top medical and military journals, and knew something about the most recent drug-and-deprivation prisoner-interrogation treatments. On his desk now, an order of medical interrogation. From what he gathered from BBC broadcasts, as well as from daily reports he received, the war was tilting in favor of the Allies, but the tilt was slight enough that advantage was crucial, including information offered up by one of Hitler's elite, a captured SS officer with direct connections to Field Marshal Rommel.

Partly to avoid stigma, partly out of efficiency, he had placed no patients in D Block. On his orders any Allied soldier showing symptoms of psychological stress was placed on a second-floor wing of the main hospital. Except for severe cases shipped to long-term treatment hospitals, the standard prescribed treatment for battle fatigued patients was deep, medically induced rest, nutritious food, and, if indicated, sodium pentothal therapy. A more personal reason he had emptied D Block of patients was because he hated the place, feared its inference of mental suffering, permanent madness. What he thought of, saw in himself, as a black abyss.

Despite his tiredness, Captain Brown could not afford to be ill or to act weak. He located Captain Hayden, gave an order that he take over his job, carry out routine rounds, review patient charts, consult with physicians, schedule necessary surgeries. He remembered to request an update on the French sniper. He then set off, with his long, deliberate stride, toward the villalike building, hidden by sinister-seeming yews. Though he had read about drugs used in interrogation, he had never administered them. He would have to decide the limits of treatment in proportion to the quality and amount of information he received. He would have to act within hazily defined legal and medical limits to gain enemy information. As a physician, he had just been given authority (orders) to devise and implement those means by which one of the Nazi regime's top officers would confess what he knew. His Hippocratic Oath—subsumed by an oath of loyalty to his country in a setting that unnerved him.

The day's design had so dramatically altered that as he strode past a shoulder hedge of white rhododendrons, the English sky pouring its perfect benefaction of sun over him, Captain Brown heard himself praying, though he was not a routinely prayerful man, that he not flinch at the task before him, that he not be found wanting in whatever courage he might need. He found himself wondering, too, if he might be able to converse with the prisoner; his smattering of German from his days at medical school, from a college literature class where he had been made to memorize and recite the formal German of Goethe and Schilling, made him wonder what, if anything, might he have in common with this man? He would have a translator in the room, an Army officer assigned to guard the prisoner; still, the notion of holding a direct conversation intrigued him. It struck him, too, as he passed the circular stone fountain, dry of water, that defined the central, formal lawn of D Block, as one of those bizarre oddities of destiny, one of history's infinite, sly vagaries, that had his own two sets of grandparents, the Browns and the Plates (formerly Plaths), not emigrated from Leipzig, Dessau, and Dresden to Wisconsin, where he had begun his life, he might well be a German, German-born, one of the enemy. Raised in Leipzig or Dresden, he might well be wearing a different uniform, defending a different nation. But for his grandparents' decision to emigrate, he might be some dreadful twin of the very prisoner he was about to interrogate.

Like his dread of madness, this thought, too, he kept to himself.

XI

He had begun his day reading Donne (he had grown terribly fond of Donne), followed by a perusal of the horticultural book, printed in London in 1929, on England's trees, her flora and fauna, a hefty, deckle-edged book the curator had delivered to him at breakfast the day before, along with a note offering to accompany Captain Brown on a nature walk anytime he liked. Nigel Wandle was not only the hospital museum's volunteer curator, he was familiar with most of the local trees and flowers, the chestnut, beech, ash, oak, and elm, the holly and hawthorn, the bluebells, azaleas, wild rose, rhododendron, plus some imported trees and flowers. England, he told Captain Brown, had once been a woodland teeming with rabbit, badger, fox, boar, and roe deer; today it bore only nostalgic traces of its pre-Roman, Druidic roots. He had thanked the curator politely, when he next saw him, for the book and answered vaguely as to the walk. He could imagine the fuss that might stir up, the rumors, if he disappeared into the woods with a homosexual museum curator. However innocent that walk might be, he was in no position to cast aspersions upon himself. Whatever he did privately must be just as capable of being seen, and honorably interpreted, publicly. His moral rectitude might bore everyone silly, but no one could fault him for any sin beyond dullness, which, in a leader, people found reassuring. Perhaps such qualities in a leader justified or excused a more lax behavior in themselves. For Captain Brown, there was no mischief or pleasure other than reading the work of dead poets and now, perhaps, learning to identify the more common English trees and flowers. It astonished him how much remained unlearned, ungraspable, how much of earthly life remained deeply, stubbornly, mysterious. The creamy, cone-like blooms, for example, that turned the enormous chestnut tree on the lawn just outside his window into a stately, gleaming candelabrum—that single tree bore a lineage far more ancient than his, a loamy, chthonic system of root life, sap, and blossom. What guileless generations, what rookeries had been cradled in those great leafy arms, what decades and centuries of human strife or peace had flared and streamed around it, inconsequential, temporal, a dream, while the tree went stolidly, impassively on in its cycles of minor eternity? Propped against the peeling taupe wallpaper with its blowsy pink blooms, in his striped cotton pajamas, it occurred to him not for the first or last time that one could walk through the world wonder-struck yet still fail to comprehend, beyond cursory naming, any of it, never venturing much beyond the tying of one's own shoe, remembering a friend's birthday, or recalling the plot to last week's novel or a scrap of family history from two years before. There were constraints on knowledge. Most people, as a rule, and if collective politics allowed, gravitated by fate or happy circumstance toward what they enjoyed most. Most people, too, lapsed into believing what it most pleased them to believe. In his case, he had followed a visceral urge to escape Plum City's complacency, its slow drift, its tenacious attachment to German and Lutheran traditions. None of these could he stand, and from the beginning, indifference to his hometown's dogged provincial habits had set him apart. Encouraged by his mother, a woman who could not escape her fate beyond the whimsy of her hats, which in their very artistry and originality bespoke her bitter confinement, Anna Brown urged him on, lived through him, her joy filtered, dilute, parasitic. At the university, he discovered libraries, then his own quick ability to memorize the interior workings of the human body. He chose surgery, then the navy, ways he thought would help him to evade a life that horrified him by its meaningless, incurious, quotidian hold. He had never spoken of this to his wife or to anyone. Captain Brown's interior mental world, arcane and yearning, was as hidden away, as esoteric as the inner body, its fascia, blood, veins and capillaries, bones, viscera. Consider two human beings, chatting amiably, visibly, all the while each is digesting, breathing, each one's heartbeats, the marrow and blood orchestrations of each plays on, unheard, until one of the instruments misfires, falters, or sounds a bleak, wrong-pitched or final note. Captain Brown's ruminations were as concealed as that, playing on in him for decades, both compelling pleasure and torment.

During lunch, he learned that the transport of German prisoners, including the captured officer, had arrived. His food seemed to congeal, look vile. He left the mess hall.

The prisoners were on the rail platform, some set to the side on stretchers, the rest raggedly queued, sullen, kept in order by army guards. He went up to the young, exhausted-looking officer in charge, platinum-haired, blue-eyed, more Aryan in appearance than most of the Germans he was guarding. The SS officer, he learned, was being held in a private compartment of the train until the others had been marched to their temporary prison camp at the far end of the hospital grounds. Captain Brown ordered the Nazi officer be brought to him at D Block within the hour; he had already dispatched men from his staff to manage the intake of new prisoners.

He carried along the English horticultural book given to him by Nigel Wandle. Its blithe, chatty talk of "the gladness of June," "careful wild-gardening; white foxglove at the edge of the fir wood," and "the cottager's way of protecting tender plants," along with its grainy, white-bordered black-and-white photographs, soothed him. Walking the distance from the rail platform to D Block, passing beneath a white, latticed pergola, his head brushing a jungle of untamed blue wisteria, stirring up a few desultory wasps, he stretched the twenty-minute walk to thirty. He longed for time to study, to name both Latinate and common names, what it was he was seeing. He yearned for a day of reading out of doors. On impulse, as if to further retard his progress, he spun on his heel with neat, unobserved grace to look back at his hospital, to gaze up at the row of windows on the third floor where he had seen, weeks before, the strange, spectral figure looking down at him. But the windows, their blackout shutters taken down, were blank as graves, bits of obsidian flashing dully, ciphered, in the July morning. No figure, ghost or human, stood observing him. He turned and made his way toward the small yellowish villalike structure, barren of ornamentation save its dry fountain and granite-pillared entrance.

It struck him again, unpleasantly, how chill the building's interior was, even in summer. A greenish stippling of mildew clung to the air, and familiar, ineradicable smells arose from the damp, aged building, a sterile antiseptic scent only half-masking other odors, blood, urine, feces, infection, pain. Human pain had an odor, as did men's fear. The place made him feel instantly ill, closed in by ghosts of war psychosis, a haunting, noiseless din of men broken and breaking, chastised and mocked. There were no patients left; the few he had found upon his arrival had been sent on to Craiglockhart, outside Edinburgh, an asylum equipped for long-term, even permanent, care. There had been suicides here and famous residents, including two poets of the Great War, Wilfred Owen and Siegfried Sassoon. If the Royal Victoria Military Hospital was a war memorial, its dead still endeavoring to live, D Block was that memorial's most grotesque euphemism, its cabinet of horrors, its curious catalog of what became of men's minds and souls, men young, ordinary or exceptional, fond of sport, of science, music, or love, marched into, and too rarely carried out of, hell.

GREAT TREES OF ENGLAND: *poplar, beech, oak, linden, elm, maple, walnut pine, ash, horse chestnut, birch, yew, lime, sycamore*

The room he selected was unfurnished but for a plain schoolmaster's desk, a wooden chair on either side. A ceiling bulb hung overhead and a window, barred and set high on the room's north wall, allowed in a square of flattened, oyster-colored light. Captain Brown paced the room before leaving to find the first-floor medical supplies room. He needed to determine that sodium pentothal and the several other drugs he required were in good supply.

The prisoner, in a filthy gray-green SS-Rottenführer or corporal's Panzer division uniform, a silk regimental scarf knotted around his neck, sat opposite him. Dark-haired and hazel-eyed, with a high forehead, sensuous lips, and a broad, pockmarked face, he eerily resembled Hermann Grossman, a boy he had grown up and gone to school with in Plum City. The captured man sat across from him, arms defiantly crossed, chin jerked high, attempting to intimidate his interrogator with a look of glacial, withering contempt. Still, he looked like Hermann Grossman, whose father had been the town's local dry goods merchant as well as a deacon in their church. No doubt his childhood friend was caught up in this war, too. And across from him, the enemy, a man who could have been Herman's twin brother. This resemblance, so striking, unnerved the captain more than any show of insolence on the prisoner's part.

He began his interrogation with what he hoped would give him the upper hand—silence. Three men (four, if one counted the hovering, immaterial presence of Hermann Grossman) occupied the small room: Captain Brown, the prisoner, and the army colonel/translator who stood, glum acolyte, between the enemy officers. Five minutes passed. Ten. No one flinched; the air remained immaculate in its silence. He could hear the occasional movements of two guards, fully armed, who stood outside, on either side of the door. He had already rehearsed the opening lines to Goethe's poem "Prometheus," a piece he had memorized years ago, and grasping a pen between his thumb and forefinger, looking at his hand and not the prisoner, he began softly:

> *Bedecke deinen Himmel, Zeus,*
> *Mit Wolkendust*
> *Unde übe, dem Knaben gleich,*
> *Der Disteln köpft,*
> *An Eichen dich und Bergeshöhn;*
> *Mubt mir meine Erde*
> *Doch lassen stehn*
> *Und meine Hütte, die du nicht gebaut,*
> *Und meinen Herd,*
> *Um dessen Glut*
> *Du mich beneidest.*

He looked up; the prisoner was staring at him. Emboldened, he started in on the second stanza . . .

> *Ich kenne nichts Ärmeres*
> *Unter der Sonn, als euch, Götter!*
> *Ihr nähret kümmerlich . . .*

The Nazi officer broke into Captain Brown's recitation, spat out the remaining lines of the second verse of "Prometheus," his precise, formal German making a mockery of Captain Brown's efforts. Still, nothing could have sounded viler than Goethe's sublime poetry rendered rote and emotionless by this being. When the prisoner started in on the third verse . . . *Da ich ein Kind war* . . . Captain Brown ordered the army colonel to tell the prisoner to stop speaking. Enough.

As it became clear that the colonel understood even less German than he did, Captain Brown suspended the interview, ordering the prisoner to be taken to one of D Block's cells, given food and water. His plan was to locate someone who spoke fluent German and return the next morning for a full medical interrogation. As the two army guards stepped into the room, Captain Brown admitted to himself that the task he had been given was formidable. Passing by, a guard on either side, the Nazi corporal, unwashed and bitter smelling, smiled wolfishly at Captain Brown, who called one of the guards back.

"Water only. No blankets, food, or cigarettes. Nothing until tomorrow at my orders. And have him here at noon."

COMMON FLOWERS OF ENGLAND: *rhododendron, azalea, bluebell, lilac, jonquil, violet, hydrangea, delphinium, lily, rose, forget-me-not, peony, primrose, clematis, daffodil, chrysanthemum*

Throughout his childhood, his baptismal certificate, *Tauf-Schein,* had hung beside his brother's in the parlor over their mother's piano—a vellum scroll, flattened and framed, with an illustrated border showing Christ being baptized by John the Baptist, the ritual recorded in flowing black ink. *Clarence Johannes Braun geb.den 15ten Januar 1895 in Plum City, Wisc., Sohn von Heinrich Braun und s. Ehefrau Anna, geb Plath, ist am 15ten April 1895 in der ev.-luth. Kirche zu Plum City, Pierce Co., Wisconsin. im Namen des Dreieinigen Gottes getauft worden. Taufpathen waren: Carl Braun, Johann Plath, and Frau Gertrud Plath, Hatchville, Wisc., Ad. Habermann, ev.-luth. Pastor.* What had he done with that certificate. No doubt Gustie knew, she was efficient at keeping family records in order. After his mother's death and the disassembling of her things, the selling of the home he had been born in, he had been so undone (and distracted, too, by his useless, drunken brother), he scarcely remembered what had happened to anything, though he had been shocked by how quickly his mother's far-flung family members had shown up to strip the house bare, except for what he had managed to hold on to as worth something, sentimentally. He had saved his and Ervin's childhood remnants, the birth certificates, the two photo albums, velvet covered, one claret, the other dark green, both fat and bursting with images of himself and his brother, some anchored in the pages, others slipping about loose among the thick, yellowing pages. The record of his birth and his school diplomas, his penciled high school valedictorian speech. . . . *Of light-souled school life we toll the knell, but not of friendship; let us still hold fast to 1907 though scattered by time's blast; In love united—Good is every state; Take heart, go forth; Obedience conquers Fate!*, a medal from the Plum City volunteer fire brigade, a single trophy from his high school's small basketball team, its second-tallest member (Clarence being the first), Hermann Grossman, physical twin to the Nazi prisoner being held without food in a grimy cell in D Block, where no doubt he was pacing back and forth, hands behind his back, thinking who knew what, harboring who knew what enemy secrets, secrets Captain Brown was determined to wrest out of him tomorrow.

BIRDS OF ENGLAND: *raven, owl, yellowhammer, magpie, nightingale, kestrel, warbler, tit, robin, cuckoo, wood pigeon, sparrow, kite woodpecker, mourning dove, kite, crow*

XII

"I understand you are fluent, Mr. Wandle. In French. I have a patient on the second floor, a woman. I've been told she is not too badly wounded, and I'd like to speak with her."

Which is how he found himself standing inside the doorway of the French woman's private room, listening to the curator, who had, quite casually, pulled up a chair beside her bed, and was sitting on it backward, his arms draped over its back. No more than twenty-two or -three, extraordinarily small and fine-boned, with large brown eyes and black, short-cropped hair, wearing a pair of men's hospital pajamas far too large for her, white with a narrow maroon stripe, she was propped against a bolster of pillows, her left arm, fractured and in a split cast, resting on another pillow, doubled over for height. The small room, stifling from the heat of a July afternoon, had a surprisingly pleasant view of the pear orchard, a benefit spoiled by a faint, foul odor coming from the metal sleeve running along the base of the walls, emptying waste into a drain not far from the captain's feet. The curator had been talking to the woman in a low voice for a few minutes, and Captain Brown found himself playing the awkward voyeur, understanding next to nothing of what was being said. The only thing he caught, in listening, was that the curator mentioned he had worked for the Resistance in Paris, a piece of information which caused her to drop some of her heavy reserve. His sense of exclusion became unendurable.

"What is she saying?"

"Oh say, sorry." Nigel Wandle took a moment to introduce his companion as *le directeur du hospital, un docteur American, un chiurgien, Captain Brown*. As Nigel spoke, she looked over at him with a gaze so direct and penetrating that his earlier feeling of exclusion felt nearly preferable to the force of this woman's personality falling on him. He smiled thinly; she smiled with unexpected winsomeness in return. He saw then that part of her intimidating presence was formed of an understated beauty.

"What she has said thus far is that she was knocked from her hiding place in a school attic by a bomb blast. This was in Saint-Lô. Two American soldiers, securing the building, found her unconscious and brought her here. Her head was cut in the fall, she received a concussion, her left arm, as you can see, is broken. She is otherwise all right and has asked when she can leave."

"Ask her her name."

"Comment vous appelez-vous, Mademoiselle?"

He heard it then. Marie-Helene. He already knew her last name, Sesiche, from her chart.

"Ask where she's from."

"She says she's originally from Paris, but has been living in Sainte-Mère-Eglise with her father who runs a small bookshop."

"How did she come to be in the Resistance? The FFI? Can she tell us that?"

He heard, translated, what she was willing to tell the curator. Her father, originally from Belgium, had come to Paris with his children shortly after their mother, a well-known classical singer, had died. He became a professor of philosophy at the Sorbonne. Marie-Helene had been attending the Sorbonne along with her older brother, Laurent, when the war broke out. Once the Germans invaded and occupied Paris in June 1940, their lives, as Jews, were in increasing danger. Laurent and his friends began a student resistance movement. Marie-Helene herself had been a member.

Four months ago, Laurent, along with five of his friends, one of whom had been her fiancé (they were to have been married this summer), were arrested by the Nazis as Jews and Communists, tortured, and executed. Because of the danger, her father was forced to leave his post at the Sorbonne and came to Sainte-Mère-Elise to open a tiny bookshop; most of the books came from his own library. After learning there were members of the FFI and the Maquis working nearby, Helene joined them and trained as a sniper. She had been wounded and was in the town of Saint-Lô, hiding in a school attic with two others, when she was found by Americans.

"What happened to the other two?"

"One Maquisard was killed, shot, the other she says she doesn't know."

"Can you ask her what she studied before the war, before the occupation?"

"French literature. She says she is a poet, one volume of poems already published. She is working on her second manuscript. In Belgium, her parents were respected in intellectual and artistic circles. Her brother had been studying medicine when he was murdered by the Nazis. Her fiancé, René, also studying to be a doctor, was her closest friend."

"Has she managed to kill any of the enemy since she joined the Resistance?"

The curator, appearing to find such a direct question in bad taste, asked reluctantly.

"*Oui.*" She understood the question before it was translated. He realized then that she understood English, some at least, and that one word, her answer, seemed to suddenly take all strength from her. She closed her eyes, leaned back, evidently tired of his questions. He couldn't stop.

"What will happen if she returns to her village? Isn't she in danger?"

"She feels the only way to go on is by fighting. She doesn't think about danger."

"Tell her thank you, and to let us know if there is anything she needs."

She opened her eyes, which had bluish hollows beneath them—part of her thinness, he saw, was malnutrition—and looked directly at him. "*Merci, Monsieur le docteur.*"

XIII

They were standing together near the second-floor lift. Nurses and orderlies passed by, some transporting patients in wheelchairs or pushing gurneys along the stone-floored corridor. Captain Brown made certain he stood a fair distance from Nigel Wandle and kept his tone neutral and cordial. He didn't want the nurses, or even the curator himself, to misconstrue their reasons for being together.

"I had heard that you worked with the Resistance in Paris."

"I have no family to speak of, captain, so while I lived in Paris as an entertainer, I was a good candidate for the Resistance. I had full freedom to come and go, and my life felt cheap to me."

"Does it still?"

The curator shrugged. "If you don't mind, captain, I may stop by later, bring her some books and cigarettes. She seems bored. I believe she comes from quite a famous family of intellectuals, and then, of course, her mother was a famous singer."

"I see. Well, I can tell you that were she more seriously injured, I would not for a moment consider her request to leave. And I should think leaving the temporary safety of an American-run hospital might cost her her life. She is terribly young."

Again Nigel Wandle shrugged, a closed gesture the captain found irritating.

"She is also exceptionally brave. She'll run risks out of vengeance as much as political conviction and think nothing of it. I've known a great many young Parisians like her. Their indifference to their own lives turns them into brilliant but doomed fighters."

"And she is a poet. Published."

"Yes, amazing, isn't it? Actually there are a lot of writers, musicians, painters, actors, in the underground. One doesn't associate an artist with courage, but I can tell you from experience that they often show the most courage of all. It is the bourgeoisie, those who are comfortable, invested, who are against risk."

As they abandoned their wait for the apparently broken lift and parted at the bottom of the stairwell near the museum where the curator was going in to finish, he said, updating old zoological records, Captain Brown took the opportunity to ask if Nigel would be available to help him in his interrogation tomorrow of the German prisoner. The army colonel, he explained, had been useless and he needed a replacement. He was careful not to let on how he guessed at Nigel's fluency in German and was relieved when Nigel readily agreed. As he wrote down instructions for the curator, he found himself doubting Captain Hayden's story about Nigel Wandle, and doubting, too, its source, Doris.

Later that night, his chronic insomnia seized hold of him. Unable to bear another minute of lying prone, he got up, dressed, left his room, and embarked on what had been his nocturnal habit these past six months, though walking was pleasanter now that it was summer and the air warmer. He debated walking outside, smoking a cigarette, and wandering, in his slippers, the gravel paths leading around the hospital's acres, a violation of curfew that promised solitude, but contented himself instead with walking the long blacked-out corridors, the darkness interrupted by the weird green glow of newly operative air raid lights installed at regular places along the ceilings. He had his cigarettes, a fresh pack, and his John Donne; perhaps he would find a comfortable place to sit and read. He found himself climbing the same stone steps he had descended earlier that day with Nigel Wandle, up to the second floor, east wing, where soldiers whose minds had been unhinged were kept, deeply sedated, on strict orders of rest, nourishment, and silence. During the night especially, that silence was sporadically broken by the howls and groans of men who, dreaming or awake, were back inside the nightmare of their undoing, sedation useless. For now, though, it was quiet.

He headed toward the west wing. He would simply look in, see if she was resting comfortably. If she was asleep, he wouldn't wake her. He had reread her chart more carefully, along with several others. Her health was good, her injuries comparatively minor; there was no reason to keep her beyond a day or two, at most.

He hung back, waiting until his eyes had adjusted to the deeper gloom before he took one careful step into the room, then another, until he was standing at the foot of her bed. It was empty. Her things were there, a full tumbler of water, a tin can cut open for an ashtray and bristling with the brown ends of her cigarettes—*Gauloises*—a cracked, black-edged bit of soap, a slender, violet-jacketed book. He picked it up. *Le Langage Sacre,* plain gold lettering on linen cloth. Her name near the bottom, stamped in the same gold. Marie-Helene Sesiche. He sat down on the mattress edge of her iron bed, opening and turning, one by one, the book's fine-grained pages. He looked at the shapes of her poems which he could not read.

Descending two long flights of stairs ending in the front hall, he came upon the Burmese elephant's brooding skeleton glowing like some massive ivory rubric in the darkness, spied the amber needle of light along the bottom of the museum door. He walked over, gently inclining his ear toward its wood surface, hearing low voices, a man's, then a woman's, conversing urgently, passionately (he thought) in French. Then he heard weeping, and the almost saccharine sound of Nigel Wandle's voice, attempting to comfort her.

He stood, his hand poised as if to knock, then dropping to his side. He felt hotly envious of Nigel, of whatever choices in the curator's life had led to his being close to this young woman, Marie-Helene, intimate enough to comfort her. The Royal Victoria Military Hospital, a place he had previously, and with secret pride, fancied as his own image in stone and marble, felt oppressive now as it grew quiet on the other side of the door, its imposing edifice no longer his image but his gaoler.

XIV

He nearly flung himself, walking, toward the orchard that could be seen from Marie-Helene's window. As a boy, he had helped with autumn apple harvests, and he supposed he was seeking comfort, some childhood familiarity, in taking himself to an orchard so late at night. These past months had depleted and drained him, and as he walked, he found himself spontaneously recalling scenes from childhood, scenes of plain work, of helping his mother or his neighbors, scenes of an uncomplicated, earlier, finer time. Heedlessly, he wore his new slippers, not yet broken-in, slippers his wife had sent him, made of tobacco-colored leather, with a yellow foulard patterned silk lining. In the moonlight, the pear trees shimmered in their gossamer, ordered rows. An orchard's beauty lay in its cultivated order, its exact rows of like trees, a green geometry to frame the subtleties of each individual tree, the snowy, fragrant blossoms, the fruit, hard, speckled green, and female-shaped. Further off, he could hear a nightingale calling to its mate and an owl, too, as he lowered his tall, gaunt frame to the ground, sat, legs outstretched, leaning against the trunk of one of the trees near the center row of the orchard, still kept neat, pruned, in the midst of this war. With his head inclined back against the tree's smooth, slightly pebbled bark, his eyes directed themselves upward, past the foliage and fragrant, swelling globes of fruit, into the quiet sky . . . a dramatic pose, yet with no one around to observe him he succumbed to it, to the tears and the ache blossoming outward from the center of his chest . . . but only for a few moments, seconds scarcely countable, for even alone where no one could see or hear him, he was so deeply stoical that even one tear was, for him, a shocking lapse in his own perception of himself, a contradiction he could not permit. He sank further down then, his head in his hands.

How long had he stood listening outside the door, shamelessly trying to understand their sentences, hers especially? He had had his hand raised as if to knock, then, fingers splayed, resting flat against the door. Would his authority be breached, would his presence interrupt them, reroute the flow of their conversation to some more bland subject . . . he had listened to Marie-Helene's weeping, to Nigel's voice, then he'd lost the whole thread of the thing. He was out of his depth with these people, their problems were not his, it was not his place to intrude, and his directive to do nothing lay, finally, in her weeping. He had lifted his hand off the door, turned, and scuffed his way back up the cool stone stairs, past the animal hides and crocodiles eternally swimming, going nowhere, and found his way outside.

And why had he wept just now and so spontaneously? His walking had not put behind him his raw sense of exile. He felt it even more here, as the dusty leaves of the trees above his head rustled, languid and pliant in the night's gentle breeze.

He had been a good boy, sensitive and eager to please his mother . . . his mother who had complained to him of his father, later of his brother, his mother whom he had heard weeping in her room at night, many nights. He had lived his life in dread of disappointing her or adding to her sorrows. His achievements had all been for her. Even when he married, it was because he felt he should, even as he moved up in rank as a naval surgeon, she was the one he exceeded himself for, obeyed his superiors for, no matter what he might have thought of them. In her later years, he had wanted her to live with him and Augusta, but both women had refused, each out of regard for the other, when truly, nothing, or so he imagined, would have made him happier.

He was the respected commanding officer of a major Allied hospital, he had played an important part in the war, yet he did not feel equal to this young woman, Marie-Helene, so gamine, deceptively fragile in appearance. With her enormous dark brown eyes and boyishly cropped black hair, she reminded him of a small, alert finch. She was beautiful, yes, he could see that she was beautiful, but beyond that she was a poet, just like the poets he had worshipped privately all his life. Yet she fought the enemy, she had killed men. Her rifle, he had seen it, picked it up and examined it, was a gun made in Connecticut in 1910. Resistance fighters frequently fought with weapons airdropped to them by Allies. She killed for her brother, her fiancé, her father, perhaps for her poetry. Could she write poetry anymore? Certainly it would no longer be concerned with the same subjects; her life could never return to its former perspective.

Nor could his.

And Nigel Wandle. He had worked for the Resistance, yet he'd had a German lover, a member of the ruthless Waffen-SS, whom he'd betrayed and then abandoned. Now, due to some hidden chapter or chapters in his story, he was home, quietly living a different sort of underground existence, a drab little curator. Like Marie-Helene, he too had flung himself passionately, daringly, into life.

Captain Brown distrusted passion. He had only seen it in his father's and brother's alcoholic rages, in their erratic and unreliable actions; he supposed he equated it with destruction, damage, pain. If he allowed himself any emotion at all, it was vicarious, diluted through poetry, centuries-old poetry at that . . . emotions further diluted by time. All his life he had cultivated a draconian plot, a barren orchard of his own emotions, controlled, ordered, bearing no fruit. Had he been so wrong, had he failed? The initial dread he had suffered, coming here, was that he would not be able to do the job. The written commendation from Admiral Stark, saying he had performed superbly, would lead to his promotion to vice admiral. His staff acted in awe of him. He should be feeling victorious and deeply confident. Instead here he was, crouched at the base of a tree, working desperately to suppress the chaos in his chest. He supposed this clumsy emotion, this little storm, was some release he was allowing himself now that the main crisis of the invasion had passed. A battle fatigue all his own. Shock of a noncombatant. He had done nothing heroic, not even in the medical theater, where he had barely bloodied his hands. He had been an administrator, a manager. Even now his choices in life, none of them badly intentioned, cushioned him. Ironically, the military protected and rewarded him. So long as he acted first in its best interests rather than his own, so long as he was efficient and dutiful, dutiful even in the hours of his sleep, he would be decorated, promoted, shielded by layers of protocol, and deeply, deeply dull. He felt passion for nothing, not even for his wife. He saw himself as an introverted, cool-blooded medical man, a military officer. That was all.

So he had not knocked upon the door because he had bitterly understood that on its other side were two people whose company he could hardly keep—two people whose lives were predicated on intelligence and passion. Both had risked, and would have given, their lives for others. He had risked nothing and been rewarded.

The encounter with the Nazi corporal had thrown him, so much so that he had postponed the interrogation by one day, thinking to weaken his subject through deprivation and isolation and to gain himself time along with a decent translator. The prisoner's murderous arrogance combined with his rapid-fire, cynical completion of the Goethe poem, his uncanny resemblance to a friend he had grown up with in Wisconsin . . . here was the first enemy he had encountered, face-to-face, and he hadn't known how to respond, and what was worse, the prisoner had seen it, taken his measure, and had only scathing, eviscerating contempt for him.

Tomorrow he would have a fresh opportunity to force out the truth from this man. Tomorrow would find him fully ready to engage in combat, off the field, to show his own bit of courage in the war.

The blood on the uniform, as it turned out, was not hers. The blood had been a young Canadian paratrooper's, under whose body she had hidden for two days and nights until it was safe to come out from hiding. She had been protected by his corpse, his blood and brain matter covering her face, her left arm fractured, her head lacerated. She had made her way to the school attic, blacked out, and been found. Nigel had told him this.

He stood and plucked down a few of the ripest pears, which he then put into his pockets. He reassured himself of his own basic goodness, calmed himself with the not unreasonable suggestion that courage was often a matter of circumstance, and that his opportunity had not yet come. When it came, tomorrow morning, he would be ready.

XV

Climbing the stairs so as not to wake anyone from the juddering noise of the barely operative lift, he found a British sergeant fully uniformed and waiting for him in a chair outside his door. Upon seeing him, the soldier, who had been dozing, stumbled heavily to his feet, saluted, then handed him an envelope.

The message inside, signed by a Major Vance Clifford, RAF, was two lines long, penned in a hasty-looking scrawl.

. . . was found hanged inside his cell in D Block at 13:00 hours this morning, July 14. Because of the prisoner's rank, the body will be shipped back to his former post of command.

"Thank you, sergeant. Does the major wish me to come over to D Block?"

"He indicated that was not necessary, sir. The prisoner's body has already been removed and placed on a transport."

He walked into his room, carefully took the pears, one by one, as if they were made of glass, from his pockets and set them down in a small, neat row upon his writing desk along with the major's message. He turned and offered one of the pears to the British sergeant, who politely shook his head.

"I ordered that nothing be in his cell. Nothing. Aside from water, I ordered total deprivation. How did he manage to hang himself?"

"His own uniform, sir. He tore lengths of it apart."

"With what? His teeth?"

"I don't know, sir. But he hung himself with his own uniform."

"He was a fool. A damned fool."

"It's not uncommon, sir, for German officers of rank, when captured, to kill themselves. In fact, I believe they are encouraged to do so. Because of that, interrogation procedures are usually done as soon as possible after capture."

"I see." Why had no one told him? Why hadn't he known? He had given himself the luxury of one day, and as a result, there was no one to question. Did he detect a faint recriminatory note in the sergeant's voice?

"I postponed my interrogation because I needed a better translator than the one I had been given."

"Hitler would kill himself before he'll let himself be interrogated. They're all trained that way, I believe, sir."

"Do you speak French, sergeant?" He needed to change the subject.

"I do actually, yes."

"Well, I speak it very poorly, so I would like you to accompany me to the room of a young woman we've got here as a patient, a sniper in the FFI. I would like to check on her and discuss her terms of release."

"Happy to, sir, though there is a fresh transport of wounded coming in from the battle around Caen, so I heard."

"Yes, I know. That will be later today. Let's get this done first."

She was sitting up in bed, a tablet propped on her knees, writing with her good arm. The British sergeant stood at attention behind him.

"Bonjour, Mademoiselle Sesiche. May I come in a moment? This is Sergeant . . ."

"Buchan, sir."

"Sergeant Buchan. May we come in a moment?"

He checked her cast, her laceration, which was iodined and healing quickly, her vital signs, which were excellent. He stood over her and told her she was free to leave the hospital at any time. He offered supplies of medicine, food, whatever she needed to get safely back to France. They could put her on a military tanker transport back across the Channel and have a driver take her home to Sainte-Mère-Eglise. Aside from her arm, which would heal in a matter of weeks, she was in good health. As he spoke, and as Sergeant Buchan translated, he noted her uniform, neatly folded and placed at the end of the bed, her FFI armband and black beret placed on top of it. Either the laundry staff had managed, miraculously, to locate a new uniform for her, or they were becoming sadly expert at removing bloodstains.

She laid her notebook to one side, stretched her legs out under the blanket, cupped her arm in its cast across her chest, and spoke in English. "I must ask you something, Doctor."

"Yes, certainly. How can I help?" He heard himself adopting a gallant tone—for the sergeant's sake.

She spoke next in French. "I need you to help my father and me to escape. Either to America or to Israel. It is extremely important."

"Sergeant? Please translate. I don't know how I can help you in that regard. Let me rephrase. I cannot do that for you and your father. I apologize but it is truly impossible."

"But you are the head of this hospital. A man of authority. Of power. Surely you can find a way to help two poor nobodies, a professor and his daughter, onto a boat or plane and out of the war."

"I can offer you supplies, food, medicine, cigarettes, even money, but I cannot do such a thing for one or two persons who ask. Everyone wishes to leave here, to escape the war."

"Jews," she said bitterly, "especially desire escape."

Sergeant Buchan translated, cleared his throat, uncomfortable with the entire conversation. "Sir, perhaps if you spoke to—"

"This is none of your affair, sergeant. I meant what I said. It is strictly impossible. Tell her I am here to tend to Allied soldiers brought to the hospital in need of medical care—not to be part of some underground railway. Say this: I sympathize with your situation, but in trying to help you and your father, I would ultimately be putting more lives in jeopardy." He did not know if what he said was true, but it shored up his refusal in an irrefutable-sounding way. He then tried to inject a bit of lightness. "And you, Mademoiselle Sesiche, have the distinction of being the sole woman casualty we have treated here. And may I say, we are all of us impressed by your bravery."

But she had already begun to cry.

"I'm sorry. I'm not as powerful as you suppose. I'm a doctor, under orders from my superiors in Washington, D.C."

She continued to weep, oblivious of the two men before her. Were the sergeant not present, he might have put his arms around her. He wanted to. Instead, he glanced at his watch.

"We are expecting a trainload of wounded soldiers from Caen. Several hundred. I will come back later today, early this evening, to check on you and make sure you have everything you need. On the other hand, you do not have to leave immediately, you can stay here safely with us as long as you like."

There it was. The salve to his conscience. The compromise.

She could stay on indefinitely. Almost immediately, he was aware of a second motive beyond the first, solicitous one—that he wanted her here for his own reasons.

"No." She had stopped crying, and the finality of her tone, the aura of tragedy that seemed suddenly to emanate from her slightest movement, frightened him. "I must return to my father. He is unwell."

"All right then, I'll be back later on to help you with supplies and arrangements for your safe return home." He was surprised by the sharpness of his disappointment and thought, at first guiltily, of his wife, then resentfully, of her tedious affection for him.

In the corridor, crowded with nurses and technicians going in and out of wards, preparing for the arrival of newly wounded men, he briefly conversed with Sergeant Buchan, thanked him, then left for his office to catch up on correspondence. As he walked, he felt strangely hollow in his own clothes, in his conscience. But that was war, wasn't it? Full of harsh decisions, cruel choices, of always having to think beyond the individual's good to that of the collective. An almost socialist-sounding thought, but there it was. Yet he felt vexed, cheated, as though his future happiness had just been snatched away. The winning of a war, he told himself, was predicated on every kind of sacrifice, including that of men like himself, officers, sacrificing themselves, their identities and desires, to duty.

The first transport arrived ahead of schedule, the first of three when only two were expected, so the rest of the captain's day was spent not in correspondence as he had planned, but in moving between triage rooms and operating theaters, supervising, consulting with surgeons and nurses, being present everywhere he could. He stopped to comfort one young soldier in the shock room, his chest and left arm full of shrapnel and shell fragments, both legs fractured. His name was Jacob Larsen, he was nineteen years old, from Arcadia, Michigan, and his slender, sweet face was remarkably like the sentimental image of Jesus that had hung in Captain Brown's bedroom, over his childhood bed, a portrait he had been made to kneel beside each night, his mother

beside him, both of them saying the Lord's prayer, *Kirchenbuch.*
Vater unser, der Du bist im Himmel. Geheiliget werde Dein
Name. Dein Reich komme. Dein Wille geschehe, wie im Him-
mel, auch auf Erden. Unser täglich Brot gibe uns heute. Und
vergieb uns unsere Schuld, als wir vergieben unsern Schuldigern.
Und führe uns nicht in Versuchung; Sondern erlöse uns von dem
Ubel. Denn Dein ist das Reich und die Kraft und die Herrlichkeit
in Ewigkeit. Amen.

Captain Brown took hold of the boy's uninjured hand, reassuring him that he would indeed live, that he would see his family and friends again, that he needed to buck up and be brave,
but the boy stared straight through him, shuddering with such
blank horror that he was not surprised to learn that after his surgery, which was successful, Jacob Larsen would be moved to the
second floor, east wing, and later shipped to a long-term psy-
chiatric ward outside London. As Jacob Larsen, possessed of the
suffering face of his mother's Savior, stared past him, unaware of
his chest bandages reddening with new hemorrhage, Captain
Brown let go his unyielding authority, which meant his distance,
his white, unused hands, and went to offer his assistance to the
chief surgeon, debriding, suturing, operating, amputating—
whatever was needed, he would do.

Before each surgery, some twenty for him that day, he scrubbed
ten minutes, then dipped his hands in alcohol, and, assisted by
a nurse, drew on a surgical cap, mask, operating gown, a fresh
pair of gloves. He began with Jacob Larsen, with the boy from
Michigan, exploring the thoracic wound first, meticulously removing any in-driven clothing, soil, devitalized tissue, bits of
shrapnel, metal, and bone fragments, followed by lavage, suturing, bandaging. As another surgeon worked from X-rays, setting spica casts for both thighs after aligning the bone ends, he
worked on the left arm, determined to save it. Glancing at the
boy's closed eyes, the faintly lavender lids, at his shock-white
ascetic's face, he recalled lines from a Wilfred Owen poem, not
the famous "Dulce et Decorum Est," but a humbler poem he
loved, said to have been inspired by a newsboy in Edinburgh:

Be you in the gutter where you stand,
Pale, rain-flawed phantom of the place,
With news of all the nations in your hand,
And all their sorrows in your face.

Hours sped by, he went from surgery to surgery without pause except to regown and reglove, and when he briefly looked up from assisting the chief surgeon with a particularly challenging but too-frequent surgery (a soldier, on hearing an incoming shell, would flatten himself against the ground to avoid being hit and be severely torn in the buttocks by shell fragments, some perhaps penetrating the rectum, abdomen, stomach, intestines, liver, kidney, bladder, spleen—each area had to be meticulously explored, the surgeon closing perforations of the large or small intestine, removing a bleeding kidney or spleen, packing any laceration of the liver, draining or closing any wound to the bladder—sometimes, too, that same soldier would require the removal of a limb, using a guillotine type of amputation, the stump left open), as he gazed blankly up from the operating table for a moment's relief, Captain Brown noticed the windows opposite him were dark, meaning it was far past the time he had said he would go check on her. This surgery required at least another hour before he could step away. He was up to both forearms in blood. At one point he had held the entrails, intestines, stomach, and spleen of this young solider in his hands, the long waves of nausea had passed and he had got on with it, not even flinching as a bright gout of blood sprayed up unexpectedly, covering one lens of his glasses, to be expertly wiped away by an attending nurse so that he could continue.

Even the most elementary observer of human behavior soon learns that human beings are complex studies in contradiction, that an individual's motives and actions shift in the crosscurrents of environment and accident. From being denied an opportunity to prove himself brave by interrogating the Nazi corporal (now a lifeless corpse, a suicide), from having to muster a reserve strength (or so he thought of it) to deny Marie-Helene her request (still, she was tough, a soldier with a gun, she had killed, been blooded and would no doubt be fiercely protected by her Maquis fighters when she returned to them . . .), and finally, by immersing himself almost recklessly and certainly selflessly in this fresh wave of casualties, Captain Brown became increasingly persuaded by the notion that he could, and would, save both Marie-Helene and her father. With his arms glazed in blood and his gloved hands helping repair or cut away flesh and bone, as the blood of soldiers increasingly covered him, he saw, in detached epiphany, the true source of human insanity. In that instant he revolted, rebelled, for her at least, as he realized that Sergeant Buchan could provide him, had indeed offered to provide him, the very answer he needed by which he could rescue Marie-Helene. He had not been unaware of the underground networks of people in England and France helping Jews escape to Israel and America, but he had not seen its applicability to his work in the hospital. Marie-Helene counted on him to help her. She called on his human, not his military loyalty.

Finished with the last surgery, he stood as a nurse untied and drew down his bloody apron. He smelled of blood, it was in his hair, his skin, that thick, half-sweet, half-metallic smell. He stripped off his reddened gloves, washed up as best he could, then took the stairs to her room, walking swiftly past the ward of shell-shocked soldiers (their numbers increasing steadily) to tell her, to announce to her he had changed his mind. His decision, decent, unselfish, exhilarated him. The courage of it especially thrilled him, though it did occur to him, on the peripheral edges of his consciousness, that in saving her, he might be able to stay in touch with her. It was in those fleeting seconds before he entered Marie-Helene's room to tell her of his commitment to her that he experienced a freeing sensation spreading outward from the center of his chest, a sense of pure, intoxicating liberation and release.

Her room was empty, the bed stripped. The window was open, the sash raised, and a warm breeze tossed the worn curtains lazily about. On the bedside table beside the ashtray, tumbler of water, and blackened crescent of soap, he saw a piece of paper addressed to him. He picked it up.

> *Dr. Brown,*
> *Thank you for caring for me in your American hospital.*
> *I fight for the hour we all live in freedom.*
> > *Respectfully,*
> > *Marie-Helene Sesiche*

In a matter of weeks he would report, as ordered, to Comnaveu in London and be sent on a new assignment. He would leave the place that had, for a time, enthralled him. The marble and stone in which he had once glimpsed his own image too painfully reflected his weakness, his paralysis of thought. Over the years, his memory of the shadowy figure in the window, gazing down at him, would become various things to him. The ghost of some soldier died or gone mad, an angel of mercy or of death, or the lost specter of himself. The Royal Victoria Military Hospital, Base Hospital No. 12, where for nine months he had fulfilled his duty, given of himself for the sake of his nation and the world, was the same place in which he had met his own disillusioning defeat.

XVI

Hotel Meurice
228 rue de Rivoli
1er Arrondissement,
Paris
June 2, 1970

Not only had they survived the war, their lives had improved because of it. During the last three years before his retirement, Admiral Brown served honorably as assistant surgeon general of the navy. Highly decorated, he remained distinguished enough in his height and bearing that men who knew him rose to their feet when he entered a room, and those still on active military duty who did not know him personally not only stood, but wholeheartedly saluted him. The Admiral's wife, Augusta, was frequently by her husband's side on public occasions. Diminutive, white-haired, elegantly dressed in navy or light gray, she was proud of her husband and of their social standing; a fashion show luncheon for naval officers' wives, with Mamie Eisenhower in attendance, was not an uncommon sort of invitation for her to receive. And the admiral was finally able to take his wife to the great European cathedrals, museums, and galleries he had once promised her in letters he'd written during the terrible years of war. Vacations in Paris, Monte Carlo, Nice, Zurich, London, all these the admiral and his wife enjoyed.

Recently though, he had been diagnosed with emphysema, a result, according to his doctor, of years of chain smoking. Augusta, too, was beginning to show signs of aging, her early dementia more noticeable now that they were traveling. They were nearing the end of a two-week vacation in Europe, and it seemed clear to him that because of his declining health and hers, this trip might be their last.

They were staying in Paris two more nights. Although he had visited Normandy ten years earlier, he correctly anticipated when he told her he would like to go again that she would not want to accompany him. The war, having made only a slight impression on her life, had never interested her. Through the hotel's concierge, he found a suitable day companion—someone to take her shopping and to lunch—while he hired a chauffeur to drive him to Sainte-Mère-Eglise. He left before dawn, with Augusta still asleep. His driver, whose name was Edgard, enjoyed talking about his own part in the war, having been a member of the French Resistance and worn the Basque beret. He'd joined at fourteen in order to avoid the hated German work deportation order, Le Service de Travail Obligatoire, or STO. He was not one of those who liked to boast that they were in the Resistance after it became politically astute to say so and no longer dangerous. No, he had really risked himself, mainly in the areas of demolitions and explosives. He'd blown up rail lines, convoys, power and telephone lines, several factories. Many of his friends had been tortured and killed. He had not been to Sainte-Mère-Eglise, though he'd heard stories, especially the one of the American paratrooper caught on the church spire, hanging as if dead while dozens of other parachutists were shot down all around him. A very famous story from Sainte-Mère-Eglise.

The Admiral was grateful for his driver's enthusiasm. It would make things easier if the time came to explain. In the years since the war, he had made up stories about her. More than anything else, he imagined she had gone on to publish more books of poetry, perhaps even moving back to Paris and achieving literary fame, though when he looked, he had not found her name in any directory.

What Nigel Wandle had told him later that night, after the shock of finding Marie-Helene gone, was that she had confessed to the curator on the previous night (presumably as he had stood outside the door, hearing their voices, hearing her weep) that during a doctor's examination at the hospital, she had been informed she was pregnant. She had wanted to escape for the sake of the child. For herself, she had told Nigel, she didn't care, she was as good as dead; it was for René's child, son or daughter, that she had begged for help. That is what Captain Brown, in his fixed, priggish adherence to rules and protocol, in his fear of consequence to himself, had denied her. But he had not known, how could he have known, was the objection that rose in him every time he thought of it. In his own defense, it was true, he had not known. Had she told him, everything might have turned out differently. Nigel had disagreed. He had blamed no one. "She didn't know you. It was too personal a matter. She'd just found out, was in a bit of shock. I think she hoped to convince you without having to go into detail."

Shortly after Marie-Helene vanished, Nigel Wandle returned to Paris to take up work with the Resistance—no one ever suspected a chubby blonde queer, he said, and after Marie-Helene, he could no longer lay low in a dim hospital museum among macabre Victorian curios. So he left. Captain Brown, ordered by Comnaveu to London in late August, would be reassigned and return home to Philadelphia in early February 1945. From there he would be assigned to Washington, D.C., serving as assistant surgeon general of the navy and finding himself frequently quoted in newspapers, medical and military journals. In photographs, he was invariably the tallest, handsomest officer. Age, rather than detracting, only added distinction to him.

He had never again glimpsed the mysterious figure in the third-floor window of the Royal Victoria—at first he'd wondered if it might have been Nigel, prone to wandering about, and almost wished he'd asked him. Instead, he let himself entertain more gothic interpretations, usually involving ghosts of dead soldiers, or, in his most far-fetched, poetical imaginings, the figure symbolized the madness of war, configured into human shape. The night after Marie-Helene disappeared, he was up as was his habit, though in a much worse state of mind than usual, walking the blacked-out corridors in the middle of the night, when he thought he saw her, the "Grey Lady," wafting ahead of him down the hallway, before floating, a silvery miasmic shape, into the Catholic chapel. Dressed in a gray fashionless sort of robe, ashen in color, as she passed beneath a green air raid light, it flickered off, then as if reluctantly, came back on.

He hadn't been frightened but he'd remembered the story— that she always appeared a few hours before someone in the hospital died. But no one had died that night, and so he discounted that part of the story, at least.

With his chauffeur holding open the door, Admiral Brown got out of the parked limousine on one side of the village square. Marie-Helene had told Nigel her father's bookshop was just off the main village square. His plan, admittedly vague, was to simply walk around the perimeter of the square until he located the shop or met someone who knew where it had once been. Sometimes he imagined Marie-Helene still running the shop with her grown child, a son named René after his father, traveling to Paris for new acquisitions, perhaps having lunch with the publisher of her latest volume of poems. He admired the life he made up for her, envied it, and lived through it as well.

It was then, as he was crossing a street, that he looked up and saw her name. Stopping on the sidewalk, alarmingly short of breath, more from excitement than exertion (as a doctor, he knew his fate: a slow, agonizing suffocation), he stood staring up, as if at a miracle. *Avenue du Marie-Helene Sesiche.* Upon seeing her in the form of simple white letters on a black sign, his heart leapt—a cliché, but it actually happened—his heart actually jumped. Eagerly, he looked around for a bookshop on her avenue, her street, but saw only a butcher shop, a sewing supply shop, and a hairdresser's salon. They went into the first shop, and having explained a little of his trip's purpose to his driver earlier, in the car, he now let Edgard speak for him. He feared his own over-reaction, and indeed, in the first shop, the butcher's, he suffered a severe coughing spell that took him outside to the curb with his hankerchief for a moment—but Edgard went on to the sewing supply shop and finally emerged from the hairdresser's salon looking for him. The hairdresser's shop, he said, with some excitement, had originally been Monsieur Sesiche's bookshop.

Arlette Boissiere was an older woman, stylish, with a short feathery haircut and a scarf of chartreuse slubbed silk wrapped around her long white throat. She spoke to Edgard in French, but once she realized the gentleman with him was American, she switched into near-perfect English.

"Yes, Marie-Helene and her father once owned a small bookshop here. The father mainly ran it; it was well known that Marie-Helene was involved in the Resistance. At one time, without her father knowing, she had even hidden guns and parachutes in his shop. One day, after having been gone some weeks working with the Maquis, she returned. She had been injured, her arm broken, and had come back to care for her father. A neighbor, a woman, a Petain sympathizer who suspected Marie-Helene of stealing her husband's attentions (the woman, a paranoid, suspected half the women of Sainte-Mère-Eglise, yet he was dead now, the husband, as was the wife, so what had it all come to?) immediately denounced Marie-Helene to the local police. They came and arrested her that night. She was jailed, tortured, and executed. It happened very fast."

"Was she shot?" Edgard asked this question.

"Much worse. We heard later from a woman who had been imprisoned with Marie-Helene but was then released. Marie-Helene had been beaten, gang-raped, mutilated, and in the end, they buried her in a field, still alive. When they found out she was pregnant, they figured the child's father was a Maquis, in the Resistance, and so they were especially brutal. I only saw her once when she and her father first moved to Sainte-Mère-Eglise, and I can remember she was very petite, intense. Pretty. Her father shot himself weeks after his daughter's capture, they found him in his bookshop. I'm sorry; it is very depressing, all of this. So many suffered during that time. Horrible, unimaginable things. She turned to address Admiral Brown. "Did you know her?"

"I was her doctor at one time."

In the end, Edgard had to lead him from the shop, sit with him on a nearby bench, bring him water, and after a time, bring the car around for him. He assumed the American man had been her lover, and he felt sorry to have brought him all this way to hear such terrible news. He did explain as they drove back to Paris that over much of France, in hundreds of villages, you can find streets named after heroes, ordinary men and women who died fighting the Germans. He tried to emphasize that it was a mark of honor, a tribute to one who had showed extraordinary courage.

They returned to Paris, to the affluent 1er arrondissement, at dusk. After paying Edgard twice the fare, Admiral Brown went inside the hotel and found his wife resting in their room. He took her to L'Imperial Rivoli, their favorite restaurant near the Meurice, the luxury hotel they always stayed in. Part of the simple pleasure in their travel was always to return to the same places each time to see how little or how much things had changed.

In the restaurant, Admiral Brown, just as he had done all his life, drew the curtain over one story, Marie-Helene's, and opened another—that of a dry martini and a three-course dinner with his wife along with light, negligible conversation about her shopping, her lunch, his impressions of Normandy (invented), their departure the day after tomorrow for Nice. When she was unable to find her way back to their table from the ladies room, when she had to be escorted back by the maître d', he could no longer deny the small, corrosive ways in which her mind was losing its fragile purchase.

Walking arm in arm back to their hotel along the rue de Rivoli, they settled for the night into their elegant suite with its view of the Tuilerie Gardens, the Louvre, the Palais Royale. Theirs was a suite on the top floor, with cream carpet, gold and white striped wallpaper, and pale blue watered-silk curtains. A large bouquet of lilies and roses, compliments of the hotel, graced the Louis XVI table near French doors opening onto an ironwork balcony. As it was summer, an amusement park had been set up in the Tuileries, and an enormous ferris wheel, glittering in the carnival's colored lights, spun slowly in fixed luminous circles until late into the night.

With his wife of fifty years asleep on her side, wearing her favorite black French silk gown, he allowed himself a thought of Marie-Helene Sesiche. Of how he had failed. He had hesitated, chosen duty, debated with himself, then revolted in favor of his heart, but too late. His driver had told him that in villages, towns, and cities all over France, you could find streets and avenues named after the heroes and heroines of the war, men, women, even children, who had died for the good of others. The thought that he could have saved her child as well, had he known—had he known! But was it necessary to know? Courage arising from obedience was limited. A young woman, a poet, had shown more courage than he had. Yet she had been terrorized, then killed, and he was now old, wealthy, honored.

He thought of his marriage. Augusta had miscarried twice, the second time dangerously, and after that, they never spoke of children. Now old, she needed him, and he, who had failed with

Marie-Helene, could only hope to love his wife in the way love most mattered. Here was his last opportunity for a kind of courage, he thought. He wanted to believe in God, it seemed to make things easier for so many people, but he couldn't find a reason beyond comfort—which didn't seem a good enough reason—so he went with Augusta to the Episcopal church on holidays, Easter, Christmas, but he went only to please her and did not receive Communion, a thing he knew saddened her but which they had also never discussed. Why had they never discussed the things that mattered? He had obeyed other men's orders, but had refused to surrender to a thing he could not see. Perhaps he had gotten things mixed up.

As he stood on the balcony, hearing a pair of lovers pass by on the street below, laughing, and watching the great wheel turn before him, its lights sparkling like gems, its passengers dark revolving shadows, he felt a constriction in his lungs, and an ugly, involuntary groan escaped him along with a wave of sickness that subsided, passing through him like a cloud or dream. His wife stirred at the unfamiliar sound, and though asleep, made a sound of her own, as if in response.

How could he forgive himself? He could not, but in her last days with him, he would turn tenderness toward his wife, a kindness that had been for too long obligatory, into something, if not redemptive, extraordinary. He could at least do that.

XVII

Near the end, he was floating in and out of consciousness. Though she shared a tiny, mostly empty room with him in the same nursing home, Augusta no longer knew her husband. Before he was taken by ambulance to the hospital, he managed to kiss her cheek, smooth a sparse bit of hair, once auburn, by her temple.

Curled on her side, weighing less than eighty pounds, Admiral Brown's wife, in her faded, chalk blue hospital gown, stared at nothing. She did not see her husband being taken from her.

XVIII

He bicycled easily along the country lane. Trellises of fragrant climbing roses brimmed overhead, and his path was sheltered, too, by a cool avenue of ivory-blossomed pear trees. England in springtime was heaven, and he felt he could ride on forever. Playfully, she came up fast behind him, first with the cheery *ting-ting* of her bicycle bell, and then passed him, the straw basket fastened to her handlebars bursting with bright yellow daffodils and bluebells . . . he cycled on, content with the sight of her ahead of him, raising her hands daringly off the handlebars as he rode back into the idle green days, into the old stories and legends of foreign lands, warrior heroes and faithful lovers, rode without haste toward a place both common and imparadised where, half-hidden in marble-arched doorways, the mothers of the newly dead waited, wishing their children home from the pain and pride of long adventure.

THE HAUSER VARIATIONS
(As Sung by Male Voices, A Capriccio)

TIERMENSCH
FERAL CHILD

Variation 1
In a narrative tone, not too fast.

I want to describe it for myself, how hard it was for me.
—Fragment from Kaspar Hauser's Second Autobiography,*
November 1828, Nuremberg, Germany

Cribbed in dirt, toed down in stone—cradle, nursery, grave, all
one, one education, one schooling. A narrow space, scarcely four
feet by seven. Not once did he think to stand, for he knew neither
how to think nor how to stand. Over his head, rough-grained
planks. On the ground he sat and slept sitting up, legs thrust
before him, back ever against the same wall, upon a thrifty mouse
nest of straw, reeking and silvered with mold. Two windows,
each no larger than the span of two starved hands set alongside
one another, were set so high that not even shadows, flitting sug-
gestions from another world, mocked him. A single low wooden
door, locked from the outside. An oven of whitened plaster,

---

* In May 1828, fifteen-year-old Kaspar Hauser, rumored to be the Lost Prince of
Baden, became, upon his mysterious liberation from the earthen dungeon in which
he had been imprisoned for twelve years, a sensation, a source of philosophical won-
derment and physical experiment, known as Child of Europe and Tiermensch. Some
months after his release, he became obsessed with writing his autobiography. Who
exactly was he? Fragments from three autobiographies all written in the same month
and year still exist. Others are presumed lost, destroyed, perhaps by Kaspar Hauser
himself, grown discouraged by the demented incapacity, the mangled idiocy of language, to ever reveal his true identity or experience.

beehive shaped, threw its meager, bullying heat at him. In the packed earth, a hole had been neatly dug for him to relieve himself. He wore short leather pants, black suspenders, a rough shirt. Since he knew neither how to dress nor undress himself, a square had been cut from the back of his pants in order that, without difficulty, he could relieve himself. So life went. Inside such a place, he slept, a thick, leviathan sleep, costive, without dream. In such a place, cradle, nursery, grave, Kaspar Hauser grew.

Variation 2
With poetic sobriety.

I had twe pley horse, and such redd ribbons where I horse decorate did.
—Fragment from Kaspar Hauser's First Autobiography,
November 1828, Nuremberg

Dank grub, cabbage vermin, white, hairless, altricial slug. It scarcely flourished in its cradle plot, its solitary necropolis, neither living nor dead, its budded tongue a fleshy club, its legs fwumped and futile. Making only the shallowest of motions in its musky ditch, eyes open or shut, lungs chuffing jaundiced, pernicious air, watered and fed by He Who Had Always Been With Him, an upright creature it never saw. The Unknown One would lace its water with opiates, then while it snored, insensate, he would trim its fingernails, toenails, hair, freshen the sad bed of straw, empty the hole of its raw, stinking slop. The windows gazed down, indifferent citizens with square, lidless eyes, somber and impenetrable. Who has endured such Nonbeing? A self minus itself, queerish slug-a-bub, ignorant of distinction between air and skin, skin the same as dirt, dirt no different from sweated flesh, salted skin, calcific stem of bone. Straw the same as cloth, all parts uncovered, exposed, interred, an austere rot, a nothing/everything —what nonsense of Being!—what distinction between It and Other, where did it leave off and things begin? Permeable, invaded, skinless, no resistance, every particle of air, dirt, straw, wood, shit, water, bread, urine interchangeable, rendered into one original universe. Two rigid black bands, suspenders, on its smooth chest, two filthy red ribbons snugged across the implacable white necks of its horses, the dearest, most darling things, breaking bread, play-stuffing their tight Trojan bellies with that which nourished, star seed of cumin, insects of anise, pale, pitted larvae of coriander, plunging stiff snouts into water poured into its own starved palm, making them snuffle from that roseate, hungry pool, nudging their carved, lipless muzzles, bidding them *Take, Eat,* from that most holy and budded cave of bread, chewed, curdled, sweetened with viscous saliva. Slug-a-bub, denied temperament or climate, was all inside a Great Egg of nothing, hueless, hucksholdered, sicklebacked, nothing had less specificity, less definition, less temperature, less calculability, than it did. A worm gyring, sepulchral revolution, an inconstant severity of air seeping from its bellowed, albescent lungs. It existed in lustless, dull stasis; waking it did not sleep, sleeping it did not dream. Devoid of the slightest qualities, thingish, possessed of no lusts no raptures no aversions no joys, not even the puerility of riddles, no solace of hymns, no scalded teat of nursery rhyme.

Variation 3
In a thoughtful, relating mood.

I will write the story of Kaspar Hauser myself! . . . I will tell you what I always did, and what I always had to eat, and how I spent the long period, and what I did . . .
                    —From Kaspar Hauser's Third Autobiography,
                                November 1828, Nuremberg

When and why was it that young Kaspar Hauser, pudding soft, quaggy limbed, a honied larva, was rudely exhumed to live a second, even more piteous life? Dug up and roused from his underground classroom, punished for making a bit too much noise as he fell backward upon his little horses, uttering a cry—in rushed the Unknown Man, thrashing at Kaspar's bare legs with a long green stick, shut up shut up shut up. And later, when U.M.

brought in the usual black bread and water he carried also a board of wood, some thin pieces of white, and an odd little stick to make shapes of gray against the white . . . sitting down, his fat legs pinching mine, he laid the board across my legs, grabbed one of my hands in his, jabbed the short stick between two of my fingers and pressed, shoving gray lines over the whiteness. Letters, he said. . . . Gripping my fingers in his large hand, pressing, shaving down shape, shape, shape. . . . Each bread and water time he repeated this, until once, when he pushed the stick between my fingers, held his hand over mine for the opening letter, K, he then took away his hand and made me finish. Thus did I learn my name and how to write it. More bread and water times passed, before He Who Had Always Been With Me rushed in loud with clothing in his arms and a letter he had written himself. He dressed me in this noisy, flapping garb, crushed the letter along with other items into my pockets. Then heaving me, like a lean sack of drowned cats, over his thick, mole-heavened shoulders, the Unknown Man carted me down high and low roads to the Big Village.

*List of clothing and various articles found upon the person of Kaspar Hauser, noted this second day of Pentecost, May 26, 1828, being a young man of approximately fifteen bodily years, found wandering in confusion near Vestner Gate, Unschlitt Square. (As noted by one Andreas Hiltel, aged fifty-one years, jailer.)

1 felt hat, round in shape, with yellow silk lining and red leather stitching
1 pair of half boots with high heels, their toes ripped, the soles hammered with horseshoe nails
1 black silk neck scarf
1 janks, or gray cloth jacket
1 coarse shirt
1 linen vest, much washed
1 long pants, gray cloth
1 red-and-white-checkered handkerchief

Miscellany: pocket rags of blue and white sprigged material, a brass key, rosary beads of horn, prayer pamphlets, religious tracts, a letter.

> *CA! CA! GESCHMAUSET*
> *Cling! Clang! Drink Roundly!*
>
> *Cling! Clang! Drink roundly!*
> *We are no feather-headed fools,*
> *Would you live soundly?*
> *Live by our rules!*
>
> *Drink today, feast today,*
> *While we're in clover!*
> *Swiftly the years away,*
> *Drinking is over!*
> —Deutsch Volkslied
> German folk song

WUNDERMENSCH
WONDER CHILD

Variation 4
Bright, lively, with humor.

(Two brothers, shoemakers named OTTO and KLAUS, or, more wittily, HEEL and TOE, discover KASPAR HAUSER wandering dazedly near Vestner Gate, Unschlitt Square, Nuremberg, on March 26, 1828, the second day of Pentecost, between four and five in the afternoon.)

HEEL. Look! What is it?

TOE. A drunkard, obviously. Look how he staggers.

HEEL. He is dressed like a beggar, yet lacks a beggar's beard.

TOE. Those boots! What a disgrace! Better they'd stayed on the hide they came off of.

HEEL. Saint's entrails! He's taken a fall. Let us go to him.

TOE. Let us step over him. *(To audience.)* I'd rather.

HEEL. No. It is a holy day of Pentecost, and our Christian duty to help him. Look. A mere child.

TOE. A youth with an overslung jaw and a letter in its hand. *(Schemingly, to audience.)* Perhaps a bit of money, too. *(Humming.)* My horse needs feeding and the dog's grown thin. . . .

HEEL. *(Ignoring his brother's greed.)* Indeed, it is a letter, and addressed, too. *(He reads.)* To the Well-Born Captain of the Fourth Squadron of the Sixth Regiment of Light Horses in the city of Nuremberg . . . well, that would be Captain von W., who lives steps from here, I repaired his parade boots just last week. Look here, what else is upon this small person . . . religious pamphlets? *(Holds them up, reading titles, one by one.)* Spiritual Sentry, Spiritual Forget-me-not, Prayer to the Holy Blood, and this last—*The Art of Replacing Lost Time and Years Badly Spent.* Oh now, brother Klaus, there's one for you to ponder. The boy is not drunk, he is a Catholic!

(The two shoemakers squat down on either side of the small figure, contemplate him and arrive at reversed conclusions.)

HEEL. Likely he is a saint in beggar's disguise. One of God's Angels, sent to test us.

TOE. He's a moron, and so are you to think anything else. Why must everything be a religious quiz for you? It drives me wild.

HEEL. Because I've kept the faith I was born with, while you lost yours in a series of hayricks with goose-eyed girls, ending with the worst, that spitfire wife of yours. Look, he's waking up. How are you, boy? Do you have a Christian name? Can you hear me? Where are you from? He's not answering.

TOE. How can he, with you yammering away at him? Clamp your jaw and let's wait.

(The two brothers sit, expectant, watching the figure on the ground between them.)

TOE.   You see? I told you. An idiot. An empty pate.

HEEL. Not at all. It's only true that we've frightened him. I'll ask again, soft this time. *(He whispers in a wheedling tone until the boy breaks forth in a torrent of sobs and wet, slurred sounds . . .* rossbuben-rossbubenrossbuben*. . . .)*

TOE.   *(Jumping up.)* That does it. A simpleton. Let's leave him and go home to our suppers. My wife has a fine blood sausage cooking.

HEEL. I couldn't agree less with you and your blood sausage, your big-mouth stomach. How can you fail to see? It's Pentecost, the town deserted, everyone off to the countryside for a holiday, and here in this empty square we've come upon a holy wonder, a Christian miracle, an angel dropped down from Heaven, speaking in tongues of fire. *(As if to prove* HEEL*'s point, the boy bursts out sobbing afresh . . .* rossbubenrossbubenrossbuben*. . . .)* It is God's test of our faith, Klaus, and you, my brother, have failed.

TOE.   I have failed nothing, Otto. It is you who, as usual, have failed to keep the common sense you were born with.

(Lugging young KASPAR, *weeping* rossbubenrossbubenross, *between them, the two shoemakers argue until they reach the door of* CAPTAIN VON W.*'s house,* HEEL *insisting they have met with a celestial being preaching God's word,* TOE *shouting back that the witless oaf, bastard son of Gypsies, should be taken off to Lugensland Tower, the proper place for vagrants, vagabonds, and debtors.* TOE *has faith, but* HEEL *prevails. There is a short, pointless debate with* CAPTAIN VON W., *who, displeased at having his supper, a halfway decent plate of pickled cod and boiled potato, interrupted, scarcely looks at the boy's letter,*

* Buben: boy; ross: horse.

addressed to him, tears it to shreds, muttering, rubbish, rubbish, rubbish, a button of cold potato fixed to his loose, indignant lower lip, and orders this floundersome pest be carted off by stablehands to Lugensland Tower. Thus KASPAR HAUSER *ascended not into any Christian Heaven or even up the steps of the nearby cathedral to be proclaimed a pentecostal messenger, but, instead, found himself hauled off to debtors' prison, given a sack of hard straw and a granite-hewn corner of the high guarded tower in which to sleep.)*

VILLAGE MONKEY o r :
M A J E S T A T S V E R B R E C H E N*

Variation 5
Brooding, choleric.

—From an unpublished account of Andreas Hiltel, baritone,
aged fifty-one, jailer, Lugensland Tower, Nuremberg

I fasten my good eye, the right, against an orb in the wood door, fashioned for the secret observation of prisoners, a hole seldom used, if I may be frank about it, until now. I see no one and, for a moment, fear the creature has escaped. Then I hear him, out of my right eye's sight but within my left ear's hearing, making piteous gibberish, slight departure from the words he repeated over and over when first brought to me from Captain von W.'s house. *"Reuta, wahn, wie mie Votta wahn is."*** Like some disconsolate, shorn-feathered parrot, he repeated himself endlessly.

Eight weeks later:

If God himself were to name my charge a fraud, as many in Nuremberg have recently accused the boy of being, I would have to contradict him. Contradict God. The child is innocent. He is a chick without feathers, a monkey without a hide, that is his only crime. He is, in my opinion (unlikely to be listened to),

---

*A crime against royalty.
**"I want to be one such as my father was."

a victim of *Majestatsverbrechen*. The boy, no more than fifteen, with the mind of a child of three or four, is rumored to be the son of the adopted daughter of Napoléon, Stephanie de Beauharnais. It is even believed by some, who claim proof, that he was switched at birth and in his place was put the sickly infant of the royal gardener, a ninth child, sure to perish. This same gardener, they say, was promoted after the child's "birth" and now lives in conditions of unheard-of prosperity. I say no more. But the boy has a gentle nature and sits on the floor beneath the wooden table, drawing pencil likenesses of toy horses, gifts from visitors. When he finishes one sketch, he sticks it to the stone wall with his spittle, strangely thick and viscous as boiled glue. Dozens of such drawings flutter whenever he gets up or moves about. His visitors arrive at all hours. It is said a visit to Nuremberg is not complete without stopping to climb the circular staircase of Lugensland Tower to see the mysterious Child of Europe. The women gawk and titter behind painted fans and silk parasols, the children roll their eyes, pull faces, and the bolder, meaner boys jab and poke at him. Worse than these children are the grown men, scientists, philosophers, doctors, and dignitaries, who cluster in somber frock coats, squint through shining pince-nez, give sober examination with cold instruments of inquiry. From Mayor Binder, pompous with his city's sudden fame, to the royal forensic examiner, Dr. Preu, to Herr von Feuerbach, the city's chief judge who has, it seems, taken it upon himself to solve the mystery of Kaspar Hauser, this crime of "soul murder," I have seen grown men, with science their excuse, run at him with a drawn saber to see if he will flinch, then hold a candle flame nearer and nearer his face until they provoke a response. He might as well be an ape in a royal menagerie, a caged hyena. No, it is not only Kaspar Hauser I press my eye and ear to the spyhole for; I wish to overhear their speculations as to the child's true identity as I watch, often with boredom (for science, manmade pursuit of truth, can be monotonous), their various tests upon him. This past Sunday, one physician, a colleague of Dr. Preu's, from Brussels, went so far as to fire his pistol straight into the air, without warning, to test the child's response. Someone else threw a lit candle at the boy's head. Both acts succeeded in terrifying Kaspar into fits of convulsion ending in a lapse of consciousness. My authority is nil; I am helpless to stop these monkey tricks. Just yesterday a philosopher from Paris came to gawk, returning early this morning with his pet monkey. He bade the monkey do tricks, delighting Kaspar initially. But as the monkey carried on, tirelessly repeating the same tricks, all at once Kaspar cried out in despair, seeing himself too much in the monkey's piteous, repetitive antics. Never have I known a kinder, gentler, more sensitive soul than Kaspar Hauser. I sometimes muse that were we all to be locked away in dungeons, suspended in our separate dreams, would our world not be the kinder for it? These are the idiot, half-mad musings of a man paid to confine other men. Oh long march of pokers-at-the-soul, keen to further their own prestige, fatten their own purses, sharpen their own reputations on the miserable story of this young man, it would not surprise me if one day I catch old Dr. Preu here yet again, scurrying off with a cold coil of the boy's stool to prise apart with metal tongs and wonder over in the profane sanctity of his laboratory. Sinful examinations! Kaspar suffers and grows weak. He eats less. I fear he will not survive such brutal, sentimental curiosity. I will speak to Judge von Feuerbach when he arrives to visit, as he does each Sunday after church, with his wife and children. I will beg him to put a stop to this monkey show. I care for this boy and wish him no more harm.

So he has been removed to Professor Daumer's house. Daumer shows rare kindness and restraint, so I am sure the change will be good for the boy. I leave his drawings upon the walls, where they faintly rustle, like pale, wintry leaves. Kaspar Hauser was the mirror of innocence. He had nothing false in him. He caused me, old fool, to take notice of things. Helped me to feel pity again.

Variation 6
In a naïve, thwarted tone.

Ich weiss nicht, was soll es bedeuten,
Dass ich so traurig bin;
Ein Marchen aus alten Zeiten,
Das kommt mir nicht aus dem Sinn.

I know not why I am so sad; I cannot get out of my head a fairy-tale
of olden times.

—HEINRICH Heine, "Die Lorelei"

La, it is I, Georg Friedrich Daumer, aged twenty-eight, poet, philosopher, misanthrope, abject and subject to black fits and outcroppings, morbid excrescences of melancholy. Former tutor to Hegel's children—imagine!—and Hegel's sometimes scribe. Herr Hegel himself, grand author of *Geist*, once my very sun and celestial fixing point, begins, of late, to depress me. Here the most recent tone of the man in a letter that I, with my failing eyesight, was made to scratch and piddle down: "—this descent—into dark regions where nothing reveals itself to be fixed, definite, and certain, where glimmerings of light flash everywhere, but flanked by abysses, are rather darkened in their brightness and led astray by the environment, casting false reflections far more than illumination."* Such talk of darkness and false reflection—think!

To counteract this recent lowering effect upon me of Herr Hegel's own depression, and driven as well by a desire to cure myself of doggish melancholy, I have developed a surpassing interest in Dr. Christian Samuel Hahnemann's astounding doctrines of medicine, his new system of Physic, Homeopathy, with its basis in philosophy, for which he has been both celebrated and reviled. One way of thinking of Hahnemann's doctrine is to consider this: two loud sounds may be made to produce silence,

---

*From Hegel's letter to K. J. H. Windischmann (1775–1839), Catholic doctor turned philosopher.

and two strong lights may be said to produce darkness. *Brilliant.* Having cultivated no thought system of my own, I am doomed to paddle in the footsteps of great men, even in the smaller, fleeter footsteps of great men's children, never to be great myself. (Though Thomas Mann himself—and by the governance of time I am not supposed to know this—will call one of my passing stabs at poetry the greatest poem in the language, and a composer, whose name escapes me, will set a body of my poems to music—so, as it turns out, I will not be entirely forgotten nor barred entrance to the thousand side-branching, tributary halls of greatness.)

I console myself with the notion that great men require an audience of nimble yet modest minds. They require men of slight genius to act as mental sycophants, cerebral slaves, theoretical devotees. I am that slave, sycophant, and devotee, mongrel croucher to Schelling, Hegel, Hahnemann (comet of controversy, double-headed pedagogue!) And now, new hope underlies this chronic gloom of mine. I have been asked by my friend Anselm von Feuerbach, a distinguished judge in this city, to house the feral boy, Kaspar Hauser, found wandering our fair city and now held in Lugensland Tower, an object of crude curiosity, a specimen exposed to merciless scrutiny. Anselm believes the youth will die of fever of the nerves or lapse into idiocy or, worse, insanity, so constantly is he held up as a freak of nature. La, the trust placed in me by such a request—consider! Staggering! My poor mind a flea, ajump with notions of how to instruct this untainted, Rousseauian creature. I drop to my knees (theoretically), grateful for the long chance at distinguishing myself, acquiring luster in the world's eyes. And—heaven have it—that low black cur, that beast of melancholy, has, I note, slunk off.

HERR DAUMER'S INITIAL ACCOUNT
(WRIT LARGE),
AS REGARDS DR. HAHNEMANN:

I have been in correspondence with Dr. H. himself—marvelous!—the famous doctor is much intrigued with my K. Hauser and asks that I begin my record as a physician beginning with the exact order of questions Dr. H. himself begins each of his patient interviews with.

1. How is it with the motions?
2. How is it with the urinary discharge?
3. How with the sleep, by day, by night?
4. In what state are his disposition, his humor, his intellectual faculties?
5. How is it with the thirst?
6. What sort of taste has he in his mouth?
7. What aliments and drinks does he most affect?
8. What are most repugnant to him?
9. Has each its full natural taste or some other unusual taste?
10. How does he feel after eating or drinking?
11. Is there anything else to be told about the head, the limbs, or the abdomen?

ADDITIONAL ACCOUNT OF KASPAR
HAUSER, BEGINNING WITH HIS
ARRIVAL AT THE DAUMER HOUSEHOLD,
18 JULY, 1828, CONCLUDING WITH HIS
DEPARTURE, 15 DECEMBER, 1829

1. Exhibition of Strange Faculties and Hypersensitivities
 a. ability to distinguish shapes of letters and complete words in utter darkness
 b. ability to "feel" someone pointing to him from behind
 c. an exquisite, mostly painful sensory apparatus: loud noises occasion convulsions, bright light is agony to his eyes, the merest

drop of alcohol or mort of meat, mixed in with other substances, creates violent sickness, difficult bowel movements, copious vomiting (thus confirming Dr. Hahnemann's belief as well as my own that a vegetarian diet and calm compassionate nature are linked)

d. speaks aloud to all creatures, all animals, cats, dogs, birds, and the like, as if they were human, like himself

e. the scent of a rose revolts him; the color red pleases him to hysterics; black disgusts him; animals, a chicken or horse or cat, for example, terrify him if they are black in color

f. music enraptures him; I have fashioned a sort of drum upon which he will beat out a tune, over and over, for long hours

2. General Progress

a. begins to distinguish between the organic and inorganic, the vital and the lifeless

b. begins to know the difference between a joke and a serious topic

c. begins to write his life story, makes numerous attempts, appears frustrated

3. Physical Progress

a. less prone to daily sickness

b. exclusive diet of black bread and water increased by a healthful cup of hot chocolate most mornings

c. whereas his face had lacked expression in repose and his lower jaw protruded slightly, and the gaze held an animal-like lethargy, his facial deformity has corrected itself, the eyes have gained human luster, and the fingers that formerly were held stiffly and straight out, fingers far apart, now flex and move with a greater naturalness. The walk, once a halting gait, a kind of lurch and stumble, is such that he is now able to accompany me on short daily perambulations outside the house.

4. Sorrows

The caging of small animals upsets him greatly. He cannot understand why people want to cage and harm, kill, roast, and then eat an animal of any sort when he himself would not harm so much as an insect. Surely, he pleads with me, all creatures wish to live free and unharmed. Just yesterday, until I freed a grouse intended by our cook for roasting, he was enraged with me. This animal has harmed no one, he wept in anger. Why not eat bread and water, as I do?

5. Of Meats and Metals

As it is well known that people are inordinately affected by substances around them or fed to them, I tested the effects of various metals and foods upon him. Forcing him to eat small bits of different animal meats (boiled beef in particular revolted him) brought him to such a prolonged agony of sickness I promised never to inflict such suffering upon an innocent creature again,* and wrote to Dr. H. to say my conscience would no longer permit me to tamper with the purity of my young charge's nature, even for a cause so noble as Science. I deeply regret my subjection of this foundling to such long and arduous experiments in metal and the eating of animal flesh. I can scarcely forgive myself. I note that the keenness of his senses has diminished as a result. I note that even language, both spoken and written, has muted his original sensitivity. The former blank slate of his soul is marred, muddied, befouled by the arrogance of man's inquisitiveness. I now believe it a Sin, man's lack of restraint in the quest of knowledge. Had I known how brief an hour Kaspar Hauser had to draw breath, I should have left off my experiments and encouraged him, instead, in his Raptures.

THE THREE RAPTURES
OF KASPAR HAUSER

I. FEATHERBED   Upon being given a proper bed of goose feathers rather than straw, the boy is in a confoundment of joyful pleasure. It was upon this featherbed, in our home, that he first began to dream, though he could not, at first, distinguish between waking and dreaming.

---

*I will later appoint myself founder of the Society of Prevention of Cruelty to Animals.

II. STARS   In August 1829, on a warm, windless summer's night, as we walked, I bade Kaspar gaze upward at the constellations. Amazed, he could not stop looking, exclaiming over and again at the bright beauty of the night sky. How was it, he wondered, he had never seen this before, why had someone wished to keep him beneath the earth, deprived of such a staggering sky? This question affected him as much as the stars, upon which he continued to gaze with woeful awe.

III. HORSES   He has received, as gifts, a great many toy wooden horses of all sizes. He never tires of playing with them, spending long hours alone, playing and talking with them, decorating them with bits of ribbon, feathers, sequins, and the like. They are like living creatures he dotes upon.

6. An Unwelcome English Visitor

One year to the day after the thwarted attempt upon Kaspar's life in our outhouse in the courtyard, the fourth Earl of Stanhope stopped unexpectedly at our home. My wife, her sister, and I welcomed him. He curtly dismissed our hospitality, asking instead for Kaspar Hauser, who was upstairs painting with the watercolors I had recently given him. Lord Stanhope further inquired if he might take Kaspar out for a ride in his carriage, as the October afternoon had only a mild wind with intermittent bursts of sunshine. Without asking Lord Stanhope's approval, I went along and was dismayed when, after only moments, the Englishman had Kaspar on his lap, caressing and even kissing him in a manner I found unseemly if not repugnant. Kaspar seemed unaware of anything being done to him, though I grew horribly disturbed. Was this, I fumed indignantly, the way of English lords, to dandle boys upon their knees and to kiss them in a most intimate manner? When I summoned him to sit beside me for the remainder of the ride, Kaspar obeyed, seeming most cheerful. Outside my home, after handing Kaspar down to my waiting wife, I coldly thanked Lord Stanhope, truly loathing the man. In a haughty manner, flicking his yellow skin gloves arrogantly, he informed me I would hear from him shortly, as soon as he had spoken with Herr von Feuerbach. He wished, he said, to adopt the boy and take him to his estate in England. He only required von Feuerbach's legal consent in order to do so. Going inside, I found Kaspar in his room, calmly resuming his watercolors. Butterflies, he was painting clouds of ethereal butterflies in fragile colors. How illusory his safety! How illusory my guardianship. I vowed I would not let him out of my sight, would plead, in a letter to Anselm, to not give Kaspar into the privileged, repulsive hands of Lord Stanhope.

7. Kaspar Taken!

My letter, suspiciously, never reached Anselm; he granted Lord Stanhope full guardianship of Kaspar. On December 15, several weeks after that carriage ride, two lawyers showed up with official documents, sealed and signatured, authorizing them to take Kaspar to Ansbach, some fifty miles distant, to stay with a village schoolteacher by the name of Johann Meyer until such time as the fourth Earl of Stanhope could arrange for Kaspar to live permanently in England. With heavy hearts, my wife and I helped Kaspar pack his few things, and with the three of us crying inconsolably, the lawyers standing drily by, we bade one another good-bye, my wife and I promising Kaspar we would come to see him in Ansbach. Perhaps he will be safer elsewhere, my wife and I tried to persuade ourselves. After all, someone had tried to take his life in our home, and certainly after that dreadful day none of us ever felt truly safe again. Yet how wrong we were to hope for Kaspar's greater safety away from us! Within one year, our young friend would be dead at the hand of an assassin. The sorrow assailing me made my former melancholia, by comparison, seem a very benediction.

DOCTOR EISENBART
Doctor Irongray

My name is Doctor Irongray,
Valleralleri, hurrah!
To cure the folks I know the way,
Valleralleri, hurrah!
'Tis I that make the dumb to walk,
Valleralleri, hurrah, hurrah!
And I can make the lame to talk!
Valleralleri, hurrah!

—Deutsch Volkslied

HASENFUSS
SISSY!

Variation 7
At a stupidly vigorous marching pace.

From the small Catechism of Johann Meyer:

I assigned a man of God to the boy after telling him that fear was to be his first lesson and God his Fearsome Headmaster. I never knew a boy not to fare better on discipline and calculated privation than on laxity and excessive praise. And this particular boy would require a sterner measure, a harsher dose, than most. Herr Hasenfuss arrived in my home pliant and pale as dough, weak as blood pudding, loose and uncooked. He had been coddled, proclaimed pure, sinless, innocent, a *"wundermensch,"* darling lamb of Nuremberg and so forth, every whim doted on—bah!—puerile whining, all of it! All his silly games of what he could and could not do, eat and not eat, what he could and could not wear, tolerate or not tolerate—pure folly! He soon caught on to my pedagogy, which was to rub his nose hard in whatever he said he could not stand, until he could stand it and stand it and stand it. To beat a boy is wise insurance against future mischief. Daily thrashing, ice-cold water baths, praying on cold stone with bare knees, fasting on Sundays, these are a few of the cures prescribed by myself, his newest master. No frivolous music, no painting of butterflies, no featherbeds, cocoa drinks, or lazy walks, meanderings leading nowhere. These had made of him a girlish, silly creature, spoiled, puling, pandered to, and I began at once by making no allowance, none, for his so-called tragic history. This fanciful talk of a lost prince, a life in a dungeon (had anyone visibly seen this dungeon?) were all false stories. Base lies. Gypsies roam everywhere, and it is well known they send their most comely brats into villages bearing fantastic and well-rehearsed tales devised to excite pity and loosen the purse strings of foolish sentimentalists, of which every village has more than one. How am I to believe he is not the wily sport of Gypsy folk? Perhaps even now he plots to murder and then rob me of what little I possess—this happened just last month in a village nearby. *Hasenfuss*. Little liar. Each morning I set out to catch my stuttering, stammering H. in his latest nest of lies. This morning, for instance, when he complained to me of being sick in the night, saying he had gone into the bathroom to vomit, I said that could not possibly be true. If his sense of smell is so keen, as he says it is, he would not have gone into the bathroom, he would have used the sink in his room. I said to him: either it is not true you have a sensitive nose or it is not true you vomited in the bathroom, or anywhere else for that matter. Choose. Either way you lie.

I am head of this boy's family now, responsible for his godly education, which I render in plainest form. It is I who must convince him of the truth that all good is rewarded and all evil punished.

Why does he not believe me?

Do you pray? I asked.
Every night, he answered.
Tell me your prayers.
I don't know them by heart.
You are lying, I said.
Thus Hasenfuss earned another day's thrashing.

Variation 8
In stern examination.

1. Do you believe that you are a sinner?
    Yes, I believe it. I am a sinner.
2. How did you obtain your knowledge thereof?
    From the holy decalogue or commandments; these I have not kept.
3. Do you feel sorrow on account of your sins?
    Yes, I feel sorrow for having sinned against God.
4. What have you deserved of God on account of your sins?
    His wrath and displeasure, temporal death and eternal damnation.
5. But do you still hope to be saved?
    Yes, such is my hope.

MORDER!!
AND THE OLD FIDDLER'S SONG

Variation 9
Atonal, with agitation.

On a wintry twilit evening, December 14, 1832, not five years after he had first appeared near Vestner gate in Unschlitt Plaza, discovered by two brothers, Otto and Klaus, Kaspar Hauser received a written message from a stranger saying news of his mother awaited him at a particular location at a certain hour. So Kaspar snuck out of Johann Meyer's icy, unheated house and hurried through a drizzle of snow to the Court Gardens in the Orangerie, where he was to look for a man standing directly in front of the statue of the poet Uz, beside a little-used bridle path. Distracting Kaspar with the supposed contents of a woman's green silk purse, saying there was a note from his mother in it, the man, with skilled aim, stabbed Kaspar Hauser in the heart, then fled. Managing to stumble back to the house where he had lived for one miserable year, Kaspar climbed the stairs to Meyer's bedroom, where he found the schoolteacher in bed reading by candlelight, a black woolen nightcap upon his head. He was reading what he continually and obsessively read, Luther's *Augsburg Confession*. Kaspar, managing to gasp that he had been stabbed, showed Herr Meyer the wound. Coolly, Meyer asked that Kaspar take him to the exact spot where he had been attacked. . . . *(I told him to quit making such a fuss, that at any rate he deserved a good thrashing for telling such a tale when it was clear his wound was slight and no doubt self-inflicted. I did not believe a word of his story and made him take me to the place of the supposed attack, which he did. When we returned home, I told him to go upstairs to his bed, that there would be no supper for disobedient boys who snuck out of houses at night. I admit, when I climbed the stairs to his room the next morning, I was astonished to find him not whining or fussing or twitching with all his usual complaints. Hasenfuss lay silent, scarcely making a sound, and when I asked if it hurt, he answered only once, in a monosyllable. This time I lectured him—then you have played a most stupid prank, for which God will not forgive you. He looked up toward the heavens, past me, and cried out—"In the name of God, God knows I tell the truth!")*

It took three days for him to die. Johann Meyer was slow to call the doctor, and when it became clear, even to him, that the boy was dying, he continued to insist the wound was self-inflicted. Kaspar Hauser was heard to whisper once and to no one in particular, for there was no one to hear him other than the doctor and the pastor, that "many cats are the death of the mouse." His last words, before he lay down on his right side and died, were, "Tired, very tired, still have to take a long trip."

By those inclined to believe in higher powers, it did not go unnoticed that on the day Kaspar Hauser's small coffin was carried to the cemetery, the sun was setting in the west at the exact moment the moon was rising, keeping perfect time with the sun in the east.

ES WOHNET EIN FIEDLER
THERE LIVED AN OLD FIDDLER

Thou crooked old fiddler,
now fiddle to me,
I pay thee with pleasure
a generous fee;
Play a frolicsome dance
the time not too fast,
the time not too fast,
Walpurgis night
has come at last.

HOHERER RUCKSICHT
SPIRITUAL MATTERS

Variation 10
Secretly.

Confession of the Unknown Man:

Death turns men honest. *Aller guten Dinge sind drei* (all good things are three). Three times I murdered you. I extinguished your spirit in a dungeon for twelve years—I cannot say who paid me. I attempted your death in Nuremberg, as you squatted in the outhouse; yes, my voice you heard beneath the black hood, my knife jumping back, failing to open your puppy's moist throat. The third time, I hid in a grove of trees, coward and spying, as one hired, drove the dagger deep. Tending you, I was richly paid. Thanks to you, my own nine children flourished. Uneasy sin, agilely done! The rarest plant, savaged. With small hope, I taught you to scribble your name, put you in pilgrim's clothes, took and pushed you through one of the city's many gates—rid of you for a time. A gardener tends life, does not murder. Your blood is on me. I am past saving.

Variation 11
Torment and hope, mixed.

Daumer's Lament:

How could I have saved you? What more could I have done? I was born a man of ideals who lacked conviction, a man of poetic dreams and no courage. I handed you over to sadists and murderers. How could I have known? I am a healthy man who no longer sees. A blind man who cannot forgive himself. A poet who writes only of you, a philosopher asking one question: why on this man-muddled earth was Innocence itself harmed?

QUODLIBET
WHAT PLEASES

Otto and Klaus, two brothers known to all in Nuremberg as Heel and Toe, sing a popular folk song as they repair and stitch, make strong for daily use, the shoes of the common man.

> *It's so long I haven't been with you,*
> *Cabbages and turnips have driven me away!*
> *Cabbages and turnips, yes, have driven me away!*
>   —Deutsch Volkslied

FINALE

> *Reuta, wahn, wie mie Votta wahn is.*
> I want to be a rider like my father. . . .

Strange, to lie underground a second time! From a dungeon with straw, lifted to a high tower, then lowered into a series of ordinary rooms (one with the bliss of a featherbed!), interred again in dirt, once more on straw, a withered, blood-drained root, unlikely to sprout or be resurrected in the same manner again. In death, as in sleep, I am all things. Like any true mystery, I am a mirror, a reflection of the self, gazing back upon itself. Buried, resurrected, shown a host of stars including the solitary sun, buried once more. And though my grave is but a small space, wondrous little, yes, a narrow patch, there is, I assure you, no end to its heights.

On a white wooden horse, I fly upward, outrace the first sorrowing fields of stars. And whether or not my life is Eternal, I cannot or will not say, but I know this, dear ones: it is you who allow pain into the world, and you, poor friends, who look away from human suffering, and in that bright, lively way of yours, break faster and faster, inching toward death, into Song.

PATRICIDE

My sister has dropped pace, fallen behind, lost heart for the trying, and it is not so much an urge to self-destruction as it is a fateful tiredness, not a simple quitting so much as an accumulation of small, quiet griefs that become one onerous fatigue, like a body so enervated by the heat and humidity of not so much a particular day in August, but of a day preceded by a hundred others just like it and the prospect of a hundred more to come, until mopping the brow, lethargic and listless, becomes an improbably vital act in an otherwise flattened landscape of both hill and heart, with energy enough only to arrive at her work in the morning and return home at night, with little nourishment and a decline even in the desire to seek nourishment, nourishment no longer being identifiable or in any quarter nearby—it was in this joyless, tired place, which no amount of rest can relieve or lessen, that I found Avis Sloane, not yet given up but nearing the end of the drained and sunless prospect her life had become.

Our reunion was to be held in an old hotel known as Linden Row on First and Franklin Streets in the historic district of Richmond, Virginia, a hotel which claimed to be the former residence where Edgar Allan Poe, as a child of six or seven, had played in the courtyard, a place referenced in his famous poem, "To Helen." After that, it had become an academy for young ladies, and for a short period, as I was to discover, a lunatic asylum for women. For the past thirteen years, it has existed as a boutique hotel with over seventy rooms.

The famous courtyard, called a garden, was, in fact, little more than a bricked-in central patio containing three round tables with dark green umbrellas, wrought iron chairs, and a number of pots crawling over with richly toothed, variegated sprawls of ivy. Difficult to imagine any child wanting to play in such a high-walled, constricted, and solemn space; perhaps it was a different garden when Poe was a child, labyrinthine, charming, conducive to young secrets.

I had no idea where I was in Richmond, having never visited the city before. My taxi delivered me straight from the airport, though I noticed on our way a group of blacks (or African Americans; impossible, these days, to keep up with proper terms of respect) making their way up the steps of a small corner Southern Baptist church, laughing and shaking hands with one another, greeting one another, the men in tightly buttoned vests, the women wearing colorful summer hats. The neighborhood itself was run down, many of the old, red brick buildings wedged tight against one another, former small businesses boarded up and defaced with graffiti. We drove next through a greener, much more spacious neighborhood, stately blocks of antebellum homes, public parks iron-fenced and verdant, with an excess of bronze memorial statues from the Civil War era, Confederate officers on horseback, sabers raised, with cars like my taxi, its occupants indifferent to such proud, defeated histories, speeding incongruously past. "If the horse has both front legs raised, the officer died in battle, one front leg raised, he died of wounds received in battle, all four legs on the ground, he died of natural causes," the driver said, the single thing he said on our hour's drive. Then I was at my hotel and saw no more of the city's surroundings that day.

We had agreed to meet for Sunday brunch in Linden Row's dining room, though I was to later learn what a long drive it had been for my sister, as I was near the Capitol building, and she lived much further out, in an outlying district of the city. She was there, however, waiting for me, so we proceeded directly into the hotel's formal dining area, a high-ceilinged room with a

Victorian decor of maroon and rich, labial pink, its tables heavily cloaked in white hotel linens, with a view of the famous but in fact quite banal-looking patio. Aside from a central table of ten, we were the dining room's sole occupants. Seated at this larger table was what looked to be a family, ranging in age from perhaps ninety to thirty-five. Their conversation was subdued, patrician, or perhaps only striving to be patrician. I particularly noted the father, at the table's head, regal in his pale blue sport coat and leonine mane of sallow white hair, fading air of privilege, presumed entitlement, faint corruption.

"They still call the Civil War a disappointing incident," my sister whispered. "They've never gotten over it, never moved on. I'm a damned Yankee in their midst. This is the heart of the Confederacy, they hold on to dead glories. Old pickles, I call them."

I studied these people, this old Virginia white family, church-dressed, evidently prosperous yet oddly dated, decades backward in fashion, the men verbally laboring, uneasy with the constraints of mixed conversation, the women uneasier still, nodding, idle and silent, with stiffened hair and expressionless faces, not a drop of mischief in them, perhaps they had never known what mischief was.

Sounding almost Southern herself, my sister said, "Don't they just make you want to shuck off your clothes and dance on every damn table? Old sacks of potatoes."

My sister has saved my life twice, both times from drowning, once in a swimming pool, an accident of youth, the second, an impulse to end things by jumping off a high cliff at night into the sea. Because of this, she is the most important person in my life, and I have always wondered if the time would ever come when I would be called upon to return the favor, to save her. But the purpose of my brief visit concerned a much more delicate, perhaps insoluble, issue. Our father, nearing ninety, has suddenly declared Avis, his oldest child and favorite (there were only the two of us), an utter failure. Because Avis Sloane had done things all wrong, not heeded his advice, he would punish her, teach her a final lesson, strike her from his will and name me, his second, and therefore least favorite, executor. Since our mother had passed away two years ago, I had taken daily care of him and was now meant, it seemed, to enjoy some late moral ascendancy over my sister. As for Avis, my father raged (set off by her latest plea for money, which, it was always understood, could never be repaid), let her stew in her own juice, lie on her own cot, suffer her life's consequence. So I had flown out from San Francisco, where I lived, to tell her this in person, as diplomatically as I could, and to try to decide what to do.

Everything at Linden Row took on a collaged, moribund cast, the dark, bannistered air as layered as any archeological site, the evocation of Poe as a child, the former girls' academy, the lunatic asylum (though I had yet to learn of it, I felt it), its current, vaguely hostile staff, even the music, playing insistently (some might say infernally), like some glaring statement of secular hope, in the parlor and dining room, songs our parents had liked and sometimes danced to, Louis Armstrong's "Mack the Knife," Frank Sinatra, diluted hybrids of jazz and Big Band music.

My room, no. 313, exercised a sort of spell over me. I felt as though I could grow old, in elegiac solitude, within its protected walls, recede, never to emerge, a creature finding, at last, its proper shell, incurved and content. I remember thinking it was very like a large, fine tomb. The walls were of a pink clay color, meaning a faint blush or flesh tinged with a hint, a wash perhaps, of gray. A solacing color, though I cannot say why. The wainscoting at the bottom was deep and white, and at the top, around the ceiling, was a paper border of deep green with a bold floral pattern of hydrangeas. The drapes, too, were floral, a deep green ground with blossoms, mainly roses, of a peach, pink, and Alice blue color. The furniture was dark Victorian—the headboard a beveled dark square like a tablet of fine Godiva chocolate, faintly polished. The bed was large and firm and had a cream damask coverlet. Opposite the

bed was a mantled fireplace of the same dark wood upon
which stood, at opposite ends, two Oriental vases, pink, with
delicate yellow collars, containing tired-looking sprays of
money plant. Above the fireplace hung a large gold-framed
print, an ornate engraving of Greek artifacts, listed, by category, in calligraphied Italian. To the left of the fireplace stood
a massive wardrobe, a chifferobe of the same blackish mahogany. A desk and chair sat between a pair of floor-to-
ceiling windows, above the desk a long oval mirror that forced
me, as I sat and wrote, to gaze occasionally upward, upon myself. What did I see? The pale face of an older woman, her face
strangely unlined, attractive but wary, guarded, with green,
deep-set eyes. In one corner of the room, beside one of the windows, was a comfortable-looking armchair, covered in that
same green floral chintz, and on either side of the bed, matching gray marble-topped nightstands, each with two capacious
drawers, each drawer with heavy, carved roses, like clumps of
hardened meat, for their pulls. The carpet was the green of
certain dark hedges, with a pleasing latticework pattern suggesting gold laurel leaves.

The bathroom had a large brown marble sink, the drain of
which was sluggish, a deep clawfoot tub, and a toilet. The walls
were papered in a pale beige linen texture, the floor made of
old-fashioned, small, hexagon-shaped tiles of a mixed gray and
white pattern, and though I studied it, I could find no order in
their placement. Both rooms, with their sober fixtures and dark
furnishings, their subdued, even staid aesthetic, calmed me. I
neglected to mention how the two windows looked out upon a
narrow gray porch with a slender white railing, beneath which
lay the famed but nonetheless disappointing Poe garden. And
by the marble sink in the bathroom was a third large window
with a deep ledge upon which I stored my various toilet articles. There was a shade to pull down at night, and over that, a
gauzy ivory panel of curtain, but I enjoyed the suggestion of
voyeurism, the idea that if someone really wanted to, was perhaps compelled, such a stranger could see bits of me, undressing,

washing, preparing for bed, or perhaps for a bath; this gave me a keen, febrile sense of excitement.

I am getting beyond the subject of my sister.

Through an oversight by a hotel staff indifferent to its reputation and less than efficient, my room had not yet been made up from the previous guest. Shortly after calling down to housekeeping, I opened the door to a tiny, hunched apparition, sickle-backed, dozens of warts, pinkish, cankered blooms, standing off her face, her grotesque hunch bringing to mind nothing other than a damp-skinned, hideous toad (I should not have been surprised if she hopped). Toad responded churlishly to my polite inquiry as to her health and the quality of her day, and I quickly received the impression that she neither welcomed nor wanted lodgers present in her rooms when she came in to tidy up (perhaps she was one of those who liked to snoop or even steal). At any rate, for this ulcerous, proprietary creature, I tried to be meek, indeed invisible, and sat at my desk, penning away so as not to disturb her, not to be in the way as she emptied bits of trash, snapped out fresh linens, patted and snugged the sheets, the blanket, the damask coverlet, audibly panting from her squat exertions. When I glanced in the oval mirror hung above the desk, opposed and distorting blocks of light cast from windows on either side lit up a face like an unwanted child's, the guilt of existence dimming the small, even features.

Toad left, not without a last, chiding glance backward into my room. I lay down, fully dressed, upon the newly made-up bed, the cream damask coverlet, and shut my eyes, to rest and to wait for my sister to ring me up. She wanted, she said, to show me her apartment and then take me to dinner. I had visited a previous apartment of hers, outside Raleigh, five years before and assumed this one would be much like it, if sparser, smaller, and slightly more threadbare, as her financial circumstance had worsened since then. What I remembered of that third-floor apartment in Raleigh was the windowed view of a hilled, perfect forest of silver spruce, which I believe she said she liked; the wind soughing through the trees at night made her feel, she said, like a bird safely tucked up in its nest. I recall how few possessions she had, things of a functional or sentimental nature from a failed and childless marriage decades before, a collection of cut-glass, silver-topped perfume bottles, a full set of antique Wedgwood from her husband's quasi-aristocratic family. She liked fine things, and if they could not be afforded, she would have nothing. She owned no television, no radio or music player of any kind. Here and there were small, elegant scraps of Florentine needlepoint she worked on in desultory yet meticulous fashion. There was a great black rocker, I recalled it from our days as children, where it had sat, stern and polished, like some great ebony chess piece, on our parents' screened back porch. I imagined she sat in that same rocker even now, reading books brought home from the bookstore she managed, review copies she was allowed to keep. Uncompromising in other respects, my sister's taste in books tended toward the mundane, not even best-sellers, but books two, three, even four notches down. As always, her tastes and mine, even in this, were widely opposed. In matters of reading, she thought me elitist. I considered her a lowbrow, but in matters other than taste, in family matters, we were profoundly united. We agreed our mother had been a snob, though too shy to socialize, signifying this only by the pretentious names she chose for us, Avis Sloane and Signe Amber. Our actual money came from father, who was careless, even profligate, with his inheritance and preferred hunting and fishing (and womanizing, we were later to learn) for days on end, leaving our mother to bury us, along with herself, in the storied ease and otherworldliness of books, expensively bound novels and, on occasion, biographies of celebrities and saints. She had been, while alive, our best advocate, defending us valiantly, if ineffectually, from the withering and vindictive ravages of our father. We had been ill-prepared for life, and now we were two sisters nearing our sixties, unmarried, childless, and exotically named, one managing an unprofitable, soon-to-fail bookstore in a middle-income mall, the other a teacher of nineteenth-century literature at an exclusive girls' school, both women of letters, small letters, marginalized and unread, except by one another.

Lying on my back, fully dressed atop the bed's stiff coverlet, I fell into a short, unpleasant sleep, which itself dropped into an oppressive, enigmatic dream of a dark, unlit corridor occupied by a straight, silent file of girls wearing identical white linen sailor dresses, each with fastidiously plaited hair and the most vacant of expressions, harmonized in mood, dress, and conscience by one great unmitigated sorrow. I walked beside this unbroken string of pearls, but not one seemed to see me as they moved in measured pace toward some unknown destiny, all in white but for a scarlet bow, a blood-adornment, at the dropped neckline of each girl's dress with its broad sailor collar and gently belling trumpet of skirt. I stood by, unable to stop their forward, dread procession, unable to avert its mysterious end, unable to wake either them or myself. A murmurous sound, as of beating wings, momentarily confused me, until at last I did wake, and the sound continued, real, not dreamt, and very near. I sat up, noting the gilt edges of the room, gossamer threads piercing the air from the half-drawn drapes, gold light wavering glumly, if light can be said to be glum, around the twilit, sunken corners of my room. I stood up quickly—I had not meant to rest so long. The sound recurred, a susurrus of panicked wings, a frenzied fluttering, then nothing. I went toward the window, parted the lined drapes, and gazed out at the white-railinged porch overlooking the dank, ivy-blackened garden. It lay motionless, on its side, ensnared between two close-set rails, its head canted awkwardly in my direction, looking toward me or the slight noise I had made parting the curtains. A vulgarly mottled pigeon, very large, its chest heaving from its own futile efforts, its feathers a fitful mix of dull lavender, dingy white, and excremental splashes, signatures, of brown. With a tremendous and frightful flap of its wings, it tried once more to free itself, nearly succeeding, then falling back, its visible eye black, wet, roving, enraged. I imagined stepping out onto that silvery corridor of porch, kneeling to grasp the frantic, palpating orb, then standing and, with one magnificent, opening gesture of both my hands, releasing it to fly a short distance, recover, then fly a further distance off, restoring its unremarkable, rather ugly life. Exhilarating whimsy, but then the drag of my own fear, my horror of lice and disease and pestilence, my dislike of most birds, set in, and I quickly drew the drapes shut, turned back into my room and, with a slight shock, though I had been expecting it, saw in the premature gloom the rubied light on the bedside telephone blinking, its persistent, hectoring rhythm signaling everything I increasingly hated and feared about the world.

She did not at first see me, Avis Sloane. Seated in a massive wing chair of broad maroon and cream stripe, one of a pair of such chairs in an antiquated parlor off the reception area, done up halfheartedly in a green and gold huntsman's theme, she was watching local news on the television, a small set secured incongruously in an upper corner of the parlor, like an insect's head. Earlier that day, as she had moved toward me, I had observed the halting limp; this time I noted the cane, a simple kind with a rubbered shoe or tip, of varnished wood, the sort one finds in any pharmacy, leaning now against the side of her chair. My sister's demeanor, from the bowl-cut silver hair, loose black pantsuit, bowed posture, and face creased by chronic pain, bespoke full retreat, certainly abdication, from a life that had proved too hard. I, too, had undergone my own retreat, withering response to recent disgrace, a school scandal that had left me ruined, a circumstance I could not bear to confess to my punitive father or even to my sister, who would surely have offered sympathy. To disclose one shame would unearth another, a secret kept from my family for over thirty years. Thus the irony of my father's naming me executor of his will, the unfairness of judging Avis's life a failure and exalting my own. In his present, deteriorating state of mind, I knew that if he learned the whole truth about me, he would call his lawyer, a bullnecked man, rapaciously loyal, and without a second thought or possibility of retraction, disown and discard us both. For my sister's sake, for hers alone, I would maintain my profile as a dull sort, reliable, virginal to the point of consecration, small, closed, bookish.

Crossing that musty huntsman's parlor to greet my sister so soon after my dream of girls moving down a shadowed corridor (a space like the wasped, glassy middle of an hourglass) caused me to have such strange emotion in my eyes that my sister, accustomed to my customary reserve, even remoteness, appeared startled.

"It's a big world," was all she said, standing up and locating, with poignant expertness, her cane, "so who decides what's news?" She was referring to a TV news story, just featured, about elderly brothers, identical twins, living together in impoverished conditions who had conspired to suffocate their eighty-nine-year-old mother in order to hasten their inheritance. The bizarre crime, which the twins defended as a "mercy kill," had seized the attention of the entire city of Richmond, pointing as it did to provocative moral ambiguities born of medical technology, as well as to heinous greed, the destruction of one's own flesh for profit. Every city has such stories of moral dilemma and crime, human dramas debated without satisfying resolution or moral surety. Surely every family, at one time or another, has had the same.

As it was late, we agreed to forgo the drive, some forty minutes in each direction, to my sister's apartment and have our dinner, instead, in the same hotel dining room where we had had our brunch earlier that day. I chose not to mention my disquieting affection for this old hotel, preferring the empty, grandiose gesture of inviting Avis Sloane to spare no expense, order whatever she liked, this was to be "my treat," though I no longer had an account, and my own savings, after months of unemployment, were gone. We were seated in a different area of the dining room, close beside a carmine-draped window overlooking the garden, dark at this hour, and forbidding. I recalled Poe's ingenious phrase for that nonbenign aspect of one's personality, the "perverse imp," a phrase returning to me from my early studies in literature. I admired Poe's uncanny knowledge of the human psyche; he understood how the shadow, the imp, given its way, its mean head, would destroy each of us with guile, cunningly, according to our natures.

Still under the spell of my dream, I inquired of our waitress, a dour thump in an absurdly ruffled, candy-pink uniform, if this building had really been, at one time, a girls' academy. "Oh yes Ma'am, the Southern Female Institute it was called, and after that it was a lunatic asylum for rich widows, closed down by fire. It reopened as a rooming house, then a series of inns, all of which failed, until Linden Row."

"Are there ghosts?" my sister inquired brightly.

"Can't say I've seen a one, though a few of our hotel guests claim to have seen a young girl dressed in white, kind of floatin' down the main staircase. According to a book on the ghosts of Richmond, the girl was a suicide, hanged herself in her room, one of the rooms up on the third floor. There's copies of the book for sale in the lobby."

"Too spooky for me." My sister gave a fake shiver and picked up her menu. "I'll have the steak Diane, I haven't had a steak in years." I followed suit, and the waitress left us, no doubt puzzled by our cutting her off so quickly, but my sister had no interest in metaphysics of any kind, or rather, she quickly became afraid of things she couldn't see.

We sat alone in the dining room except for a young couple, prematurely afflicted with a malignant contempt for one another. Our dinner became a source of great interest to both of us, particularly as we ordered second drinks, a martini for my sister, scotch on the rocks for myself. I asked about her limp, and she explained about the most recent treatment she was receiving for her condition (a painful osteoarthritis in both knees), monthly injections of a substance made from rooster combs, adding that she could not afford surgery so she got injections, a treatment expensive in itself for someone with as little health insurance as she had. My sister had other health conditions as well, all chronic, for which she took numerous medications. Her life had been a string of minor misfortunes, bringing her little joy. Unlike my father, I did not and never had seen this as her fault, her doing.

"So who the hell else do you know who goes around wearing a bit of cock in both knees," she joked, and we splurted with ungainly, relieving laughter . . . how rebellious and fine it felt to laugh! "Aren't you the cock of your walk," I added, and we sniggered and snorted, reckless, ill-behaved children. When our lavish dinners arrived, we settled down, first to our food, then, more reluctantly, to the real point and purpose of my visit, our reason for seeing one another after five years. I described our father's insidious dementia, marked by paranoia, rage, and the recent decision to strike her from his will and name me sole beneficiary and executor. Afterward, we sat saying nothing. "Life sucks," I finally said, sounding ridiculous, sounding exactly like one of the stupider girls I used to instruct in the slow, entropic decline of English literature.

"You don't look well," my sister finally spoke. "You seem smaller, have you lost weight?"

"I'll fix this," I said. "His mind is going, but I'll find a way to fix this."

Years ago, a former bishop of our parish had been accused, though never convicted, of criminal acts of a sexual nature. A diminutive, puckish man, prone to stammer; after such public disgrace, he contracted even further into himself. One of the visible effects of public shame, I have discovered, is to literally shrink a person. Shame had done that to him, and now to me, though he had claimed innocence, and I knew I was blameless, though if one could be convicted on thought alone, I should be hanged. My life and reason had been usurped by a fourteen-year-old girl named Annie Girard, who possessed loveliness of a kind I had never seen before and had no defense against. Not usual beauty, no; it is far too easy, as the Marquis de Sade is said to have complained, to love those of ordinary beauty, for such loveliness, upheld in a common awe, turns dilute and harmless, becomes the stuff of sentimentality. Annie was ethereal and corrupt, fey and spiteful. Initially capricious, she turned vengeful and now her power knew no bounds; a second teacher had just been named and had also taken leave as Annie's story grew ever more panoplied, convoluted, and shocking. A disturbed child, she proved a magnificent liar, fabricating sordid details that made of my shame a true thing. Shame corrupts, makes one rank from the inside, and what I suspected had just been confirmed by my sister's observation that I looked unwell, smaller, shrunken into myself, contracted.

My sister, Avis Sloane, had twice married the same man or cut of man, cinematically handsome, melancholic, incapable of fidelity, prone to depression and a sporadic, lashing cruelty, a man irresistible to types of women prone to martyrdom and impervious to self-esteem. Our father, I suspect, had been such a man for my mother. Beautiful, Irish Catholic, stubbornly devout and clinging to her rosaries, she stayed with him until the end, her end, a demise riddled and wormed from within by disappointment, betrayal, and an unsaintly rage. Was it our mother we had modeled ourselves so disastrously after, choosing either rebellion or variation? And who was I but a private-school teacher accused of "inappropriately touching, fondling" a fourteen-year-old student, a charge so shocking and false I left school on indefinite leave a full month before I was fired for openly admitting that Annie, transferred midyear from another school, had enraptured me, though I had done nothing wrong, nothing of outward consequence? It was she who courted me, pursued me, studied my subjects as though they meant everything to her, created reasons and situations for us to be alone. But for Annie, youth provided her absolution.

At twenty-four, I had married a probate attorney, divorced, then, years later, carried on a painful, protracted affair with a

fellow teacher, a woman ten years my senior, eventually choosing to live alone, vowing never again to let cupidity, lust, mar
my orderly life. Despite my best efforts, because of Annie Girard, I was without work, bright with scandal, and soon to be
entirely dependent on my father's charity. Never a generous
man, he was now suspicious, choleric, and vengeful. Of late,
as my depression worsened, I found myself portioning out his
medicines, preparing those foods he could or would still eat,
and wishing him thoroughly dead. At times I would literally
shake my head as if to clear it of its suffocating atmosphere,
its violent musings.

Contrary to popular symbology, life cannot be symbolized by
an hourglass. It is, at most, half an hourglass, waste funneling
through the tightening neck, like a corridor of girls, white-
frocked, virginal, spilling seeds, seeds bursting, products of an
infinitely cruel, indifferent profligacy. It had been my job, my
self-proclaimed mission, to make each girl as elegant and resist-
ant to sin as possible, my duty to suppress youth's natural
ardency. Discipline, celibacy, and devotion to dead literature
were my attempts, I suppose, to save them.

As I watched my sister's lips bunch into a moist, slitted red
purse as she ordered the most extravagant dessert on the hotel
menu, I suddenly loathed her appetite, or hated myself for urg-
ing her to indulge herself, the bill being mine, or rather (a lie)
the school's. When the dessert arrived, a wide, warmed slice of
fudge pecan pie with a freshly shaled ball of pecan ice cream, a
Richmond specialty "to die for" my sister said, we giggled, *yes,
to die for*. I plucked up my small, heavy dessert fork and ate fully
half its nauseating richness.

*Do you admit you touched her, Ms. Leach? Do you admit you
touched Miss Girard in the ways she has said? Did you tell Annie
Girard you loved her? We have evidence of a letter, handwritten
by you, thirty-five pages in length, addressed to Annie on the occasion of her fifteenth birthday.*

I have always lacked courage, sought refuge in books, stories
about others. As my sister excused herself to go to the ladies

room, I stood and went out into the courtyard. I felt a new reluctance to return to my room, perhaps because of the dying pigeon, or the toad-maid who had hopped in to clean and to disapprove, as if she knew exactly who and what I was and wished me some terrible harm.

I saw it then, glimmering faintly across the courtyard, the pigeon, a filthy mound on the bricks, fallen to its death directly beneath my room. I imagined it would lay there, trivial and swelling, in a ferment of its own putrefying gases, until someone saw it and, with an utterance of distaste, removed it, on a muddied spade, to oblivion.

> *But out of this our cloud upon the precipice's edge, there grows into palpability, a shape, far more terrible than any genius or any demon of a tale, and yet it is but a thought, although a fearful one, and one which chills the very marrow of our bones . . .*
> —EDGAR ALLAN POE, "The Imp of the Perverse"

Who knows when an evil idea takes firm root? In my case, the plight of my sister, her troubles at work, her obvious pain without means to alleviate that pain, her history of twice saving me, my own loyalties deepening on one side, thinning on the other, being invisible in one city, flayed by scandal in another, all added to Poe's brilliant notion of perversity, his dark tales and mysterious death, presaging, I surmised, my own hideous end, and all these things fell together, attached themselves to one another, breeding a new creature in me, one who would plot murder for what she thought an honorable or at least justifiable motive. Linden Row, too, played its part, increasingly overrun by its female ghosts, pathetic, malicious, insane. No one spoke of the asylum it had once been, of the tormented madwomen it had housed, then set ablaze. My father had become a cartoon, exaggerated and rakish, of the awful man he had always been. Only money, medicine, and my increasingly resentful ministrations kept him alive, while my sister suffered on without hope. Out of all these arose the evil idea, if it was evil, of patricide. Our father must make way, and which would be the worse, I wondered, to be caught and punished for a crime, or go undetected and "free"? It seemed essential to answer this so as not to sabotage my own actions. The ancient Greeks thought it the most fascinating question in human ethics: what was the consequence of someone committing evil (say murder) for a higher good? One hundred and fifty years ago my father would have died at least twice by now. Only modern medicine and my own sense of duty kept him alive now, propped up, and, so far as I could see, he was neither grateful nor happy about it.

> Today I wear these chains and am here! Tomorrow
> I shall be fetterless—but where?
> —EDGAR ALLAN POE, "The Imp of the Perverse"

Who can name the instant madness first blooms from a disordered mind? Stripped naked, I drew a bath for myself in the deep white tub, hot, greenish water thundering in from the thick, curved spout. Spreading the curtains wide, leaving the shades carelessly raised, daring anyone, inviting anyone. I had seen the shallow depression my body left on the ivory damask coverlet, the merest indentation, much like the memory of a life growing fainter over time. I had listened to my one message from the day nurse I had hired, father doing well, eating well, not noticing my absence.

Climbing the staircase, a shell-like spiral rumored to be haunted by a schoolgirl who had hanged herself, I thought of how I had just stood beside my sister on the sidewalk outside Linden Row, waiting for her car to be brought round by the valet, as she spoke again, as if fascinated, of the old twin brothers who had murdered their mother, desperate for profit. Outside the door to my room on the third floor, I understood all at once Avis Sloane's indirect order, her veiled directive, my sister's cry, at last, for help.

After my bath, which lasted until I became frightened by my clothing, discarded and resembling a corpse, frightened still more by the transparent specter standing in the doorway of my bedroom, I rose up from the porcelain nest of my bath, rose naked from the cold, muscled water and sat, aging, unclothed, at my desk, leaving every light on, every curtain and shade widely drawn. I found several blank sheets of Linden Row stationery in an otherwise empty drawer and began to write, not to Annie Girard, not to myself, not to my sister nor to the craven authorities of the school where I had given my life for the sake of shaping young girls. I wrote instead to the spirits of Linden Row, schoolgirls in white hanging by frayed ropes, women widowed and gone mad. I addressed Poe, who had been found semiconscious, incoherent, in a gutter in Baltimore, wearing rags not his, a victim of foul play or poor health or his imagination's own protean, scabrous power. I wrote on and on through that night and into the morning, scratching, scratching as one possessed, never hearing the short, peremptory knock, nor the door opening, as behind my chair appeared an apparition, a lumpy, warted toad, arrived, I suppose, to ferry me across the rising waters of self-depravity and murderous fancies. Harpie, imp, *go,* her face floated in the mirror directly above mine so that we were one hellish vision, twin-headed—*go,* so I might remove all trace of you—but no, this was wrong, for she was followed in small procession by others who surrounded me, crying out over the ruined desk and my old nakedness, blackened with scribblings of ink, and when ink had run out, scrawlings of feces, and when feces had dried, bright cuttings in blood—expressions of horror and what, in a more gracious, generous era, might have been called *ruth,* upon their vague, inhuman faces.

THE ODDITORIUM

Mr. Rip-Li
(Astounding! Supernal! Ghostly Appendage!)

Who, you ask? A third or fourth leg of Swiss-Austrian descent? A shrunken head schooled in Krakow? A Friday night cranial hopper? If you collect junk long enough . . . ("Get rid of the junk or get rid of me," said Beatrice Roberts after two months of connubial stress. An evening gown competition winner in the Miss America pageant, Beatrice went on to star as Azura, Queen of Magic in *Flash Gordon's Trip to Mars* and had a fling with Louis Mayer of MGM, gravitating from one set of junk to another. She was a different kind of human cork, the dime-a-dozen kind, female corks who cling to moguls like Mayer in order to stay afloat in their own mediocrity. Bah! Enough of a studio actress who died alone in her North Hollywood bungalow with no greater distinction than having been a villainess and Robert LeRoy Ripley's wife for less than nine embryonic weeks. The junk stayed and she ventured on.)

What is the Mark of Cain?
Answer Next Sunday
—Ripley's Believe It or Not,
the *King Features Syndicate*,
June 10, 1945

As Mr. Ripley's Astounding! Supernal! Ghostly Appendage, I can, with authority, compare him to Stambaugh's great ball of string:

A recluse named S.S. Stambaugh for several years collected eight-inch lengths of string from a local flour mill in Tulare, California. By knotting and winding the pieces he was able to build a three-foot-diameter twine ball in less than two years. Upon seeing the huge creation, a friendly visitor calculated that Stambaugh had tied 463,040 knots in nearly 132 miles of twine to make the 320-pound ball. (March 22, 1938)

That was Ripley to a "t." He couldn't roll into a room without rolling back out again covered with the shortest lengths of ideas and the tightest knots of objects in there. Beyond Beatrice, he wouldn't let go of a thing. Including me.

If an Appendage may be allowed an opinion, here is mine:

Given an era of less anxiety and more discretion, take away the Great Depression and two World Wars, and Ripley might have been your run-of-the-mill suburban crackpot. A plastic bag sorter, hoarder of stoppers and snaps, jam jars, jawbreakers, broken ping-pong paddles, push mowers, racially perverse lawn ornaments, waffle irons. He was simply a man at ease with bizarre objects, weird bibelots, fantastic freaks of nature that made him feel, by association, less odd. He would turn antsy, visibly peeved around "Joes and Janes," the people, he complained, who lacked verve. He reddened and chafed under the constraints of circumstance and possessed a genius for malleability, a gumby-like elasticity always bending him in the direction of Fame, that disco ball of collective Yearning.

Watch our for the bashful ones! The stutterers, the stammerers, the timorous and whey-faced. The ones whose dreams (in this case, to be a world-class ballplayer) collapse early on. Watch the prune-lipped wallflower, the school dropout, the amateur sketcher with a knack for cartooning upside down. Stand back for the homely ones! Mr. Ripley was no looker. Melon-headed, with no more hair than the tines on an oyster fork, bucktoothed (his overbite part fang, part awning), he gained glorious ground wearing bat-winged polka-dot ties, knickerbocker pants, argyle socks, two-toned spats, pith helmets, and Panama hats, natty togs in lurid, eye-stabbing colors. At the pinnacle of his celebrity, he sported maroon silk Chinese robes and multi-tasseled monkey caps around BION,* his twenty-eight-room mansion in Mamaroneck, New York—retreating on occasion to his favorite "curi-oddity," Mon-Lei, a Chinese junque fitted out with twin diesel engines at cross purposes with its billowing, painted sails, so that Ripley was often forced to bob around the harbor outside his home or just sort of spin in a lazy figure eight out there, sipping gin from a Buddhist monk's yellowed brain pan, part of his human skull collection.

This was a kid from Santa Rosa, California who loathed himself early on, called himself freak-o, fats-o, and dunce-o. Who feared being called fail-o. Deserting his first job as a tomb-polisher, he catapulted from San Francisco to New York, went from "Champs and Chumps" to "Believe It or Not," from LeRoy to Robert, from poverty to the gilt patronage of William Randolph Hearst who underwrote Ripley's globe-trotting excursions in search of the fantastic, the grotesque, the terrifying. With each boiled Amazonian head he dangled like a key chain before his hungry public, each Nuremburg Iron Maiden he ghoulishly invited rub-berneckers to step into the spiked embrace of, with each giant, man-eating clam he posed beside for snapshots, with such infi-nite stores of plundered oddities, Ripley grew whole, hale, greased with the oil of self-adulation. His obsessions were serenely democratic. They entertained, quasi-educated, helped people thrill to the world again. Ripley opened the spigot on the American penchant for useless ingenuity on a staggering scale. Ripley was Walt Whitman's mud show.

---

* BION: acronym for Believe It or Not

No one had the faintest idea who was behind all of this. Who made it happen? I'll tell you who: The Astounding! Supernal! Ghostly Appendage. Otherwise known as the fact checker.

**How Old Was Moses When
Pharaoh's Daughter Found
Him in a Basket?**
Answer Next Sunday

Eighty million yawning, sad Americans rattled open their newspapers every morning to read about: *Liu Ch'ung, the double-eyed man of China!* or *The long-tailed shrew, smallest mammal in the world, breathing eight hundred times a minute!* or *Kuda Bux, the man who walked on fire through a twenty-foot-long bed of charcoal without a single burn on his feet!* or *"Three Ball Charlie," who could put three balls in his mouth and whistle at the same time!* or *A seventy-five-year-old petrified apple!* or *Laurello, the only man in the world with a revolving head, who could walk forward while looking backward!*—all this set Ripley fans agog, agog enough to forget there were no jobs, the dough had dried up, and a wholesale slaughter called war was taking place on a never-before-seen scale . . . forget it, readers could marvel at the Human Slate, the Human Flag, the Human Belt, the Human Pincushion, the Human Cork, the Human Autograph Album, glimpse wider possibilities for themselves in the ice sitters, the one-legged lawn mower hoisters, the upside-down writers and readers, the waitress from Clayton's Café in Tyler, Texas, who could carry twenty-five cups of hot coffee in one hand, or Johnny "Cigars" Connors of Roxbury, Massachusetts, who rolled a peanut with his nose from Boston to Worcester . . . if you were unemployed, wearing week-old newspapers for your shoe soles, if you were tempted to drown yourself in a teaspoon of something awful, you could always try stacking quarters in your ears, playing the piano with the tip of your nose, knick-knack-paddy-whack your mutt-dog into telling time while puffing a cheroot, remove nails with your teeth, lift your sister on your chin, be like Dr. A. Boinker, jumping backward from a train going twenty miles an hour, or outdo James Weir of Weirton, West Virginia, who could hold a half dollar in his eye, a pencil between his upper lip and nose, another pencil between his lower lip and chin and a cigar between his teeth all while moving his scalp back and forth and singing. This was no time to die!

Under the reign of Ripley, America became more wonderstruck than beautiful, and in 1929, when his Believe It or Not column in the *New York Post* declared that America had no national anthem, the consequent uproar resulted in the official adoption of "The Star-Spangled Banner" (Francis Scott Key penning the words to an old English tavern ballad during the 1812 siege of Fort McHenry) as the nation's paen to itself. Rip-o-mania kept people awake nights, kept folks writing letters, millions upon millions, three thousand a week, the envelopes addressed in Braille, wigwag, semaphore, Morse code, upside down and backward or sometimes with just a single rippley line. America's hunger for whimsy, for petty invention and pointless stunts, the vanity of the human mammal, that "mute creature of the breast," performing feats of repetitive idiocy; Ripley had struck upon it like a bottomless seam of black gold pluming skyward, a geyser coating him and everyone else with slick tomfoolery and genuine amazement. Life was fun again.

Believe It or Not.
I have had as many as 50 different pins and needles stuck in my body at the same time without causing any pain. And it is no trick.
   —B.A. Bryant
   600 Hook St.
   Waco, Texas

Dear Sir:
Would it interest you to know I have a young lady living with me that can lap her tongue over at the tip about an inch and it will remain there.

Try yours, see if you can do it.
> *Respectfully,*
> *Elise M. Buck*
> *R.F.D. #3*
> *Burlington, N.J.*
> *c/o The Nook Lunch Room*

Mr. Robert L. Ripley, New York City,
Dear Sir, I am sending 3 of my Pictures. There is one of them showing me lifting a 12 lbs. Hammer by my Nose. I have lifted as much as 25 lbs. that way. But I thought the Hammer would make a good Picture.

I can also lift 10 lbs by my Earrings. The one Picture showing me lifting a Granite Rock was taken up on the Summit of the Sierra Nevada Mountains. The weight of the Rock is 115 lbs.
> *—Angels' Camp, Ca.,*
> *Feb 5, 1938*

Hockley, Texas
May 11, 1932
"Tex," a part bulldog and part birddog, weighs 120 pounds. He is only 22 in. high and is 44 in. around his body. Everyone that see "Tex" considers him the fattest dog they have ever seen. "Tex" will not go to his bed at night without a bag of cookies. He is owned by A.A. Forek of Hockley, Texas.

I am enclosing a snapshot of "Tex" as proof. He is holding a box of lemon snaps, his favorite food.
> *(Miss) Irma Jane Forek*
> *Hockley, Texas*

**How old was Adam
when he died?**
Answer Next Sunday

The Human Fact Checker:

FACT: In 1923, a wispy, unassuming man from Tarnow, Austria, educated in Krakow, master of fourteen languages, was hired by Robert Ripley and the King (newspaper) Syndicate to research facts for Believe It or Not. For the next fifty-two years, Norbert Pearlroth toiled at the New York Public Library, ten hours a day, six days a week. Eighty million readers demanded that Believe It or Not's outlandish claims and hyperbolic statements be backed up by facts, making an odd duck like Pearlroth an indispensable appendage.

Norbert treated his wife, in fifty years of marriage, to one vacation in 1933, to the Chicago World's Fair, the Century of Progress as it was billed, to attend the opening of Ripley's first Odditorium, an occasion marked by 2 million visitors, hundreds of whom fainted dead away, hit the ground, stiff as planks, at the sight of the two-headed baby, the corkscrew man, and little Betty Lou Williams, a four-year-old with a parasitic sibling consisting of two legs, one tiny armlike appendage, a more developed arm with three working fingers, and the head of her twin embedded deep in her abdomen. Mr. and Mrs. Pearlroth were also present when the FIJI ISLAND MERMAID, purchased by Ripley from P. T. Barnum, was publically declared a hoax, not a half-woman half-fish at all, but the blackened head of a one-year-old Rhesus monkey crudely sewn onto the preserved body of a swordfish.

If Robert Ripley was, as the Duke of Windsor unimaginatively dubbed him, a Modern Marco Polo, traveling over 24,000 miles and two continents, Norbert, whom nobody knew, was the Marco Polo of the New York Public Library, circumnavigating 7,000 books per year, 364,000 books in fifty-two years, in his hunt for hard-boiled, irrefutable facts. While Mr. Ripley trotted the globe by boat, plane, donkey, camel, train, elephant, and rickshaw, visiting over two hundred countries, the names of which most Americans had never heard, hauling back souvenirs of the terrible, the thrilling, and the bizarre, wearing his signature pith helmet and kneesocks, complaining about his "bum dogs," Mr. Pearlroth sat rabbinically at desk number 3, chair number 3, in the Rose Reading Room, beneath ceiling murals of azure skies and gold-limned clouds, a Maxfield Parrish heaven, with his wax-papered sandwich of liverwurst and lingonberry jelly on dark rye, sitting so long he received the same carbuncles, the same ass stigmata, as Karl Marx. Charting infinite stacks of reference books, bibliographies, dictionaries, encyclopedias, indexes, and monographs, rowing through oceans of milky white pages with his slim pencil-oar, wearing a boiled wool cardigan, rumpled shirt, limp dungarees, and leather slippers the color of fossilized camel dung, he uncovered and confirmed such facts as Charles Dickens's cat alerting Dickens to his bedtime by snuffing out the candle on his desk, or Rajah, the sacred ox from Katmandu, born with an arm, hand, and fingers attached to its left shoulder. (This was how Pearlroth first conceived of himself as a similar appendage to the body of Ripley: an arm, hand, and fingers paid to nail down facts. He called it Rip-Li.) The world's most invisible man labored anonymously for the world's greatest celebrity, a Believe It or Not character attracting absolutely nobody's attention. Norbert Pearlroth rode on the subway from his home on Newkirk and Sixteenth Avenue, Brooklyn, to Manhattan every morning at the exact same hour, wore the same lumpen clothing, ate the same liverwurst and lingonberry jam sandwich, sat on his blazing rump at the same burnished oak table beneath the epiphanic light of the same bronze lamp, a biblio-badger, scarcely moving except to turn pages with whiskered, pursey sounds, jotting notes as dry, dark, and wizened as ferret droppings. Over decades, in true Ripley fashion, Norbert Pearlroth, Appendage, turned square, silent, deep-shelved: half man/ half book.

Routine was Pearlroth's ballast, habit his anchor. I repeat, he sat so many years on the same steel-hard oak chair, he grew mean, cauliflower-like boils on his buttocks. His wife of five decades said in the single five-minute interview she granted upon his death that Norbert might as well have been paralyzed and mute for the little he moved or spoke in his life. He was discovered deceased in his customary chair, his head on a biography of Nostradamus; the rubber-soled librarian had left him alone, presuming the man asleep, but by nightfall, when he was found, unmoved and alone in the two-block room with its rows of polished tables and gleaming bronze lamps, it was confirmed he was no catnapper but, (*in fact!!*) a corpse, his blue, ink-grimed fingernail pointing to his final fact-checked article: *Ripleymania hits Luverne, Alabama!, "the Friendliest Town in the World," on May 3, 1933, when an unprecedented number of townsfolk turned up in City Hall to compete for Believe It or Not contest prizes. One farmer showed off his four foot eleven inch snake cucumber, another a hand-shaped Danvers carrot, another gentleman owned a horned rooster named "El Diablo," and a woman a footless Peking duck, an elementary school math teacher named Mr. Bubb demonstrated holding a pencil under his ear, the painter's wife held a one-gallon varnish can between her shoulder blades. Presiding over the melee was Miss Annie Rainer Shine, banana plant grower, locally famous for having been mentioned in a special Believe It or Not column devoted to unusual names. Wearing a handmade, homegrown skirt stitched entirely of banana leaves, Miss Annie Rainer Shine awarded first prize to a Miss E.E. Smith for growing her own hat, an Easter bonnet crocheted out of hair from her own head. Second prize went to Mr. Waldo Rasmussen, who ate and regurgitated a live albino mouse patriotically named FDR.*

Slow as a snail, dun and small, Pearlroth tracked a wavery but resolute pearl-slime through 364,000 books. Listen: if you put your head down and turn your right or left ear against the very spot where Norbert perished, against the residue of his finger oil, hair oil, and scalp drift, you may hear, much like the sound of the ocean surf inside of a conch shell, the whisper of bizarre facts, odd facts, terrifying truths, that never found their way into the public newspapers as grist for the American maw with its naïve, carnival appetites. The truth was: Norbert censored, withheld,

198 | MELISSA PRITCHARD

pulled out, refused to disseminate. He had come to know truly terrible things about the human race, about the future, and believed it his sacred duty to tell no one.

DISCOVERED IN MR. PEARLROTH'S BRIEFCASE
FOLLOWING THE APPENDAGE'S DEMISE IN THE
ROSE READING ROOM OF THE NEW YORK PUBLIC
LIBRARY:

—presumed notes for his alter ego Rip-Li's autobiography.

12. Proclaim: The Human SlateTheHumanCorkTheHumanBeltThe-HumanFlagTheHumanAutographBookTheHumanPincushion-TheHumanUnicornTheHumanMusicalChair (a three-legged Sicilian mandolin player)—put the word *Human* in front of anything and people are spellbound. Ditto the world's largest broom, widest frying pan, tallest man, etc.

13. Train an animal to ape humans, produce a time-telling horse, a cigarette-smoking duck, a roller-skating Chihuahua, a typewriting rooster, a fat, pie-guzzling dog . . . and you have the country's ear.

14. Seek out feats involving time: world champion chicken picker "Buck" Fulford of Port Arthur, Texas, who could kill, pick clean, cut up, cook, and eat a chicken in one minute and fifty seconds.

15. Ferret out the improbable tinged with the pathetic: World's Busiest Man: a one-armed paper hangar with hives.

16. Unveil the Shocking and Horrific Stunt: El Gran Lazaro, El Indio de Baracoa of Havana, sticks a needle in his eye socket and pulls it out of his mouth.

17. Deliver up the Born-Odds: the extra-limbed or no-limbed, the hole-headed, the quadruple jointed, the dual sexed, the gleeful midgets and glum giants, the one-eyed and triple-tongued, the albino, the bearded, the conjoined, the parasitic, these cause the self-haters, self-loathers, self-cringers, and self-abusers of the world to pluck up, to perk up, put a spring in their step, hey, at least I'm not YOU.

18. In a singular category, proclaim: "El Fusilado," The Executed One, who faced a firing squad, received eight bullets through the head and body—and in a coup de grâce—LIVED!

Was Nostradamus Right?
Are we in the End Days?
Apocalypse: 2012!
Answers Withheld

My employer, Mr. Ripley, to whom I was deeply attached, invisibly appended, would not talk on the telephone for fear of electrocution. He owned boats by the score, his bathing costume consisted of a pith helmet, droopy swim trunks, and a dog-eared bathrobe, but he refused to immerse himself in water. He owned the world's largest fleet of cars but refused to drive. He rotated harems of beautiful women but, beyond Beatrice, never married. He kept a twenty-eight-foot pet boa constrictor in his mansion, BION, on instruction it be granted one milk-fed mouse per day, dangled from sanitized fingertips by its rubbery, ballerina-pink tail.

As Mr. Robert Leroy Ripley beheld the scope of the earth, its vast peculiarities, its human epic of horrors, its animal, mineral, and vegetable incredulities, his own little worm of self-hatred shrank, shriveled, gave up the ghost. This is my opinion only.

I never met Mr. Ripley in my life. It would have been a superfluous gesture.

"The world is all a fleeting show, for man's illusion given."

For every navigator, a compass. For every farmer, a seed. For every doctor, a symptom. For every actor, a play. For every charlatan, a fool. For the body of Robert Ripley, there is his supernal appendage, Mr. Pearlroth of the carbuncled bottom, here now, talking to you.

ANSWERS:

Mark of Cain: Some scholars say God gave Cain a dog for protection. Others say God gave him a disease such as leprosy. No one knows the factual answer.

Age of Moses: 3 months

Age of Adam: 930 years

Nostradamus, End Days, Apocalypse: See Miles Stair's Survival Shop, Urban Suvivalists, or Frugal Squirrels.

end

THE NINE-GATED CITY

Oh babu, without beggars how will people wash away their sins?
—ROHINTON MISTRY, *A Fine Balance*

New Delhi, January 2007

Sidonie Recoura remained sexually attractive to men under certain lights and conditions, although after a life spent beneath the gaze of men, she had of late grown tolerant of her diminished effect, seeing it not as loss or punishment or lapse, but as a wide, empyrean freedom. Becoming older, less visible, left her breathless, lungs starved, faintly exhilarated. To do as she liked. Behave as she liked. Lose herself. Her surface chipped, worn, she nearly looked forward to decay, then death, the certainty of being stripped to the core. And what was Sidonie's core? She wasn't certain, though her essence, she knew, harbored a contradiction easily parodied, an unending row between hedonism and the inclination to martyrdom. Her life, up to now, had been a string of sporadic gestures, grand to minor, mirroring this paradox. She was a creature of largesse, quick to both defend and to defy the sybarite, and most of her adult life had been consumed by this argument. Unresolved, still simmering, this essence, spirit, whatever it was that lay beneath the given name and physical body of Sidonie Recoura, was preparing, tempted at least, to die.

Past fifty yet often mistaken for a woman in her early forties, with alabaster skin and long reddish-gold hair, small boned, ethereal, lithe, Sidonie had come on business to Delhi, booking a room at the five star Imperial Hotel. A part-time journalist, she was here to meet Aruna Kumari, a woman dedicated to stopping the sex trafficking of young girls from Bangladesh, Nepal, and other parts of India into big cities like Calcutta, Bombay, and Delhi. She had a morning interview with Aruna and another, the following day, with a State Department official at the U.S. Embassy.

Sidonie's affairs of the heart, poisonous confections, had all ended badly, until only opulence remained, her loyal consort and companion. Seen from the perspective of envious friends, her life as an affluent, peripatetic writer appeared independent, exotic, brave. They did not experience life as she increasingly did, tormented by loneliness and empty consumption. They did not see as certain men, narcissists, were drawn to her beauty and limpid intelligence, to an elusive, gazellelike quality that catalyzed their predatory instincts, men who sought themselves in her enigmatic gaze until they encountered the barb of her conscience, her social indignation—saw her humanitarian sleeve unfurl, her moral garment show forth and shock—and like a sudden frigid current in an otherwise warm gulf stream, she turned alarmingly, catastrophically principled. They would back away then, offering polite admiration expressed in teasing monikers like "cashmere saint," or "wandering soul," feeding Sidonie's own hope that indulgence and sacrifice could coexist, though her largely ineffectual life seemed testament enough to that fallacy.

When she was not travelling, she lived in the Sonoran Desert and loathed the cold. Whenever she did travel, she kept her hotel rooms overheated. With her beauty sustained and age camouflaged by designer clothing, Chanel cosmetics, an artful hair colorist, and a diligent regimen of Pilates and yoga, Sidonie clung to the privacy and insularity of wealth even as she felt increasingly reckless in her concealed desire to somehow fling herself into the vortex, the drowning void, of common suffering. No wonder, she sometimes thought wryly, she was alone. No wonder those paid to maintain her bathysphere of comfort found her vulnerable to rote blandishments. *(May I pour your tea, Madame? Good morning, Madame.)* No wonder she had chosen the Imperial, been given a suite of marble and cherry-wood, with Porthault linens, Ayurvedic bath oils, and a tranquil view of an Asian courtyard with a serene and shallow ornamental pool at its center. The sole public encroachment upon her peace was the television, tuned now to the morning news. Four big stories slowly spun, as if on a crude flywheel, on every channel, whether in Hindi or English—a series of gruesome child murders in the Noida district of Delhi, riots by peasant farmers in Bengal, a forty-five day spiritual festival at the Ganges River called Ardh Kumbh Mela or "Half Grand Pitcher," and the cruel cold snap affecting all of Delhi, especially the homeless.

As she dressed, Sidonie, who considered herself at best a dilettante journalist, kept a semi-professional eye on these latest stories. She would be interviewing Aruna Kumari for a speculative magazine piece on sex trafficking in Southeast Asia. The word itself, *traffic*, suggested to Sidonie lanes and intersections, vertical signage, red, green, and amber lights. Traffic, a thing light or heavy, congested, jammed, or at a standstill, making one late.

Sidonie changed her clothes twice. She had begun with a white silk blouse, a navy cashmere pullover, designer jeans, brown leather boots, and a burnt umber silk scarf bought in the hotel's gift shop after breakfast, overpriced and probably imported from the crowded, filthy outdoor emporium around the corner. She scaled down into an Amnesty International T-shirt, its sleeves still knife-edged, a Christmas gift from an activist friend, dark gray with an orange mandala across the chest, the AI logo at its center, a single candle flame encircled by a barbed strand of prison wire. Over this an ivory silk and cotton jacket suggestive of safari, and the same orange silk scarf for a stripe of elegance. She wore plain silver hoop earrings and around her neck, strung on a black silk cord, a Tibetan silver amulet of protection given to her by a Buddhist friend. Supposedly it contained a seed, blessed by a protector deity known as the "State Oracle" (a term sounding vaguely socialistic to Sidonie, who was not a Buddhist).

Standing before the carved, gilt mirror, knotting and unknotting the scarf, indecisive about her hair, Sidonie wondered why it took longer and longer to achieve any truly satisfying effect. The hotel phone shrilled unpleasantly in the cool marble room—a box of beige and ivory, of calm, impenetrable surfaces . . . *(At the reception counter where she had waited to check in, a nondescript little man, puny, British, loudly decrying the ugliness of his room . . . drab little box! he'd shouted, no style at all, beige, for crippled Christ's sake, my own blind grandmother could have painted it . . . yet he was the very avatar of drabness, all wispy rodent whisker, hair a sparse, taupe nest, skin like uncooked biscuit . . . his tantrum met by the patient, nonplussed looks of the young Indian staff, ambitious graduates of hotel school, quick to disguise their contempt.)* The phone rang a second time, a jarring note in her pristine jewel box. The message was from Aruna, just arrived in the lobby, pleased to spend the day with an American journalist writing an article on trafficking. Fitting this interview into her typically jammed schedule suggested that Aruna might be hopeful for support from rich Westerners of conscience, for fresh donations to keep her foundation solvent and her rescued "daughters" afloat.

Making her way down a marble staircase softened by a runner of intricately figured Persian carpeting, Sidonie caught an unstudied glimpse of herself in an oversized mirror on the second-floor landing. Perfect, she thought: adventurous, original, tasteful. Rechecking that she had her notebook, camera, cell phone, she stepped into the high-ceilinged, imposing lobby, its marble flooring polished to a watery gloss, like the unblemished surface of a lake, its chandeliers sparkling and palatial, its majestic palms and oversized arrangements of white-tongued, luminous orchids, its blood-dark Persian carpets running the gleaming lengths of hallways extending off the enormous lobby into alcoves and sitting rooms furnished with elegant, virginal white couches evenly lined with pillows in slubbed, pale silks, the effect one of pure splendor, of British Raj, of Colonialism as atavistic aesthetic.

Post-Christmas, post–New Year's, the hotel was fully booked, a favorite with American and European celebrities. Historically, the Imperial had been a watering hole for artists, politicians, the old and nouveau riche. Mahatma Gandhi had met here with Lord Mountbatten and Jawaharlal Nehru. Somerset Maugham, a favorite British author of Sidondie's second husband, had stayed here. The effect was to make one feel in the thick of things, among people who mattered, to suggest importance by mere association. This morning, however, as she searched for Aruna, a woman she had never met, the majority of guests looked American: entire inelegant families, disheveled, slouched, spoiled. Sidonie gazed in vain around the lobby as hotel staff swarmed officiously, young Indian women in long red skirts with short black woolen jackets, their black hair austerely knotted, young men in red topcoats with gold braiding and black pants, speaking with soft, extreme courtesy, *Yes, Madame, no sir, of course, certainly*. The manager strode about in his rat-gray Western suit, dyspeptic, frowning from the impossible strain of matching servitude to satisfaction. No one, Sidonie thought, watching one of the Imperial staff, a slick-haired young man with brittle style, bow before a disdainful-looking couple—no one could prostrate themselves like that before another human being without hating himself and the object of his false obeisance more than a little.

As an afterthought, she glanced into one of the intimate, pillared rooms off the lobby. There, sitting alone on one of the immaculate sofas, bizarrely out of place waving her over, was Aruna. Crossing the room, Sidonie was aware of the turbaned Sikh man eyeing her over his sprung newspaper, of the hyperexercised blond shawled in a silk pashmina the color of faded violets, coolly appraising the Indian woman, plain in her bearing and dress.

A squat woman in her fifties, round as a bellied urn, Aruna wore loose flowing pants and a matching *kurta*, or tunic, of an indeterminate winter fabric the color of roadside dust, of the bristled dogs Sidonie had seen scavenging the city in sun-whitened, feral packs. Her cropped black hair was equally mixed with coarse silver, her only ornaments a pair of black-rimmed glasses and tiny rose earrings, incongruously delicate, feminine, pinkly sparkling against the fleshy lobes of her ears. A cell phone hung from a black cord around her neck, an es-oteric black amulet in the center of her broad, sloping chest. Speaking on the phone in soft, rapid Hindi, she gestured for Sidonie to sit. Waiting, then, on an adjoining sofa, Sidonie looked down at Aruna's callused feet, the square, unpainted toenails, the worn leather sandals slipped half off. Aside from the fairy glitter of her earrings, Aruna dressed with monastic, masculine rigor. Sidonie's own attempt at plainness seemed fraudulent in comparison to the real roughness of dress Aruna brought into this impeccable white hotel.

As Aruna snapped her phone shut, she introduced herself to Sidonie, her low, husky voice congested—allergies, she apolo-gized, waving a crumpled Kleenex. A rote, summarial history followed: how long her nonprofit foundation had been in exis-tence, how it had begun in response to the horrific revenge mur-der of a sexually abused child of eight Aruna had personally taken into her own home. She was married, had one grown daughter who worked at the United Nations in New York, and yes, as a professor of literature at the University of Delhi, she still taught classes. She traveled constantly, speaking at various international conferences on the relation between sex traffick-ing, *kothas* (brothels), and HIV/AIDS, a subject on which she had become grimly expert. Standing with some difficulty, Aruna excused herself to take one more call, while indicating to Sidonie that they should be on their way.

The Imperial had two massive sets of entry doors made of glass, gleaming wood, and mirror-bright brass; uniformed staff waited beside those doors, swung them open for guests, bow-ing from the waist as they did so. Theater of the rich, all gilt sham, yet Sidonie had, until this moment, enjoyed the pretense.

Accompanying Aruna—whose sandals scuffed along the marble floor, her heavy-rimmed glasses lending an owlish, intellectual look—Sidonie felt the disdain of the door attendants, who looked away as they dutifully opened the doors. Outside, beneath the white-columned portico, carpeted and aisled with potted palms, a scarlet-turbanned attendant, his beard mink-dark, ushered guests into and out of hired cars with aplomb, as if each was heir to some obscure but august lineage. She noted the flash of contempt he directed at them. If Aruna seemed oblivious to the waves of disapproval rising in her wake, Sidonie clearly felt the staff's resentment—the hotel itself a social entity, haughty and high-nosed—of one of their guests keeping company with a beggar or one who cast her lot with beggars. *You are making a mistake—your naïveté, your American innocence, is dangerous.*

Still, she felt excitement once they had climbed into the backseat of Aruna's hired car with no help from the Sikh, who stood beside a black limousine, lavishing his trained courtesies elsewhere. Their driver, Govind Singh, would be taking them first to the University of Delhi, where her "daughters" were learning to operate a small cafeteria given to them a month before as a Christmas gift. Afterward, they would drive out to Aashray, an extended family home for about sixty of her children. Sidonie mentioned she needed to return to the hotel by five o'clock, although she really had nothing to return for, and though they had barely left the hotel, she already felt tired. Excited one moment, exhausted the next; Sidonie wondered what was wrong with her.

Govind was Aruna's permanent driver. If one had any money at all, she explained, one hired a driver. Delhi traffic was lethal, a scrumble of auto and human rickshaws, motorbikes, bicycles, pedestrians, sacred, straying cattle, elephants and wild monkeys, rogue dogs, horse- and camel-drawn carts, crowded buses, trucks heaped high and swaying like great, painted elephants, all set to a chronically snarled and angry-sounding blat of horns. Far better to let someone nerveless and certified, transport you safely from place to place. Even as she spoke, their car became stuck in traffic; Aruna rolled down her window to speak to a street beggar of eleven or twelve who floated up beside the car, a tray of cheap trinkets slung around her neck. As she spoke, the girl shook her head vehemently, turned, and darted away through packs of cars immobilized, sluggish, as though sickened by their own jaundiced and stinging exhaust.

"What did you say to her?"

"I promised that if she was ready to leave her life, if she got into the car, right now, I could offer her food, a safe home, education. I promised she would never be harmed again."

"What did she say?"

"That she wasn't ready."

"Has anyone ever accepted such an offer?"

"Never. They would rather suffer what is familiar than get into the car of a stranger and possibly face worse difficulties. It is completely understandable."

Sidonie had never seen anyone roll a car window down to offer sanctuary to a street child. Everyone in India (and everywhere else in the world, she supposed) kept windows rolled tight, transparent barriers against the stream of ravaged faces, the rush of piteous cries—*beggar etiquette,* she had heard someone describe it.

Govind left the congested thoroughfare to turn onto a relatively quiet street, the car wending along a road lined evenly with light green leafy trees. University classes had not yet started; it was still winter holiday, so the campus was largely deserted, except for Aruna's girls, learning to run the canteen. Govind parked in front of a one-story brick cottage with a deeply shaded, unfurnished porch. Sidonie followed Aruna up several steps into the canteen's shadowy, unlit interior. Inside, the air felt frigid, weighted, and the large, simply furnished canteen had an old-fashioned, if icy, feel to it. The walls were painted and tiled in a cool mint green, the plastic tables and chairs a syrupy brown. Tinsel garlands and limp foil chains in gold, fuchsia, green, and blue, looped crookedly along the glass shield of the long aluminum serving counter, behind which two luridly tinted posters, one of Lord Krishna, another of Ganesh, stamped the green wall space. Following her gaze, Aruna commented, "We need other artwork on that wall . . . not just Krishna, that's only Hinduism." Her dislike of religion was not confined to Krishna or Hinduism. Earlier, in the car, while bitterly recounting the story of a failed adoption from one of Mother Teresa's orphanages, Aruna had called herself a nonbeliever. "My children are my religion. They are what I believe in."

At once, these acolytes of Aruna's faith appeared from here and there to welcome her. As she introduced her guest, "the American writer," each girl bowed, hands steepled in prayer, saying *"Namaskaar,"* the greeting traditionally given to someone older than themselves. Wearing uniforms of black pants, white blouses, and long denim aprons of alternate dark and light blue striping, they lined up for Aruna's inspection. Regarding them with sternness, Aruna paused now and then in her unsmiling address to her daughters to translate for her guest. "I've told them they must properly iron their shirts and aprons each morning. They must always look crisp and neat, completely professional. I've had them all trained by a five-star chef, and professionalism is very important to their success. This one is the money counter, she is also certified as both an ambulance and a taxi driver. Several of the girls have their taxi licenses. These three are still in school, finishing their education, doing very well. The master chef who trained them volunteered his time, as did Sanjay." An older man with short gray hair, wearing khaki trousers and a perfectly ironed khaki shirt, had just stepped into the canteen to say hello to Aruna. "Sanjay is the university's head horticulturalist. He has visited our Family Home, Aashray, several times to show the girls how to manage their vegetable gardens properly." She spoke briefly with him before turning back to Sidonie. "These girls are not victims. I detest that emphasis. They are survivors. Ah, here comes Kanta. Kanta Dhungana is Nepalese, only twenty years old, and very, very active in the rescue of girls. She goes with me to speak at conferences, she is in charge of everything at Aashray, she is also an expert in martial arts. She has learned to have no fear, going straight into the brothels. Once she returned, disguised in a burqa, to the *kotha* on G. B. Road where she had been kept for five years, to rescue other girls." Aruna spoke to Kanta in rapid, businesslike Hindi as the others drifted back to work. Shivering in the aqueous light, Sidonie gratefully took the hot chai offered to her. Then came a partitioned aluminum dish of white dumplings, three great, rough pearls, floating in a watery orange curry, with a side dish of light green coconut chutney. She thanked the girl who placed the tray in front of her. The aluminum fork felt light as air as she pressed down and took a bite. The dumpling was dense, bland, the sauce fiery. Aruna told her what the dish was called, but Sidonie immediately forgot. She wasn't hungry and the foreign taste and smell slightly nauseated her, but, determinedly, she ate most of what she had been given. Another girl brought out a second plate with a single plain dumpling on it; apparently, Aruna's tastes and preferences were well known. Taking a few bites, she pushed her dish away, explaining more. "Time is precious for these girls. It is critical that they learn cuisine, beauty school, martial arts, gardening, computer, and driving skills—whatever each one likes best—that is very important—they must like what they do so that they can be successful and self-sufficient. Education and training will give them confidence, self-respect, economic security, then they will be able to help other girls."

Feeling warmer from the hot tea and curry, Sidonie requested a tour of the kitchen. She followed Aruna behind the serving counter, through a doorway into a tiny, nearly empty pantry, through the narrow cooking galley with its stacks of enormous blackened pots and pans, and stepped into the canteen's walled courtyard. The girls who accompanied them were solemn yet eager to answer any questions Sidonie might have, though she had none. For an odd moment, she felt like some minor government inspector, and tried to think of what to ask, though all she really wanted to do was—what? She wasn't even sure, she just felt at peace, being where she was. In the courtyard, yes, that big mixer, churning and wrapping pale, elastic-looking bands of dough around its great beaters, that was the *chappati* and *dhosa* mixer. A rough wooden table stood heaped with whole bursting heads of cauliflower, cabbage, broccoli, other vegetables, shrouded with a length of white muslin cloth. Parsley, coriander, and other herbs she didn't recognize sprouted vigorously from giant clay pots, and as they passed back through the slip of dark kitchen, the dingy supply pantry with its two great burlap sacks of flour, everything, by Sidonie's Western standards, appeared to be fifty or more years behind. Yet sunlight filtered lacily through the young trees in the courtyard, the girls followed, anxious to please Aruna with their accomplishments. In less than two weeks, their cafeteria would be filled to capacity, noisy with students and faculty.

As Sidonie finished taking photographs of the girls, lined up along the porch, a lanky older woman in a deep green, tangerine-bordered sari stepped off the graveled path outside the canteen to speak to Aruna. "That woman," Aruna explained later, as they waited for Govind to open the car doors, "recently learned that her husband has a second wife and five other children. He has abandoned her for this secret family, so now, tragically, at her age, unskilled, she struggles to survive. He has also beaten her on more than one occasion. I am helping her find work at the university so she can feed the children he abandoned." As Govind prepared to drive off, Kanta dashed down the porch steps, ran around to the passenger side, and hopped in beside him, turning as she did so to speak to Aruna.

For the better part of the next hour, as they headed toward Delhi's rural outskirts, Sidonie looked out on scenes of poverty so brutal she could scarcely believe what she was seeing. Aruna, seemingly inured, reminisced about her childhood in the mountains of West Bengal. Her father, a highly ranked police officer, had fallen in love with the beautiful daughter of a feudal lord, Aruna's mother, who had ridden out of the forest on an elephant to meet her new husband. Chafing inside her overly sheltered childhood, possessed of a wild, rebellious nature, Aruna joined the revolutionary political group NAXL and, when traveling to remote villages as a young teacher, had slept alone in a thatched hut in the middle of a cemetery, a machete by her side and a guard dog at the door to ward off assault.

Staring out the car window, absorbing Aruna's fantastic tale, Sidonie took in hundreds of fragments: starving dogs, maimed beggars, gaunt, ashen-skinned children, the homeless, hungry, and lame, all crowding the same space, egalitarian, anarchical, laboring, unrushed, resigned. Poverty as color, she considered, looking out at the bright pinks, turquoises, oranges, and greens on buildings and clothing, on everything that moved or refused movement. (The Imperial, by contrast, was all cold, white wealth.) She tried to slow the blur, seize on vignettes: a man squatting, naked but for a loincloth, beating away on a huge patched metal dish with a sort of hammer, repairing it, she supposed. Ramshackle tea stalls. Parched trees, and beneath them, small tables with mirrors, each with a single wooden chair—outdoor barbershops—field upon field, barren, stubbled, home to great horned cattle. Carts of woven sticks and rotting wood, drawn by stunted, tough-limbed horses and even goats, wearing circus-like headdresses fashioned of gold foil, gaudily feathered and beribboned, crowning their bowed, burdened heads. Women whose saris dully gleamed in the chilly sunlight, stepping around an old man asleep on a cot crudely made from leather strips and branches, perhaps not asleep but dead, or nearly dead, and when dead, would he be a matter of large or small consequence?

Aruna reached into her purse and handed Sidonie a gift bag made of lavender paper. Inside, a calendar with photographs of Aruna's children, a pamphlet of narratives, written by some of those same children, each telling how she had been abducted, sold, sexually enslaved, rescued. Two bracelets of dark blue hemp and cowry shell, an address book covered in burlap, framed with strips of cheap satin. Opening her gifts, she pricked her finger on a staple; Aruna produced a Band-Aid from her purse and doctored Sidonie herself. But first, the single scarlet bead of blood, so empty of personality and contradiction! Looking out the window, Sidonie imagined glossed, silent rivers of blood, secret tributaries flowing through all people and animals as they slept, cooked, ate, scavenged, cycled, walked, washed themselves, the blood slowing, stopping, as they died. Did everything exist democratically, perdurably? And the oceanic, pulsing calm beneath the surface squalor: was this fatalism, faith, or the lethargy of disease? Depression or metaphysical serenity, *samsara*, the wheel of life and nothing one could or even should be bothered to do about it? Human beings and animals flying along to who knows where, cars and bikes and buses, point counterpoint, swift between them. Now the car turned off the main road, and Govind was taking them down a rural lane. They stopped before a high white metal gate. Stepping down, Govind pounded until the gate creaked open with slow precision and a small boy of perhaps six, barefoot, wearing only shorts, responsible for such a great action, emerged, waving.

Aruna gave a prolonged, satisfied sigh. "Aashray. Home."

A two-story concrete building, L-shaped, white as a yacht, with chalk-blue ironwork trim, Aashray was stark, utilitarian, yet not unpleasant in its spacious setting. Sixty-two girls, aged sixteen to twenty, along with several younger children, lived at the Family Home. The compound was walled, gated, secure. The house stood along one length of the property, divided and hidden from a parallel vegetable and herb garden by a dense ribbon of hedging and a sere strip of winter grass. Stout-hipped terra-cotta pots of yellow and lavender chrysanthemums and white alyssum stood in symmetrical rows along the concrete walkways. An American philanthropist, after having heard Aruna speak at a conference, had written her a check for a vast sum, and with that, she had built her paradise.

Now, she climbed down from the car and, with Sidonie barely

keeping up, headed straight for the garden. Despite her shawled bulk, Aruna moved swiftly along raised dirt footpaths between dozens of squared, individual plots of cabbage, eggplant, tomatoes, coriander, parsley, chilies of different types. At the far end of the garden, near the compound's rear wall, stood a brick storeroom, empty and in disrepair. Aruna pronounced it Aashray's future bakery. Nearby, stood two fragile-looking peach trees, saplings, symbols of a future orchard.

"The girls run everything themselves. It is their home, not mine, and they must manage it properly."

Emerging from the garden through an opening in the hedge, they stood on the lawn near an empty swing set, watching girls bloom from inside the house and run straight for Aruna, crying "Mummy, Mummy." In the pale January light, on the winter lawn, striped brown and green, one of the girls set down two plastic chairs while another carried out a small table with a scrubbed and faded wooden top, placing it between the chairs. A third girl stood nearby, holding a round tin tray with two glasses of plain, uniced water. "This water," declared Aruna, sitting down and inviting Sidonie to do the same, "is absolutely pure. It comes from our own well and is safer to drink than the water at your hotel." As Sidonie gratefully drank the clean cold water, a fourth girl appeared with a mismatched tea set, a floral-patterned teapot, and two chipped cups without saucers, arranging each piece upon the worn table as if it were the finest bone china. The dignity of her movements affected Sidonie unexpectedly, almost violently. Embarrassed, she politely ate several of the little brown and white "wheel" cookies with vanilla filling, the spicy, dry shredded potato and green raisin mix. These treats were quickly followed by dishes of spinach leaf, potato, and mushrooms fried into egg-battered shapes like golden flat envelopes and served with chutney. Sidonie ate as much as she could, noting that Aruna, as before, barely touched the food and instead swatted at a fat fly lazily circling. The tea was weak, the sandwich cookies of a cheap packaged sort, and the unsalted vegetable fritters tasted oily and of smoke, yet Sidonie felt she had rarely tasted anything so satisfying. As Aruna conversed with those girls who approached her with their private, saved-up concerns, others sat nearby in a circle on the lawn, doing home-work, talking quietly, writing in their notebooks, glancing over now and again with mild curiosity. Then, as a bird might, one of the girls, schoolbook closed on her lap, tilted back her head and sang in a sweet, true voice:

You are my sun, you are my moon. You are my existence.

More girls emerged from the great white block house. Like the others, they wore long skirts with sweaters, jackets or tunics, woolen caps and scarves. Several wore Western blue jeans. Aruna purchased new clothes for her children once a year, refusing cast-off, donated clothing. Though all the girls attended local schools, she regretted not having funding to send them to British-system public schools where they would receive a far bet-ter education.

When she groaned that her left knee pained her, one of the girls darted off and returned from the house with a chair for Aruna to prop up her leg on. Another stood behind her, massaging her shoulders. A red-capped, unsmiling girl of three or four ran up, and Aruna lifted, then set her down on the sore knee, the child's weight a comfort, her legs, plump in scarlet tights, swinging back and forth. In the chilly winter air, girls flitted like butterflies, gos-samer and fragile, landing around Aruna, draping themselves around her shoulders, along her arms, at her feet. Aruna intro-duced Sidonie one by one to her Muslim and Hindu daughters—Hasina, Jyoti, Razna, Seema, Sultana, the rest—each murmuring *"Namaskaar,"* as their anxious, adoring eyes darted to their mother. *This one is my spot of trouble, doesn't care to study in school, but she wants to learn beauty culture, this is our basket-ball star, here is our smart one, she has just received another scholarship, ah, this one has been depressed lately, she needs a little extra love, come here darling. I wanted to have eleven chil-dren, and now, see, I have sixty . . .* They pressed close in the dusky light, one showing "Mummy" a small cut on the hand *(this*

one is my best cook, she loves to cook) or a bruise on the shin
(one of our fine traditional dancers) or simply throwing arms
around Aruna's neck, kissing her cheek (*ah, this one doesn't pay
attention to her studies, but she has a very big heart).* Later, on the
drive back, when Sidonie asked about fundraising, Aruna would
answer, curtly, that she had no time for it. She depended on donations, on what was given without asking. She preferred to
spend her energy, her time, rescuing trafficked girls, testifying in
courts, speaking at conferences worldwide.

Only hours ago, Sidonie had been breakfasting in the gold-
and-blue-glassed atrium of the most luxurious hotel in Delhi.
Now she was somewhere in the Utter Pradesh countryside, sitting on this winter lawn in the fast-fading light beside Aruna Kumari, a small child wearing black-and-white checkered trousers
and a red woolen cap, perched on Aruna's swollen knee, her little arms thrown about "Mummy's" neck, her head nestled
against the broad, soft chest. Above the garden side of the compound's wall, the rounded dome of a temple appeared to float,
albescent, against the clear violet sky.

Hoping a walk might warm her, Sidonie, shivering now, asked
if she could see the garden one more time. Aruna sent for Kanta.

Aashray's garden was plotted into neat squares like a long,
variegated, hand-sewn quilt. The sprawling green plants looked
vigorous, and the soil had a whitish film over it, a matte glaze,
underneath which, breaking through here and there, was dirt of
such a pale, churned brown that it looked, in the light by which
Sidonie now saw it, grayish pink.

Kanta walked, wordless, on the footpath in front of Sidonie.
Her black trousers, white-collared shirt, shiny black athletic
jacket, black hair buckled into an oiled knot at the nape of her
neck, her black-rimmed glasses, exactly like Aruna's, all gave
the young Nepalese woman a scholarly, grave air. There was
an intimidating force to her quietness. Aruna was grooming
Kanta to be an expert speaker, bringing her to conferences to
speak not only as former sex slave and survivor, but as a legal
authority on sex trafficking. The silence lengthened as they

came to the far edge of the garden and stood beside the brick outbuilding, Aashray's future bakery. When they finally spoke, it was of roses.

"In July we have roses here."

"They must be especially beautiful."

"I once saw a black rose."

"Black?"

"Yes, a single black rose."

Sidonie remembered the White Rose, a small society of university students in Munich who had openly opposed Nazism in 1942. By 1943, all of them had been imprisoned, including an eighteen-year-old girl, executed along with her brother, founder of the White Rose. But she said nothing; there seemed no way to talk about a young German girl's bravery in relation to Kanta's courage. They walked back to Aruna who stood, a dowager queen, wrapped in a navy blue shawl, waiting.

"The girls wish to dance for us." It was like watching a bright scatter of doves, flying low, dipping and wheeling—the girls, skimming from the house to the lawn, disappearing back into the house again.

The ground-floor room was overrun with mismatched couches, pushed to the various sides of the room, and one low coffee table. Sitting down, Aruna, with a pained sigh, raised her left leg, rested it on the low table in front of her. She lifted up another of the smaller children, unaware of her role as a healing property, to perch on her knee. Instructing another girl to reposition the space heater's glowing orange coils nearer Sidonie, Aruna leaned over to drape her shawl around Sidonie's shoulders (*you did not dress for the cold*). Layers of warmth, both from the shawl and the heater, felt blissful.

Kanta stood beside a portable cassette player, somberly selecting tapes from a loose pile scattered along one windowsill. Seven dancers lined up before their little audience, hands set on narrow hips, giggling. "A Muslim song," Aruna said as the music began. With heads held high, clothing mismatched, feet bare, knit winter caps askew on their heads, they danced. Each girl, Sidonie thought, weighed no more than eighty or ninety pounds. The other girls, lined up along the couches and on the floor, seemed to relish the familiar dances, holding the younger ones, barely two and three years old, on their laps.

A Nepalese song followed, then a Hindi folksong that began with each girl holding a proud archer's stance, one arm drawing back the string of her invisible bow, poised as though to shoot an arrow, the dance ending with that same arm outstretched and holding not a bow, but a lamp, shielding with her other hand its invisible flame.

> *I am that woman*
> *Who has been abused for so long.*
> *Now you will see how strong I am,*
> *How finally free.*
> *I am that woman.*

Sidonie signed a worn red guestbook, noting, as she did, the delegation of church visitors from Sweden and Norway who had preceded her. Kanta toured Sidonie through the Family Home, showing her several large, unheated dormitories with simple cots covered by thin Indian cloth blankets, the dining room and kitchen, the library with two outdated computers, a glass-fronted cabinet with a haphazard collection of donated books, the pink-tiled communal shower, study hall, infirmary. All of Aashray's interior walls were gray concrete, bare of adornment.

At the entrance to the house, girls clustered to say good-bye and pose for photographs. From inside the car, Sidonia turned a last time to see them still waving, faces shockingly forlorn. The normal sadness of leave-taking had been eclipsed by older, unexpunged sorrows, surfacing and set like a seal on each girl's face. She turned back around, ashamed of her small, secret eagerness to return to the warm privacy of her hotel room. The drive back would take more than an hour over the same roads; it was evening now, the shrinking band of sunlight against the horizon washed a last deep gold over everything.

Aruna's phone was switched back on, and in between taking and returning calls, she continued to answer Sidonie's interview questions. She had first met her husband thirty-one years ago. They had a mutual tendency, both being equally stubborn, to engage in ridiculous, dramatic arguments. For example, the time they were in the car arguing about their new driver's terrible navigation skills, shouting so loudly at one another that first one vowed to get out of the car, then the other, and there they both stood, by the side of the road, Aruna and her husband, arguing pigheadedly, while Govind (whose skills had since improved considerably) waited stoically for them to get back into the car. But no, her husband thoroughly supported her work and her travels, whether to Thailand or to Holland, Sweden, the Netherlands, New York, or Washington, D.C., all places she had recently been invited to speak. Her biological daughter donated most of her salary to support her "sisters," her mother's cause.

Nearly ill with fatigue, drowning in Aruna's loquaciousness, Sidonie gazed out the window at street scenes unreeling, a filmstrip in reverse. A silver-haired woman in a black sari with a red-embroidered border, a basket of laundry balanced on her head, stepped matter-of-factly around a corpselike figure curled in a fetal position on a rush mat on the sidewalk.

"Where do you get your energy to do all of this?"

"Energy? My daughters give me energy."

"I ask because I feel so tired, trying to keep up with you for even one day."

"I will tell you something. Last night my husband woke me saying I was shouting in my sleep again. Often, when I am asleep, I carry on entire conversations with my daughters, so I do not always get proper rest. I am also in the car many hours each day, traveling from here to there, one destination to another, so I have learned to sleep while in the car. In fact, I will tell you something. I have been asleep just now."

"You've been asleep this whole time we've been talking?"

"Yes. Absolutely. I am able to carry on a perfectly lucid conversation with half of my brain while the other half sleeps. You could say I am asleep all the time, at the same time as I am awake."

"I wish I could do that." Sidonie felt envious. Was it possible then, life being but a dream? Something about India, she thought, made one into an amateur philosopher. "My last question, for now at least, is about the relation of sex trafficking to the increasing rate of HIV/AIDS in India's population."

"Very grim, of course. We are one of the few social agencies to have made the direct link between sex work and this raging epidemic. What is the good of India's information technology boom if we continue to be indifferent to the suffering of our children, our young girls, sold, raped, HIV infected, dying at younger and younger ages? Ah, here we are, your hotel."

This time, an attendant opened the door so suddenly that Sidonie managed only a hurried, clumsy thank-you. As she started to unwind the shawl from around her shoulders, Aruna stopped her. "No, my dear, put it back on. Put it back on. It is a gift. You must keep it."

The Imperial's great doors swung open. *Good evening, Madame*. She made her way up the marble stairway, down the silent carpeted hallway to her room, where, without even bothering to turn on the lights, she fell across the bed, succumbing to a state more like unconsciousness than sleep. Hours later, she woke disoriented, still entangled in the folds of her blue woolen caul.

In a fairy tale, such a cloak would bestow magical powers, invisibility, bravery. Sidonie merely felt ravenous. Light from the courtyard below her window threw funereal shadows around the smooth-surfaced, gleaming room. Sunken in its cherrywood armoire, the television's gloomy eye stared, baleful, into the room.

She would order room service, watch the news as she ate, draw a bath, prepare for her interview at the U.S. Embassy the next morning. Adjusting the shawl around her, she crossed the icy marble floor to flick on the portable space heater she had ordered earlier from housekeeping. Consulting the in-room menu, she called down for dinner, noting from the digitalized, ice-blue numbers at the bottom of the television screen that it was past ten o'clock.

The heater's intestinal coils warmed the room by degrees as she perched on the bed's firm edge, surfing from channel to channel. She stopped at each English-language broadcast: a bitter cold snap in Delhi, the worst in thirty years, affecting thousands; the "Tata" riots in West Bengal with poor farmers outside Kolkata protesting the giant corporation's intention to move in, encroach on land tilled by the same families for generations. The CEO of Tata and the head of the West Bengal Communist Party standing together, assuring everyone that an auto factory will, by offering jobs with decent wages, lift the local economy out of its abysmal slump. A modern, globally engaged solution to chronic poverty. A way to save a dying city. Thousands of poor farmers marched by torchlight, shouting into news cameras, waving banners and farm implements, protesting the corporate takeover of their land. Additional police had been called in to restore order, ward off bloodshed, by bloody force if necessary. Sidonie switched to another channel, to the other big story, less political, more sensational—a lurid, local tragedy unfolding by the hour. A wealthy businessman (born and educated in Delhi, spotless reputation, graduate of the best private schools in the city) whose palatial home abutted the slums of Noida, accused of luring children from the miserable streets of Noida, sexually assaulting, dismembering, and burying them in pieces around his property. Up to thirty or forty known victims, the horror of dozens of children buried in bits who knows where, bones, skulls being unearthed everywhere. Grieving families, mostly immigrants from Nepal and West Bengal, having no legal identity or voting rights, "nobodies," weeping, holding worn snapshots of children up to news cameras, children missing weeks, months, some even years. The valet, implicated as well, shown being carted off to the police station, jacket hooded over his head, a

222 | MELISSA PRITCHARD

murderous mob kept at bay by a phalanx of police. A gruesome, grisly crime, and now the police were being upbraided
for turning away the poor victims' families who went to them
for help. Journalists, social workers, psychologists, heads of
government agencies were trotted on the air to comment on
the morally bankrupt state of India today. What good is it if
India strives to be a global competitor in information technology when the poor are disposable, invisible, dismissable,
their children sacrificed? The entire collective conscience of
India was being flayed by "Children of a Lesser God," as the
crime story was being referred to by one prominent news station, "India's Shame," by its rival station.

She had ordered an American cheeseburger, french fries, a
small bottle of red wine, an apple tart with vanilla ice cream.
She opened the door to let in a handsome young man, crisply
uniformed, bearing a large silver tray. Setting it down on the
bed as she requested, he took his time, lifting the silver dome
from each dish with a practiced flourish, filling her wine glass
from the small, uncorked bottle while asking if there was anything else he could do for her. "No," she answered, scrawling
her signature at the bottom of the bill, aware of his proximity,
his youth, wondering what he must think of her. This same
young man had been sent to her each time she had ordered or
requested anything. His name was Vikram Singh, and so far,
he had brought up her dry cleaning, delivered and taken away
her many room service trays, plugged in the space heater, an-
gling it toward the bed as she had asked (she simply could not
see paying for a room in which she was cold; cold temperatures
made her unreasonable). He was outrageously handsome, with
the great brown eyes, thick, clean black hair, and the even features of a 1930s matinee idol. Really, why had he been assigned
to her? It was incredibly awkward, having to disguise her awe
each time he broke, with princely courtesy, into the lonely intimacy of her room. Each time he knocked, she would dash to
the mirror before opening the door. Tenacious vanity! Had it
been her own wishful imagination, how he seemed to linger a

bit longer each time, asking questions, eager to talk, standing
about, gazing at her? Each time she had to rethank him force-
fully so that he would go. What did he want? Her red hair and
pale skin? Her presumed affluence, her independence, a Western woman boldly on her own? Her cynical side suspected the
hotel's management of acting, in a nonsubtle way, to insure she
was provided everything an attractive, possibly lonely Western
woman might want. So she scarcely looked at him (except
when he couldn't see her looking, then she stared openly, greed-
ily, envying his lover, whoever she was, or he—who knew anything these days?). She kept her transactions with Vikram brief,
impersonal, generous. He was a service, an extension of the
hotel, no different than the Indian masseur she had paid for her
first night at the hotel as her room was being changed (she had
objected to the room she had been given, overlooking the service area's parking lot where the hotel's cooks, maids, and drivers idled on their breaks, smoking, talking loudly). The whole
shape of the room had felt wrong, cramped, so while they were
finding her a better room, she had gone down to the beauty
salon and requested a masseur, sat in a velvety white robe at a
mirrored counter while an older Indian man with one missing
front tooth gave her an Ayurvedic head massage, kneading and
knuckling and rubbing her scalp, her ears, her neck and shoulders with slick, fragrant, warm oils. As she smiled at herself in
the mirror, the masseur's reflection, in a limp, slightly frayed
white jacket, asked how she liked it, *Does that feel good,
Madame?* Given over to sensation, she could only nod. Any
guilt she felt about being waited on, her money affording her
this luxury, was assuaged by an awareness, almost self-righteous,
that she was supporting him after all, his family, his relatives . . .
weren't her needs and desires helping all of these people who
waited on her? It was an uneven equation, but it hardly paid to
impale oneself upon too fine a moral point.

Now, devouring her hamburger down to its greasy, limp leaf of
lettuce, quelling some dietary homesickness, Sidonie suddenly saw,
as if on an imaginary split screen, the masseur with bad teeth

grinning eerily into a mirror to ask how she liked his touch, and on the screen's other half, one of Aruna's daughters, offering food from Aashray's garden. She pushed back from her linened tray, a bit sick; she had eaten too quickly, even sloppily, with her fingers. A young Bollywood actress was being interviewed on the television. She had exquisitely made-up green eyes, long glossy hair, her features so perfect as to defy reality. What must her young, unmarred life be like, one could only imagine, and why was Sidonie in such an anxious, panicky toss about hers? A gorgeous actress, serene, adored, while Sidonie drank alone in her room, in some decline or other. She felt a spasm of envy for the young woman, mixed with a sudden, unwarranted repugnance for herself. Men who wanted her were increasingly compromised, older, less attractive, the latest one married and expecting her to subsist, gratefully, on what crumbs he parsed out. Perched cross-legged in the center of the enormous empty bed, she finished off her glass of wine, restlessly switching channels, stopping at an in-depth news feature on the forty-five-day religious pilgrimage occurring every twelve years in Allahabad, called Ardh Kumbh. Resting against a bulwark of down pillows, she reached over and splashed the remaining wine from the small bottle into her glass. Her room had grown so warm from the heater's neat coils glowing in the corner that she was nearly sweating. Ardh Kumbh was the world's largest congregation of spiritual pilgrims seeking purification, release from the cycle of reincarnation by taking a dip in the holy Ganga or Ganges River. Over 70 million men and women, *sadhus*, clad in orange or crimson or naked but for loincloths or *dhotis*, their brown limbs, faces, and long tangled hair smeared with white ash, all bathing in the holy river. One group of *sadhus* protested the filth in the Ganges, threatening *jal samadhi*, or ritual suicide, if the government didn't do something, as it had promised, to clean the sacred river.

Stretched out in her warm bath scented with cedar and orange Ayurvedic oils, Sidonie raised one slim white leg out of the water, studied it, lowered that leg and lifted the other. Flesh. A raised vein on her right knee that had never been there before. The water, like a glistening, ragged fringe of blown glass, fell unevenly from the length of her bare leg. In India, water was dangerous; one was not to drink it or eat anything washed in it. In India, water brought death. She stood up from her cooling bath, the dull headache from too much wine already beginning. Wrapping herself in one of the hotel's plush white bath sheets, she padded barefoot across the too-warm room (lovely, soporific sensation of damp feet on smooth marble), switched off the heater, the television (some sort of scandal involving a cricket match), called downstairs to be woken at eight, then slipped beneath cool sheets with their silken, soothing pattern of white-on-white stripes. Alone in the overheated darkness, fragmented images—the festival of Ardh Kumbh, villains, child murderers, wailing parents, farmers brandishing shovels by torchlight, a beautiful, sloe-eyed actress tilting her perfect chin to comment on her latest romantic musical, all swirled and dissolved into an anxious sleep as the identity of Sidonie Recoura slipped off like a sleeve, a loosening skein of foreign, peripheral self.

Another massive white edifice! What was it in Delhi (*place of the heart*) that held to such blindingly white statements of importance—the political, the historically sacred, the opulent—the Presidential Palace, the Taj Mahal, the Imperial Hotel, the United States Embassy (even Aashray was painted white, trimmed in dull blue)? Ice-white structures that pierced and hurt the eyes. With Bhavesh Motwani, the embassy employee who had picked her up at the hotel earlier that morning, she walked past a faded blue, circular pool, a nondescript fountain burbling tiredly at its center, and entered the security room in front of the embassy. Purity, innocence, hymenic virginity, cleanliness, holiness. In some indigenous cultures, the color white stood for death. Perhaps on a continent subject to extremes of heat, dust, monsoon rains, and ruinous floods, white offered cool, hygienic, otherworldly relief.

The uniformed security guards grimly checked first Sidonie, then Bhavesh, who remarked, standing in socked feet, arms extended, as the guard's wand brushed first one pant leg, then the other, that since 9/11, and especially since the Iraq war, embassy security had to be maintained at the highest level. As the contents of Sidonie's purse were emptied and diligently examined, she found herself staring up at uninspired, official photo portraits of President Bush and the Secretary of State, Condoleeza Rice. Finally they were cleared (the cell phone and camera confiscated) and permitted to walk into the open, atrium-like courtyard. Finding the embassy's main entrance, they walked along carpeted corridors and office cubicles, passing people on one task or another, moving with brisk importance. The air smelled moribund, decades-old, everything run-down and enervate, a cross between outdated office decor circa 1960 and the mediocre architecture of a chain hotel lobby. From the tired atrium with its large-leaved, flaccid green plants to the uninspired interior colors of beige, maroon, and brown, the whole place felt drained, depressed. Government, Sidonie thought, trying to keep pace with Bhavesh, a small man in a brown suit with a blue sweater vest, moving with amazing alacrity past dozens of offices and around blind corners until he stopped before a pebble textured, opaque glass-windowed door with the black lettered title: First Secretary, Office of International Narcotics and Law Enforcement Affairs.

Sidonie sat at one end of a harsh-textured, crocodile-green sofa, Bhavesh at the other. From behind his untidy, hurricane-struck desk, the First Secretary, Capper McNair, half rose to greet her, before squeezing around and sinking opposite her into an office armchair upholstered in a dull, nubbled mustard. He seemed to both welcome and resist this diversion from the blizzard of paperwork covering his desk, and probably judged her as one more meddlesome, morally outraged American with no clue as to the policy quagmires and bureaucratic ineptitudes he wrestled with every day. (*I am glad you care about these issues*, Sidone felt him thinking. *I, too, used to care, yet I abhor your*

ignorance and envy your ability to take notes and be ferried
back to your fine hotel, while I am pinned beneath lassitude,
lies, byzantine laws, and caste systems, my progress as an out-
side moral policeman measured in centimeters at best.) With the
brusque, taurine manner of a high school athletic coach, Capper looked underexercised, sleep-deprived, and poorly fed. His
ideals, even his pragmatic ideas, had taken a beating, yet Sidonie
nearly liked him as he sat answering her questions about trafficking with more depth and sensitivity than she had expected.
"We measure our success by small victories," he repeated several times, doggedly, as though he wanted to be quoted saying
that if nothing else. In India, yes, sex trafficking was acknowl-
edged as an enormous problem, yes, it was on the government's
list, but it was not at the top of that list, matters more urgent
preceded it, so that in the way of top-heavy governments
strapped for time and money, the issue did not get the attention
or legal action it deserved. Yes, the NGOs, the nongovernmen-
tal organizations, were helpful in calling attention to the issue,
but they succumbed to territorial competition, sabotaging their
own effectiveness. What was needed, and badly, was a unified
coalition of NGOs. The other problem—he spoke slowly,
watching Sidonie scribble in her notebook—was that the State
Department had cut much of the funding allocated to fight
human trafficking. Funding was essentially gone, the money di-
verted to the war in Iraq, yet Washington expected the same re-
sults. He was squeezed between two governments, one wanting
to see measurable success while drastically cutting aid, the other
burdened with too many concerns and lacking funds to address
any of them adequately. It was a miracle when anything happened at all. Capper glanced at the watch on his burly wrist,
stood up, apologized; he had another meeting scheduled. The
First Secretary (were there, Sidonie wondered, Second and Third
Secretaries?) had come to life only once during the hour she had
spent with him, when he told her about individuals helping to
fight trafficking in specific ways. A man from the United States
who had moved to India and founded a traveling activist the-

ater. An American businessman who had built a school for girls and was in the process of building another. People who stepped in with ideas and made them happen. In the grip of twin neurasthenic governments, entrepreneurship cheered him. When Sidonie asked if he knew Aruna Kumari, he said he certainly did. He said nothing more.

It had been an unsettling interview at best, mottled with half-dead figures of speech, grim statistics, and the ugly, parasitic chancre of cynicism. She and Bhavesh did not discuss any of this, walking through the tropical-foliaged courtyard, the air humid, pocked with bird cries, reentering the drab security station, where her cell phone and camera were returned to her. Instead, on the drive back to the hotel, he suggested she might wish to come back one day as a guest of the State Department, travel through India and speak to select audiences about the epidemic of trafficking. He gave her his card, and on the back wrote the name of someone she might contact in Washington, D.C. She had Bhavesh's embassy card now, as well as Capper's, handsome white cards embossed with gold seals and raised black lettering, meant to bestow power and the authority to change things—and yet how little changed, how wide and fixed the gulf between government offices and streets.

Back at the Imperial, Sidonie spent the next two hours in the hotel's handsomely appointed "business quarters," reading and answering e-mails from her editor and Laurent, the elegant Parisian she had met on her layover in Hong Kong, president of a major airlines, married yet openly desirous of an affair. Laurent's note was flattering, calculated, intelligent, but it would not be difficult to decline a romance that would mainly benefit him. The message she had most wanted to find, from the one man she was deeply in love with, also married, was strangely prim, fussy-sounding, beginning with how he was writing in "frenetic haste," was "on the fly," how she was a brave girl (girl!) to be off on her own in India, he had a busy weekend before him, taking "the children" (they were teenagers!) to museums, the theater, church. Many tender and passionate kisses for his brilliant lady, et cetera. There was a hollowness to his words that caused her to panic. Was he taking advantage of distance to disengage, expertly, gently, so as not to risk threatening the unhappy marriage he couldn't seem to leave? She stared at his message, and for the first time in the year she had loved him, left it unanswered. He could not afford to be interested in what she was seeing, thinking, feeling; it might topple the equilibrium of his wealth and privilege, his several homes, the convenience of a wife who, suspecting infidelity, never questioned him, or if she did, accepted his lies. And wasn't Sidonie herself slowly perishing in the secret, airtight compartment he had devised for her? The French airline president, handsome, educated, at cultural ease with having a mistress, was of the same ilk. Depression, brought on by this unsought surfeit of reality, crashed over Sidonie with a nearly audible roar. Hotel guests, tapping away at other monitors, bent over their own secret tasks, seemed not to notice her disequilibrium. She signed out, left. Her business here was finished. What would she do with the rest of her time? How to find relief from the sinking awareness of her lover's cooling toward her, signs of yet another failure? What time was it? She should go to her room, change, have a late lunch, and from there, decide on her evening. As for tomorrow, she could prebook a day trip, through the hotel, to the Taj Mahal.

Sidonie revived at the sight of Vikram, poised at the end of the hallway, as if waiting faithfully for her return. His white pants impeccable, his red Nehru jacket with its black sash accentuating his broad, neat shoulders and narrow hips. "Madam." He smiled, bowing as if his existence had been dormant until this moment. "Good afternoon." And when he might have said, "Is there anything I can do for you?" he rose from his little obeisance, saying, "How are you today, Ms. Recoura?" Sidonie suddenly imagined herself touring Old Delhi with Vikram in handsome tow, the historic Red Fort, Qutb Minar, Old Delhi's bazaar, and Humayun's tomb. Ridiculous. The mind, she thought, is full of sophistry, chicanery, hunger.

"Fine, just fine, thank you. I'll try to find some lunch down-stairs." She thought of something. "Actually, I do have a ques-tion. Do you know how far it is to the Ardh Kumbh?" His face registered bafflement. He tried to pronounce "Kumbh" as she had. She tried to help. "The festival at the Ganges . . ."

"Oh, yes, Madame. You mean Ardh Kumbh, yes? In Alla-habad?"

"Yes, yes, that's it, sorry, I didn't know how to pronounce it. I'd like to go there, perhaps tomorrow, instead of to the Taj Mahal."

Vikram's thoughtful expression was slowly overtaken by a solemn disapproving one. "Oh no, it is terribly far, perhaps ten hours' drive, and it is also . . . very crowded, *lakhs* and *lakhs* of people from everywhere . . . villagers . . . poor people . . . very unclean, perhaps even dangerous . . . it would not be at all safe for Madame. Not for Madame, no. Something else perhaps, the Red Fort, President's Palace? With a guide, of course."

Was he offering himself? Of course not. He was simply con-cerned for the safety of a hotel guest. She was his responsibility, and he took that responsibility very seriously indeed. Sidonie was irritated.

"Thank you, Vikram, I suppose you are right. Thank you for your honesty. And now"—she lifted up her notebook—"work to do." She smiled briskly, indicating she was an independent, suc-cessful Western woman, her time and intelligence very much in demand. Impersonating some version of herself. A staff manager, dressed in sober black, rounded the corner. Both she and Vikram stiffened further into their roles as guest and servant. The woman passed, glancing at them as Vikram, aware of being assessed, bowed with exaggerated deference.

"Very good, Madame, have a most pleasant afternoon." He walked away, quickly catching up to the small woman in black, his boss. Ingratiating himself.

How she loved her gold and white room, serene, pure, beauti-ful! Her laundry had been neatly hung in the cherrywood armoire, a fresh flower arrangement and plate of fruit placed invitingly by her bedside. She set down her camera and notebook, settling for a brief washing up, as she did not have time to change. She unpinned her long hair, brushed it, and, pleased with her face in the bathroom's soft lighting, reapplied a neutral lipstick before heading down to lunch.

The Spice Route was as famous for its cultural ambience as for its exquisite South Asian cuisine. Designed to reflect the journey of spices from Kerala, India, through Indonesia to Thailand and Vietnam, its museum-quality sculptures and murals, painted with subtle vegetable dyes, covered the walls. The candle-lit restaurant was empty at this hour but for the table nearest her. As she was led to her table, Sidonie glanced at the other diner. A middle-aged Indian man, corpulent, wearing a mud-brown Western business suit, head bent low over his plate of food, a large snowy napkin tucked into his shirt collar. A reclusive gourmand, she thought, noting the fussy concentration with which he ate, in curious contrast to his drab, elephantine bulk. He raised his graying head, empty fork poised, napkin like a nationless flag of truce across his chest. She looked down at the menu, knowing he would ask her to join him. After all, he would say, two people alone in such an exotic atmosphere, such a shame, et cetera. . . . And because she was flailing, caught in the vertigo and instability of loneliness, well-hidden of course, she also knew she would join him.

As the waiter drew out a second chair for her, this time at the gentleman's table, her new companion deftly plucked his napkin from his chest, patted it across his lap, then signaled the sommelier, who stood nearby, to recommend a wine for his guest, whom he regarded dotingly as she opened and began to study the complex menu. "Anything you like," he said. "The food is excellent. I know. I have eaten here nearly every day for ten years." He extended a large, beautifully brown, manicured hand. "Siddharth Gupta, call me Sid."

Sid? What a vulgar contraction for the mythically glorious Siddharth. Sid, the exact same ugly-sounding, loathsome nickname she had been burdened with as a child: Sid, Sidney, Sidney

Bean. She took his hand, "My name is Sidonie Recoura." They laughed then, at the pleasant absurdity of two strangers, named Sid and Sidonie, meeting.

Peering at her through thick black glasses, as though she were some honeyed mort to be savored at the end of his meal, Sid produced a business card, setting it with a snap on the pale pink tablecloth in front of her. "I am chief engineer, in charge of Medi-City."

As the waiter returned with her Chardonnay, she noted her companion had no wine glass, that he drank only water. She approved her wine, sipping a bit too gratefully as Sid explained that his project, Medi-City, was the largest medical project of its kind in India, perhaps in the world. The first of a planned series of surgical cities, serving patients flying in from everywhere in the world for first-rate procedures. The finest hospitals, five-star hotels, helipads, an entirely self-sustaining, luxury medical community. As she listened, Sidonie thought of the protesting farmers from Nandigram, in Bengal, the murdered children of immigrants in the Noida district of Delhi.

As for Siddarth, he had grown up in Delhi, attended exclusive public schools, enjoyed, still, international travel. Slab-jowled, glasses pinched halfway down his broad, brown nose, graying hair thick with pomade, nothing about Sid Gupta appealed to her, yet his eyes were not unkind, and an aura of complacency pulsed around him, both irritating and compelling. He was proud of his wealth, his status, his curt, first-name familiarity with the waiters; right now, he seemed determined to impress her with a hasty, formulaic courtship. From nowhere he produced a gold foil box of chocolates sealed with a garish pink ribbon. "For you," he said. "You must like chocolate, all women do." (She had seen those chocolates in the hotel's gift shop. Did he keep a box handy in the event of running across someone like herself?) "You are a beautiful woman. Do you enjoy sweets?" Lonely Sid, unsubtle, esurient. Yet here, in the empty, exotic setting of the Spice Route, under his myopic gaze, she felt newly seductive, her allure restored, extant. Even while she looked at him with distaste as he droned on about his next Medi-City project in Mumbai, she pictured jetting around the world as Mrs. Sid Gupta, Western wife of a billionaire Indian engineer, his wealth underwriting her chimerical charities. A winning team, Sid and Sidonie, Sid and Sid. She became so distracted by this fantasy of marriage to a toadish, plump stranger, a union providing her, at last, the means by which she could reconcile her hedonism and philanthropy, that she failed to see him leering at her.

"I'd like to see you again," he said, staring at her breasts. "Dinner this evening?" They agreed to meet in the hotel lobby at eight o'clock and decide then on one of the other superb hotel restaurants; he knew them all, they all knew him. Working a clipped sheaf of money from his back pocket, he thumbed through the paper bills, extracting the proper sum for both their lunches.

The restaurant had closed; they had to wait for the door to be unlocked. As they walked along the hotel corridor, past expensive boutique shops, Sid Gupta towered above her, reminding her, in his brown suit, of a great male sea cow, his shape bloated in the middle, tapered at both ends, bumping indelicately along the bottom of the sea floor, frightening off smaller creatures. Lugubrious, torpid but not unpleasant. Or a snail, *l'escargot*, toiling along in his mottled, monied shell. What was he saying? "What kind of Indian clothing do you like?" The question threw her back to the memory of a retired Russian brain surgeon, a widower, who had made her wear his dead wife's clothing whenever they went out. She guessed that Sid, faithful to his recipe for seduction, intended to buy her something. "Shawls," she answered. "I do like the shawls I have seen women wearing." He pushed his glasses up with one finger, irritated by her choice. "Those are not even from this region of India. The pashmina is from the Kashmir and Nepal." Beside the stairs in the lobby, Siddharth reconfirmed their dinner date, then ended by whispering in her ear that they perhaps could take a walk together afterward. She pictured

234 | MELISSA PRITCHARD

him strangling her on the hotel grounds, leaving her body stuffed beneath some remote hedge, his innocence upheld, like the businessman/murderer in Noida, by caste, wealth, and an unimpeachable family name. More likely, rather than strangling her, he merely wanted to steer her behind some pillar or palm and fondle her breasts. She climbed up the broad staircase and, from a hidden place on the second-floor landing overlooking the lobby, watched him move ponderously, sad sea cow bumping along the marble bottom of his golden aquarium, a man who had eaten his lunch in the same place every day for the last ten years, a widower with two grown and distant sons. She could marry him if she chose. Within months, even weeks, she could be an Indian billionaire's wife. Palaces, jets, servants, first-class travel. The thought dismayed her. He was dull, incurious; he had been arrogant with the waiters, impatient with her. She drew back from the balcony, ashamed of having entertained such a cheap fiction.

Back in her room, Sidonie's anxiety, her black panic, as she called it, returned in a great, sickening wave. Calling for a driver, she said she would be downstairs in less than twenty minutes. Keeping one eye on the television news, she changed into a chestnut cashmere sweater, jeans, and sandals. The same stories, further embellished: the ghoulish Noida murders (more childrens' bodies, parts of bodies), millions of Hindus arriving for Ardh Kumbh. An Australian couple, close up on camera, sweetly earnest and sunburnt, going on about their guru, their changed, purified lives, oblivious to the procession of pilgrims passing right behind them, some stopping to gaze openly into the news camera. Behind them all, the glinting thread of silver, the holy, befouled Ganges. On the way out of her room, almost as an afterthought, she drew Aruna's dark blue shawl from the back of the desk chair where it had been draped, an added layer against the cold.

To get off the grounds, she lied, telling her hotel driver that she wished to see the Red Fort, a seventeenth-century Mughal emperor's palace, a walled fortification of red sandstone stretching for several acres along the Yamuna River, an aggressively touted tourist attraction she had seen far too many bad photographs of to be truly interested in. Much more fascinating was her driver, Mahadev, an exact Indian replica of the American actor Robert Duvall. As she introduced herself and told him where she wished to go, Mahadev nodded, closed the door behind her, and got into the car himself. *So, an American tourist wanting to see the Red Fort, would she care to see the Presidential Palace as well?* Certainly, she lied a second time, settling into the backseat of the little compact car, her true destination spelled out on a piece of paper, concealed in her hand, written down for her the day before by Aruna.

The dashboard of Mahadev's car was lined with miniature statues of the Hindu gods—Ganesh, Vishnu, Krishna—while the roof above this mobile tableaux shimmered with green and pink foil streamers. Hunched over the steering wheel, alert to traffic, Mahadev passed through the hotel's ornamental security gates, navigating the crush of late afternoon traffic in Delhi. A sallow nimbus, a vatic, vaporish pall of gold-suffused dust lay over the city, both gilding and obscuring the long, straight avenues of trees and the formal symmetry of government buildings. Sidonie, who had just begun, before bed each night, making her way through an annotated version of the Bhagavad Gita, recalled one Hindu scholar explaining that the chariots driven by Krishna and Vishnu were symbolic of the soul's fleshly vehicle, and the conch shell, held aloft and blown upon, was an ancient call to battle. In the tangled, poisonous maze of Delhi traffic, cars turned into modern-day chariots and the blatting of horns became one long, sonorous, war blast.

The moment they had left the hotel grounds, beggars (she knew no better word) pressed hard against the sides of the car. Whenever traffic slowed or, worse, came to a standstill, women in saris, holding up wailing infants, beat softly on the window, emaciated faces inches from hers, exhausted eyes pleading, lips moving soundlessly, one hand opening and closing to indicate hunger, or touching one breast to show a need to feed her child. Children of five or six rushed up to the car, selling paper pin-wheels and fans, snow globes—useless, cheap toys. Sidonie did what even travel guides insisted was the only practical response to such unpleasantness: she turned away, even as small hands pat-patted the window with sticky, percussive obstinacy, as singsong voices pleaded tirelessly, causing her to hate herself, and even them, a little. Relief from such venial agonies came only when the traffic surged forward, bearing her away. She remembered Aruna rolling down the window for the girl who had approached selling trinkets, offering a home, education, safety, even handing her a card with her phone number, telling her to call anytime she was ready—how the child, frightened, had backed away, vanishing into a hard sea of stalled cars.

Mahadev skillfully backed the car into an empty space beside a curb. "The Presidential Palace," he announced with equal pride and ennui. Straight ahead. He urged her to get out, walk the short distance, peer through the immense black and gold painted iron gates, up the imposing tree-lined avenue, at the distant end of which stood yet another massive white architectural statement, this one housing the current rulers of India. To appease him, she obeyed, even giving Mahadev her camera to take a picture of her, posing, dwarfed, before the remote, scarcely visible outline of the palace. How many pictures had he taken of tourists standing in front of this utterly boring sight? Well, she had cooperated, been one of them. Getting back into the car, sitting in the front seat this time, she moved a scattered handful of cassettes aside and handed him the slip of paper. "Can you take me here, please?" He took the slip of paper, read it, looked at her in astonishment. She was quick with her answer. "I am writing an article for an American magazine, and I must visit this place before I return to the United States. It is an important article; it will help many young girls. Please, Mahadev."

He looked at his watch and stared out the window. Pondering. She had no idea how far the city's major *kotha*, G. B. Road (also known as Gandhi Baba or Garstin Bastion Road), was from the presidential palace, although common sense would suggest a respectful distance. Later, she would find it was on the edge of the Old City, less than seven kilometers from the palace. Wiping his glabrous, shiny forehead, sighing heavily, Mahadev returned the paper to her. "Let me make a call," he said.

Mahadev paced on the sidewalk a few feet from his car, talking into his cell phone, talking, she supposed, to his wife, how he would be late, an unusual customer, she must be patient, he would earn more money this time.

Resignedly, he got back into the car. Yes, he could take her there. After little more than ten or fifteen minutes, he pulled the car, with a jerk of the brake, alongside another curb, switched off the car's engine and stared straight ahead. The car's windows, grimed and gritty, stayed rolled up. "G. B. Road?" she asked. He nodded to the left, toward an ordinary street, the same as dozens of others they had passed on the way here. "You can take a very good picture from here." To prove his cooperativeness, he rolled down his window.

"Oh no, Mahadev." She pointed across the street. "I need to go in there. Walk around, take photos. I have to do that."

In an almost comical gesture, Mahadev smacked his palm, a damp flat sound, against his shiny forehead.

"Madame, I do not recommend you go into that place. It is not at all safe. No."

"Go with me, then. We will just walk down a few of the streets. Ten minutes, I promise. Look"—she pointed upwards for emphasis, though not far, as the sun was sinking faster in the sky than she had anticipated—"it is still light out." He sat unmoved. She brought out half of the Indian currency she had tucked into her purse. "Here. And I have plenty more. Plus credit cards. It's very important." She paused deliberately. "If I have to, I'll go in alone."

He let out a painful sigh, shaking his head at the offer of cash, as if offended on top of everything else. She had made him miserable with her crazy request. A devout Hindu, a married man, and she was asking this of him. Then bribing him. He got out of the car, came around, and, not looking at her but up at an un-cooperative heaven, opened her door. As they crossed the busy street, threading between cars, she raised her voice. "I am doing this to try to help these girls." His expression of bilious misery did not change. "Just for a few minutes, Mahadev. I am completely grateful."

The main thoroughfare of G. B. Road was crowded with the urgent clamor and commerce of merchants, bicyclists, cars, human rickshaws, motorcycles, street vendors, pimps, beggars, and clients, set apart by the way they moved, in doglike packs, boisterously hiding their sly, common prurience in a reddish brown haze of lust. Girls, Sidonie could hardly estimate how many, lined both sides the street, lounging in uneasy clusters by the doorways of what she could only assume were the brothel houses. She walked beside Mahadev, gripping her purse a little too tightly over one shoulder, feeling the shadow her easy liberty cast as she walked between two aisles of girls, each one for sale. For relief, she looked up at the brothels themselves, at the scabrous, arrogant remains of outmoded colonial architecture. Ironwork balconies, bellied, ornately scrolled, ran like permanent black lace veils along the outsides of the bleached pink, blue, and green painted exteriors of the three- and even four-storied houses, giving a carnivalesque air, as did the bitterly bright, tinsel-colored saris of the prostitutes. With Mahadev beside her, stocky and solid, his sunglasses adding impassivity to his already stony face, she walked down alley after dingy alley, each with its eerie frieze of blank-faced girls in stilled postures of oppressive boredom shot through with sharp, animal wariness. Many looked no older than fourteen. Turning down one alley, deserted and empty, they passed the rain-beaten remains of a paper temple, leftover from a *puja,* or religious procession. A portable shrine made of willow branches, painted in gaudily swirled psychedelic patterns, studded with hundreds of diminutive electric bulbs, like dull-lustered pop-beads. Eroded by sun and rainfall, degrading into nothingness.

At the end of the alley, they nearly tripped over twenty or thirty children, bunched, jostling, drawn to something in their midst, a thing Sidonie could not see until she deliberately pushed in and found the object of the children's derisive, simple curiosity. A small black bear, hunched into a rough mass, knuckled into itself, a man desperately tugging on it with a filthy hemp rope, the rope's crude, handmade harness lashed around the bear's short, conical muzzle, the hair chafed off, the rope-seared skin turning a raw, mossy, infected tan. Some of the children hurled sticks, refuse, hitting the bear's parched black coat, as the man, frustrated, yanked on the rope, struck the animal about its head with a short stick. He wanted the bear to dance; he needed to feed his family. The bear would not move, and the children jeered at this dismal excuse for entertainment, one more sore disappointment in their lives.

Backing away, Sidonie searched for Mahadev. She found him half a block away, visibly angry, swatting people off: pimps, begging children, food vendors. She relented. "Okay, I've seen enough, Mahadev."

They still had the entire length of the main G. B. Road to walk down. It was nearly dark, lights were coming on, and men jammed the streets now, many in white business shirts, like frenzied moths, rapacious in the failing light. The stench of liquor was overpowering. Near an arched doorway, standing apart, was a tall, exceptional-looking girl wearing a long maroon skirt and tight-fitting orange T-shirt, her full lips stained the same red as her skirt, her black hair sculpted into a polished, heavy bun at the back of her slender neck. Her up-tilted chin defied the filth of her surroundings; she had a haughty look, as if awaiting the person arriving at any moment to rescue her from this place. As Sidonie passed by, the girl turned her gaze directly on her, her kohl-rimmed eyes bright with tears. Sidonie hesitated, and then, as if her legs could not obey her conscience, as though her sole imperative was to catch up to Mahadev, who had quickened his pace as he came nearer the end of the street, she hurried past. Waiting to cross the street with her driver, suddenly afraid of the tumultuous traffic, Sidonie recalled a line from a Tagore poem she had lingered over in her annotated copy of the Gita that morning, addressed to the Great Mother Goddess, Kali.

Mother, I shall weave a chain of pearls for thy neck
with my tears of sorrow.

Back inside the gaudy sanctuary of Mahadev's car, Sidonie looked out of her window. Weak electric bulbs, like loosely strung garlands of fireflies, threw a ghastly glow over row upon row of stalls selling vegetables, dishes, clothing, kindling, meat, the endless, negotiable jig between scarcity and purchase. She wondered how upset he was with her.

"Are you hungry, Mahadev? May I buy you dinner?"

"No," he shook his head. "I am fasting today."

Her crime grew worse. Not only had she asked a Hindu on a holy fasting day to accompany her to G. B. Road, a place of such impropriety he could not tell his wife or children about it, she had just invited him to eat with her.

"Mahadev, how far away is the Ardh Kumbh?" Because of Vikram, she pronounced it correctly. "I saw it on television back at the hotel."

He glanced sharply at her. "The Ardh Kumbh? In Allahabad?"

"Yes. I want to go. Will you take me?"

"Now?"

"Tomorrow."

If Mahadev had looked miserable before, he was now in a near contortion of despair. Speechless.

"I have more money," she said. "Much more."

His shoulders slumped as he careered along in a fresh storm of honking. This one wanted him to go first to a brothel and now to the Ardh Kumbh, a place he himself, despite his life's devotion, could not go.

"Madame, he said, "it is many miles away, in Allahabad, at least ten hours. It is impossible, and for you, a woman tourist, an American, very unsafe."

She had meant to offer him the Ardh Kumbh as a gift. Or an apology.

Holding up one of the cassettes, she asked if he would at least be willing to drive her around the city for an hour or so. She wasn't ready to return to her hotel, to her dreaded dinner date with Siddharth Gupta. Sid. Mahadev nodded, took the cassette from her and inserted it into the player.

"You like songs of Krishna?"

"I'm sure I will."

As *bhajans* shook the tiny, festive interior of the car, he explained that he had just returned from a pilgrimage to one of Krishna's temples. He had taken his entire family: wife, children, grandparents. Turning up the volume, he chanted along, as cheerful now as he had been dour before. Idly, she wondered where they were going. She thought of Siddharth, waiting for her to join him for dinner or for life, entrapped by his syrupy wealth. Her small bravery, walking along G. B. Road, had made her feel buoyant, a bit mad, as if she had escaped something inevitable. It was fully dark now, the traffic a great stubborn beast, uncoordinated, slothful, the cacophony of horns unending. Sidonie laid her head back, neck and shoulders aching. Eyes closed, she saw the bear, captive and unmoving, the men squatting in a circle on the sidewalk, gambling. Her camera had remained hidden, unused. Pulling a notebook and pen from her purse, she began to scrawl details, her handwriting awkward, scarcely legible in the weak light of the city streets, the sporadic, flashing headlights of cars.

Content with aimlessly driving about the city, Mahadev grew chatty. "You have been to Agra, to the Taj Mahal?"

She slipped her pen and notebook back into her purse. "I am supposed to go tomorrow." One of the wonders of the world, and she didn't care about seeing it, though the tale surrounding the Taj Mahal was romantic enough: a seventeenth-century Mughal emperor, Shah Jahan, building the temple as a tribute to his second wife, Mumtaz Mahal, after she died giving birth to his fourteenth child. But Sidonie also knew there were no jobs in

Agra, that begging had become a horrible scourge, and she really couldn't stand the idea of empty-bellied children tapping at her, pulling on her skirt or purse strap as she gazed upward, snapping redundant photographs of a four-hundred-year-old mausoleum erected by slaves at the sentimental whim of one man, once a mighty emperor, now dead, deprived of appetite, emotion, ambition, desire.

Mahadev drove Sidonie around the city to the sounds of the tabla, sitar, bells, a chorus of male and female voices, hypnotic, sweet. Krishna, Krishna. With her eight o'clock dinner date successfully aborted—she had been detained in traffic, surely the most legitimate excuse in Delhi—Sidonie sat spellbound. A fine white mist hung in the air, strands of lights looped along the jerry-built stalls lined up one after the other, an unending, tilting bazaar of doorless shops. Motorized rickshaws with rain-slicker-yellow tops, elephantine lorries, lumbersome and destabilized by their cargo of sweet potatoes or cement or God knows what, buses bloated with passengers to cartoonlike proportions, motor-bikes, women in saris riding sidesaddle behind the driver, like butterflies alight, the jewel-colored hems of their saris rippling backward. If she rolled down her window and stretched out her arm, she could touch the edge of that woman's sari, or put her hand inside the car beside her and touch the solitary passenger, or with her hand catch at the bicyclist or pedestrian or street vendor darting expertly through traffic, the hard cacophony of horns the one rule of navigation.

As she and Mahadev waited in yet another snarl of traffic, a girl sidled up to the car, nose pressed against the glass, less than an inch from Sidonie—her piquant, gamine face clowned with black paint, greasy blocks cubed on her tiny cheeks, polka-dotting her forehead with crude gaiety. Poking out her cat's tongue out at Sidonie, sticking her thumbs in her ears and waggling her fingers, she jumped back toward the sidewalk and launched herself into a rapid-fire series of backflips and cartwheels, graceless contortions fueled by the desperate need to impress before traffic started up, taking her audience with it. Wearing hot pink spandex capri pants and a too-small, paler pink T-shirt baring, like a cincture, the brown expanse of her midsection, the child catapulted into even more perilous-looking acrobatics, causing Sidonie to wince. She noticed a small boy of three or four, the girl's little brother perhaps, sitting nearby on a mat, dressed only in a pair of little shorts in the freezing winter night. Behind the boy, a ghostly urban forest: tall, spindly eucalyptus trees with dozens of wiry rhesus monkeys clambering up the shaggy, peeling branches, their pinched, old faces turning, at times, her way. Mahadev, phone cupped to his ear, was deep in conversation; Sidonie rolled down her window to better see the monkeys in their arboreal gymnasium, backdrop to the girl flipping and wheeling, a pink, febrile blur, the black patches on her cheeks ghoulish. Seeing the car's glass barrier go down, the child shot over to Sidonie, a mad, amphetamine glitter in her eyes. Gasping for air, her shirt streaked with dirt, tiny breasts peaking up under the faded Western-looking logo, shiny pants torn and tight, her face, up close, inches from Sidonie's, looked prematurely aged. Shoving a bundle of rupee notes along with her unopened water bottle into the girl's hands, she noticed the monkeys staring, their hairlines, like toupees, sliding low around their wrinkly pink faces. Horns blared at the girl as she grabbed Sidonie's money, vaulting into a final handstand, a hot pink, mercurial hiero-glyph in the city street, hands planted in the filthy road, the money, as if by sleight of hand, already gone. Righting herself, the child darted to the open window again; Sidonie thrust an-other soft bundle of rupees into her street-blackened hands. Scrambling back to the sidewalk, crouched beside the boy, she waved at Sidonie. Behind them, golden-haired monkeys, tails curled in tall, wild apostrophes, peered out from their eucaly-pus forest with grave and cunning eyes.

Mahadev's car moved away. Within blocks, they were overtaken by a milky fog that erased cars, people, buildings, billboards. Keeping her window down, letting the cold vapor trail in, Sidonie, looking out, saw a rat, oily black and feline, slip between buildings, its life more certain than that of a child turning cartwheels on the street. Beneath the titan clashing of car horns, beneath the spontaneous libretto of hunger and commerce, breathed some not-quite-holy viaticum of calm.

Above the scrim of mist, luminous neon signs and giant billboards floated past: Luxury Apartments, Airtel, Jewelry Museum. The shops, she realized, were arranged into districts, chemist's shops, jewelry and butcher shops, clothing, cell phones, computers. And though it was past eight o'clock, nothing of the noise or press of traffic had lessened. They had been driving for more than an hour, and Sidonie's head was beginning to ache from the burning smell of exhaust, the rancid pollution in the cold, humid air. She turned to Mahadev. "I'm ready to go back now." Keeping one eye on traffic, he turned toward her, nodding pleasantly as he made an aggressive right turn which took them onto a broader, quieter avenue leading back to the government district. Parklike, secluded, luxuriant, with whole blocks of mature trees, lawns, and an ordered skyline of pale, formal buildings, the district's calm made it hard to believe that surreal skirmishes of poverty and traffic went on only blocks away. Sidonie's eyes burned, her lungs felt poisoned, but still she sighed with pleasure at the fog-heavy green around her, the spaciousness. Even Mahadev looked content as he put down his cell phone and simply drove. She had signed up for a tour of the Taj Mahal tomorrow, a four-hour drive to Agra, the hotel van leaving at 7:00 AM. It had seemed a requisite, to visit a world wonder, but really, how requisite was it? She could cancel, not show up, spend her last day in Delhi relaxing, doing what she liked. What would she like? She didn't know. She didn't want to see Aruna Kumari again. Something beneath the surface of the woman's benevolence disturbed Sidonie, and she didn't want to know what that something was.

Mahadev gave a harsh cry, slamming on the brakes. Thrown forward, they were both forced to regard the sight before them: a white horse, one of its back legs broken at the hip, staggering, disoriented, in the middle of the road. As they watched, the horse, its leg at a hideous angle, vanished into the fog.

A sickening sight, they agreed—such a poor, beautiful animal, with no one to put it out of its misery. Sidonie felt lightheaded, as though she might faint.

"Your hotel, Madame."

Mahadev parked beneath the now-familiar portico as a red-turbaned attendant rushed to open the door for her. She paid Mahadev double what the meter showed, and wished him and his family well. In the lobby, Sidonie went up to the reception desk and asked if it was too late to book a massage at the hotel's spa. "Of course, Madame, let me check for you. Yes, there is one appointment left, at 8:30, in fifteen minutes . . . would Madame wish to make that appointment?" Yes, yes. She felt a huge, stupid relief.

In her freshly made up room (the walls hung with colored lithographs depicting Delhi's colonialist history, variously titled "Raj," "British Royalty," "The Mughals," and her favorite, "Beating the Jungle for Tigers"), orchid blossoms floated in a shallow bowl beside her books and magazines, all neatly rearranged. The bed linens had been changed, the bed itself turned down. With the curtains drawn and lights dimmed, the room was glowing, amber-colored, its perfection marred only by a bundle of brown paper, set across one corner of the vast bed.

She opened the folded shopping bag, noting it was from the local bazaar. The pashmina was of fine, light cashmere. As she held it up to admire the subtle paisley, the muted colors of rose, beige, and black, a business card dropped to the floor. She picked it up. A note on the back, penned in Siddarth Gupta's spiky, masculine hand. *Sidonie, best wishes for your article. There is always a next time. Love, Sid.*

She pictured him in the lobby, waiting, awkward with his shopping bag, calling up to her room, then by 8:30 conceding defeat, writing the note, requesting that the hotel staff deliver his gift to her room. Leaving then in his ponderous, sea cow way.

The red light on her phone blinked; two messages, a hotel reminder about the Taj Mahal tour (no, she would not go), the second from her lover, his smooth voice, familiar endearments, (his honey-sweet girl), one of his stolen moments, he'd hoped for a chat, he missed her. One year in, and it was a long series, a concatenation, of such stolen moments, as he liked to call them. She felt it with sickening clarity, the marginal pleasure she gave him, an obviation of marital boredom, how complacent he was to go on, risking nothing, gaining everything, never thinking of her hours, nights, and holidays spent alone.

The silent, carpeted hallway, its long row of tall windows reflecting the black night, the honeyed fragrance of jasmine, the pale niches with softly glowing candles—she walked down the pathway to a temple. Everything leading to the holiness of the body. The spa was empty but for her masseuse, a tired-looking, older Thai woman in a white, pajamalike uniform. She handed Sidonie, her last client, a folded white robe, asked what incense she would prefer (frangipani), what tea she would like after her massage (ginger). Removing her clothes and slipping on the robe, knotting it lightly around her waist, Sidonie walked into a dim-lit sitting room where the masseuse, kneeling, placed each of Sidonie's naked feet into a deep glass bowl of warm, scented water, its surface blanketed with white orchids. Soft music soothed her as she leaned back, naked under the plush, pristine white robe, her feet in the warm, white-flowered water, trails of frangipani incense perfuming the air. The masseuse dried her feet, slid them into straw slippers, brought her to a spacious room, to a massage table draped with an exquisite blue and green paisley fabric, stepping tactfully from the room as Sidonie slipped off the robe and lay beneath the cool length of cotton cloth. On her stomach, eyes closed, she opened to receive this woman's touch: delicate, expert, instinctively strong. When she turned over onto her back, the masseuse folded the sheet down past her bare hips and began to knead and sweep her small, strong hands over Sidonie's stomach, around her breasts. In the privacy formed simply by closing her eyes, she surrendered especially to this. How long had it been since her breasts had been touched? Her lover had been unavailable for months, with constant business travel and family obligations, yet she had held herself loyal to him. Tears slid from beneath her closed eyes, her chest felt a knot of grief—then an inchoate, cresting sadness as the woman's hands slid with timed intimacy along the insides of her thighs, across her stomach, drawing layers of sorrow out of her body. She wished the stranger's expert hands would never stop, that she would feel nothing but the soft stroking of skilled, impersonal hands on her bare flesh.

But it did end and, like most pleasures, had to be paid for. She sat in her robe, sipping from a celadon cup of pale ginger tea, hearing the masseuse, Lily, in the next room, quietly cleaning up. Minutes later, after thanking her, Sidonie padded back to her room in clean straw slippers, white-robed and hooded, holding a small cloth sack of her street clothes.

She had scarcely put her clothes away when there was a knock at her door. She had forgotten the hot chocolate she had ordered earlier. Unlocking and opening the door, she stepped back so the young man—sadly, not Vikram; it would have cheered her to see him, who knows, she might have invited him to sit with her and talk—could wheel in the linen-draped cart with its silver tray, pot of chocolate, dish of chocolate-dipped madeleine cakes, a vase with one fully opened white rose. Glowering, the young man, Arijit, almost angrily poured a stream of cocoa into her cup, then held out the padded receipt folder for her to sign the bill inside. As she scribbled her signature, he stared insolently, as if picturing her naked beneath the hotel robe, all that separated her body from his contemptuous, young gaze.

The cocoa, in its gold-bordered cup, was rich, velvety. Sidonie sat cross-legged in the center of her vast bed, sipping from the British-made china, watching television news. Updates on the same stories, fresh riots by the Bengali farmers, more murdered children, up to 70 million Hindus converging in Allahabad despite concern over a possible fatal stampede.

The phone shrilled. He would leave a second message, wondering, in his seductive, patrician voice, where she was other than halfway around the world, his sweetheart, liable to disappear. She had nothing to say to him. She watched saffron-clad, ash-smeared *sadhus* bathe in the muddy water, revered them, imagined herself stepping off the foot-worn steps of the *ghat*, wading up to her hips in frigid river water, perfumed and rotten, soupy with offerings, rough pulp of coconut shell, orange marigold blossoms, the scum of white ash, food, waste, necklaces of cowry shell, effluents from factories, sewage, hypocrisies, lies.

She turned off the television, cutting short the roundtable discussion of scholars and actors chatting self-importantly about *Kalyug*, the current dark age or cycle in Indian history, a history of endless cycles, golden and dark, wheels large and small, set to spinning by hundreds of deities, from blue-skinned Krishna to Kali, to gods and goddesses lesser known, unknown, not yet born. Shedding her robe stained with scented oil, she stepped into the marble bathroom, turned the handles of the bath until water in a fine, hot spray issued from the heavy brass showerhead.

She left the curtain undrawn, her white body reflected in the vanity mirror, half-hidden in the rising steam. Tilting back her head, feeling her hair grow heavy halfway down her back, she opened her mouth, letting water sluice down her throat, seep into her nostrils, pool into her ears, flood across her opened eyes. She sat down in the rising bathwater, let its foulness and purity rise over her legs, enter her vagina, her anus; she lay back, her eyes open underwater, let all nine gates, various portals to the body, be cleansed.

Great Mother Kali, I shall weave a chain of pearls for thy neck
with my tears of sorrow.

Alone in her large bed that night, Sidonie dreamed she was at the Taj Mahal with Mahadev. As they stood barefoot within the spectacular architectural gloom of Shah Jahan's tribute to his queen-become-dust, as they waited in the long, single-file line with other tourists passing through this monument to conjugal love, pressed in upon by beggars, most of them children, Mahadev answered her questions. Yes, his marriage had been arranged between his wife's parents and his own . . . that was how it was done. Yes, an astrologer had been consulted. In the West, she told him, we choose whom we marry, but it doesn't work so well, half of our marriages end in divorce, and most of the other half cheats. Perhaps letting the stars and deities or even one's parents choose is better? Mahadev laughed. I have a good life, very fortunate. And you still love your wife? she asked. Oh yes, entirely.

Then, in the way of dreams: *Here we are, Madame. Your hotel.*

It would be important, though an ultimately fruitless matter, that the manager on duty remember Ms. Recoura checking out one morning earlier than indicated by her reservation, and asking for a hotel driver to take her to the main train station in Delhi. When the manager inquired, as a matter of courtesy, as to her next destination, she had said Wildflower Hall, a luxury resort in the Himalayan mountains, the former home of Lord Kitchener. Assuring her of her excellent choice, he asked if she had plenty of warm clothing, as it was very cold this time of year in the Himachal Pradesh region. She had said yes, she did.

The driver, too, had done nothing wrong. He had taken her to the station, she had paid him, everything perfectly in order. He did recall one unusual question—she had asked if he or someone he knew might drive her to Allahabad. He had told her he could not, that as a hotel employee he drove only short distances within the city, and he warned her of the drivers standing around their old, filthy cars outside the station. Extremely unreliable, even dangerous, he had told her. Do not go with any of them, though naturally they will all offer to take you. You must ignore them.

American Tourist Found Dead

A female tourist from America was found dead in the Ganga River near Allahabad early yesterday morning, an apparent drowning victim. Identified only by a hotel receipt found in her jacket pocket, no other possessions were found on her person or nearby. Authorities are investigating the death of 58-year-old Sidonie Recora to determine if foul play may have been involved. Police speculate she may have been taking part in the Ardh Kumbh Mela, a spiritual festival held once every twelve years. "It is definitely tragic" said Scottish tourist Rory McBride, 29, a self-described "world pilgrim," who discovered Ms. Recora's body. "You come here to lose yourself and gain everything. The Ganges is the bridge between life and death, and they say once you bathe in it, you are released. Free. That's why I'm here, and I'm guessing that's why she came here, too." Allahabad and Delhi police inspectors are now attempting to locate Ms. Recora's relatives in the United States.

That morning, as every morning, a copy of the *Hindustan Times* was left, impeccably folded, outside the door of every occupied room in the five-star Imperial Hotel. Vikram Singh, who had been deeply and secretly in love with the American lady, who had hung her fine clothes in the armoire with reverence, who had lifted up and put back her perfumes and cosmetics, leafed through the books by her bedside, tracing with his fingers their fragile, pencilled, foreign notations, who had found it difficult to leave her presence, wondered how many of the hotel's guests would bother to read that day's paper, much less the small, misspelled article on the inside page, a death, an accidental drowning, so much less interesting than the Noida sex murders, or the rising death toll from the cold snap, or the violent takeover of farmlands by yet another mega-corporation.

Who besides God, he thought, knew who really loved whom, who would bring such permanent release to herself. Or why.

ACKNOWLEDGMENTS

With thanks to David Morley, Maureen Freely and Louise Doughty for welcoming me to London and to the MFA Program at Warwick University. To Jewell Parker Rhodes, Piper Endowed Chair, and to the Virginia G. Piper Writing Center, Arizona State University, for the opportunity to teach at Warwick University and for Fellowships in 2006 and 2007. To the Hawthornden Foundation, Midlothian, Scotland, for a 2008 Fellowship, and with special thanks to Anjana Appachana for recommending that I apply. To the Bogliasco Foundation and Liguria Study Center, Italy, for a 2011 Fellowship, and to my sister, Penelope Byrd, for her selfless support of my work.

To Frances B. Clymer and Mary Robinson, McCracken Research Librarians, Buffalo Bill Historical Center, for your kind assistance.

To Professor Mario Materassi, enduring bridge to Italy, I cherish our friendship and your faith in me.

To generous friends and colleagues Cynthia Hogue, Marshall Chair in Modern and Contemporary Poetry, and Alberto Rios, Regents' Professor and Katherine C. Turner Chair in English, for helping to fund trips to India, my heartfelt thanks.

To editors and authors Sven Birkerts, Bradford Morrow, Brigid Hughes, Gregory Wolfe, Zack Bean, Ian Stansel, Michael Louie, Richard Burgin and Ben George, thank you for publishing these stories in your literary journals and magazines. To Mary Kenagy Mitchell and Anne McPeak, I am grateful for your friendship and incomparable editing skills.

To the brilliant Erika Goldman and perspicacious Leslie Hodgkins, who take the risk with élan!

To artist and writer friends Sarah Twombly, Kristen LaRue, Darcy Courteau, Tessa Stevens, Heather Poole, Jillian Robinson, Charles McNair, Laura Tohe, Berkley Carnine, Markus Armstrong, Rachel Malis, William Akoi Mawin, Laurent Recoura, Dave Hunsaker, Robert Clark, Rohit Dasgupta, Bishan Samaddar, Roma Debabrata, Melissa Walker Glenn, Federica Paretti, Stefano Vincieri, Susanna Casprini, Simona Lumachelli, Simon Ortiz, Gyorgyi Szabo, Brad Watson, Robin Hemley, Rachel de Baere, Masha Hamilton, and Kristy Davis for uplifting my spirit in countless, invaluable ways.

To healers and seers Soken Graf, Deana Marie Howlett, Pat Donovan, Robert Romano, Clara Darby, Rosemary Carey, Silver Rose and Susanne Wilson . . . you have kept me well.

To Jess and Noëlle Pritchard Barkley and to Caitlin Skye Pritchard and Gabriel Rushing—love immeasurable.

To Simon, tiny dachshund, merry sidekick, humbler of egos.

In memory of my grandparents, Walter and Louise Rose Reilly and Vice Admiral Clarence J. Brown, USN, and Augusta Duwe Brown and my parents, Clarence J. Brown Jr., and Helen Lorraine Reilly.

In all your names, lie the best part of these pages.

Finally, in memory of Air Force Senior Airman
Ashton Lynn Marie Goodman, USAF,
1987–2009
These stories are for you, beloved friend.

ABOUT THE AUTHOR

Melissa Pritchard is the author of three short story collections, *Spirit Seizures, The Instinct for Bliss,* and *Disappearing Ingenue;* three novels, *Phoenix, Selene of the Spirits,* and *Late Bloomer;* and a biography of Arizona philanthropist Virginia Galvin Piper, *Devotedly, Virginia.*

Her short fiction has won the Flannery O'Connor Award, the Carl Sandburg Literary Award, the Janet Heidinger Kafka Prize, a PEN/Nelson Algren Honorary Mention, two O. Henry Prizes and two Pushcart Prizes, the Ortese Prize in North American Literature from the University of Florence, and has been cited and anthologized in *Best American Short Stories, Best of the West, The Pushcart Prize, The O. Henry Awards, The Prentice Hall Anthology of Women's Literature, American Gothic Tales, The Literary Ghost: Great Contemporary Ghost Stories,* and *The Inevitable: Contemporary Writers Confront Death.* She has won the Barnes & Noble Discover Award, been chosen for National Public Radio's Annual Summer Reading List, and received fellowships from the National Endowment for the Arts; the Hawthornden Foundation, Scotland; the Bogliasco Foundation, Italy; and the Howard Foundation at Brown University. A number of her works have been translated into Spanish and Italian. Pritchard teaches in the MFA Program at Arizona State University, and is founder of the Ashton Goodman Fund, The Afghan Women's Writing Project.